D0463629

PORCUPINES AND CHINA DOLLS

PORCUPINES AND CHINA DOLLS

A Novel by **Robert Arthur Alexie**

Published in Canada in 2002 by
Stoddart Publishing Co. Limited
895 Don Mills Road, 400-2 Park Centre, Toronto, Canada M3C 1W3

Published in the United States in 2003 by
Stoddart Publishing Co. Limited
PMB 128, 4500 Witmer Estates, Niagara Falls, New York 14305-1386

10 9 8 7 6 5 4 3 2 1

To order Stoddart books please contact General Distribution Services
In Canada Tel. (416) 213-1919 Fax (416) 213-1917
Email cservice@genpub.com
In the United States Toll-free tel. 1-800-805-1083 Toll-free fax 1-800-481-6207
Email gdsinc@genpub.com

www.stoddartpub.com

National Library of Canada Cataloguing in Publication Data
Alexie, Robert Arthur
Porcupines and china dolls: a novel
ISBN 0-7737-3305-1
Indians of North America — Northwest Territories — Residential schools — Fiction. I. Title.
PS8551.L4739P63 2002 C813'.6 C2002-900574-4
PR9199.4.A44P63 2002

Jacket design: Angel Guerra
Text design: Tannice Goddard

We acknowledge for their financial support of our publishing program the Canada Council, the Ontario Arts Council, and the Government of Canada through the Book Publishing Industry Development Program (BPIDP).

Printed and bound in Canada

If there's one thing I've learned, it is for everything there is a reason. We are all at this moment in our lives because of everything — good or bad — that has happened to us so far. We are here and now because of the choices we've made, or haven't made, or in some cases, choices that were made — with or without our permission — for us. To that end, I'd like to dedicate this to those who've supported and enhanced my goals and ambitions . . . and to those who didn't.

To those who did —
To Mom and Dad, and to my sister, Gladys.
To my uncle, Robert, and my friend, Chief James.
To my friend and confidante, Doug.
To my children: Krista, Brandon, Travis and Caroline.
And to my wife, Renie.

Prologue

There is at least one moment in all our lives when we are faced with a decision that will forever change our future and the future of those around us. It is at that moment, whatever our beliefs or lack thereof, that we look to the heavens for an answer, or a reason.

The Ultimate Journey to Hell

He stood alone beside the highway in the Blue Mountains like he'd done so many times before. His tall, dark figure looked foreboding against the dark clouds. His black leather jacket glistened like blood-soaked armour from another time. His scowl told everyone and everything to keep their fucking distance. He looked like Death ready to go on a rampage.

The hills and mountains were in their autumn splendour and the gravel highway cut across the land like a rip in a painting. It was as though he was seeing it for the first time. It looked like a dream. And who knows, maybe it was.

He spread his hands, then lifted his head to the heavens as if to ask a question. What came was something he didn't expect: the hate, the rage, the anger and the sorrow. They burst from his tormented soul and ripped a hole in his chest and were given a voice. They sounded like a million deaths rolled into one. They spread out over the land of his People, shook the sky, then echoed off the distant mountains and disappeared into hell, where they belonged.

After a lifetime, he looked to the sky again and asked the question. Six billion people must've looked to the sky at one time or another. Six billion people must've asked it at least once in their lives.

Why?

He waited for an answer. Six billion people must've heard it at least once in their lives. It was silent. It was nothing. He felt as if he were the last person on this cold, desolate planet. He then realized he had one option left and had no alternative but to take it.

He took the gun from his truck and loaded one bullet, then returned to the side of the highway. He closed his eyes, then lifted his head to the heavens. This time he asked the Powers That Be to take him instead. They didn't. He told them he'd do anything they wanted. They wouldn't. He told them to fuck off. They did.

Then it came to him. He'd always been alone. He'd always be alone. He then did something he'd thought about and tried for a million years. But this time, he knew he'd do it.

All in one smooth motion he got down on one knee, put the barrel in his mouth, then pushed the trigger. He watched the hammer fall and closed his eyes. He tensed, waiting for the explosion. After a million years, he heard it: metal on metal. It was the loudest sound he'd ever heard. It shook his whole body and deafened him.

He took a deep breath, dropped the gun, then exhaled. He heard it: the peace and the silence.

He waited for his ultimate journey to hell.

Part One

The Dream World

One

Legends, Beliefs and the Newcomers

In order to understand this story, it is important to know the People and where they came from and what they went through. The story begins with the Blue People and their legends and beliefs in the time before first contact.

The Blue People are one of the aboriginal peoples of Canada's western Northwest Territories. They got their name from the fact that they lived in the Blue Mountains to the west of the Mackenzie River in a land of majestic mountains, rolling hills, wide-open valleys and tall-standing trees.

Like all indigenous people of the North, the Blue People have an oral tradition rich in stories and legends. One of their legends tells of their Creation. It is said that the Creator took some red soil from one of the valleys in the Blue Mountains and created the Old People from whom all Blue People have descended. It was because of this that the People brought their dead to the mountains to be burned in the belief that their bodies would return to the land and their souls would continue on to the Old People, who still lived in the mountains.

The legends also say the Creator provided the Old People with the Old Songs that were sung soon after Creation. From these songs came the animals, including the caribou, which were revered and respected because they provided food, clothing, shelter, tools and weapons. Wolves were also held in high regard. The People believed they followed the caribou north each spring to the Arctic Ocean and brought them back to the mountains before the winter winds came.

The People did not have an easy life. Theirs was a daily struggle for survival, and starvation was always the enemy. In the summer they fished along the rivers, then moved into the hills to harvest the caribou in the fall. Theirs was a nomadic existence; they moved from one camp to the next, from the mountains to the rivers, from where game was scarce to where it was plentiful.

And so it was that for thousands of years the People lived, usually undisturbed, in the Blue Mountains. But things were about to change; the future was unfolding, as it should.

The future came in the form of intruders, or newcomers. The first of these arrived in the summer of 1789: a white explorer by the name of Alexander Mackenzie. There would be other explorers, but they are not important to our story.

In 1840, the fur traders arrived, and with the approval of Chief Red Jacket, a permanent post was set up on the Teal River. This would later become the community of Aberdeen. Another community would be established in the 1930s on the Mackenzie River just east of Aberdeen. This community would be called Helena. For the first hundred years, the only way in and out of Aberdeen and Helena was by river, but that would change. Things always do.

The fur traders also brought other things to the People: the fiddle and new dances called jigs, square dances and waltzes. The People took to these as if they were born to them.

In 1850, the missionaries arrived. They would have the greatest impact on the People, but no one knew it at the time. The missionaries, called Anglicans, baptized the Blue People, then took away their drums, songs and funeral practices. They told the People that burning their dead was barbaric and uncivilized and that their drums and songs were the devil's tools. They also frowned on having more than one wife, and this practice soon disappeared. The drums, songs and funeral practices went underground, at least for a while. By 1875, most of the People had been given Christian names and were bona fide Christians.

In January of 1877, Chief Red Jacket realized too late that the newcomers had brought something else: diseases for which the People had no defence. He sent more than twenty of his People home to the Old People and led the rest into the safety of the Blue Mountains to escape the epidemics. That fall, he reluctantly came into Aberdeen to trade. He did not stay long and he did not leave alone. Four months later, he and thirty-seven of his People were sent back to the Old People. As was the custom, his eldest son, Thomas, became Chief Thomas.

In 1903, a fourth group of people arrived: the Yellow Stripes. They were so named because of the yellow stripes they wore on their pants. The white people called them the North West Mounted Police. They established a post in Aberdeen, enforced the white man's laws and never left.

In 1920, Chief Thomas passed away and his son, Francis, became Chief Francis.

In 1921, the last of the newcomers arrived: the Treaty Party. There's a lot of controversy about what was or wasn't in the Treaty, but most are not important to this story. What is important is that the government and the People agreed that the Treaty contained a clause that states: "His Majesty will pay the salaries of teachers to instruct the children of the 'said Indians' in a manner deemed advisable by His Majesty's government."

Even back then the People realized the value of the white man's education, and they didn't make a big fuss about it. They just didn't realize how it was going to be done. They put their faith and trust in His Majesty and His Majesty's government and believed their "said children" would be cared for.

What they didn't know when they put their X on the Treaty was that the church would be given the responsibility to educate their "said children." It sounded like patronage and it is still a contentious issue to this day. It probably always will be.

Soon after, the first mission boat arrived in Aberdeen, and thirty-five children were herded out of the Blue Mountains and dragged off to mission school. The People have no words in their language for mission school. The closest anyone has come to it is "hellhole," but that's beside the point. The point is that years later, twenty-four of the thirty-five would return. But more importantly, eleven wouldn't. It had begun, but no one knew what "it" was. Things were beginning to change; the future was unfolding, as it should.

Two

The First Generation

It could be anytime in the 1920s or 1930s. A young boy and his sister, seven and six respectively, have spent all their lives on the land. They have never known a day without their parents or grandparents and have never spoken a word of English. They wake up when they have to, eat when they're hungry and sleep when they're tired. Their parents and grandparents tell them the stories and legends, and they've never been punished in their life. Their future, up until that moment, is a known certainty: he will become a hunter and trapper and she will become a wife and they will spend their lives in these mountains until they are returned to the Old People. That's the way it's been for countless generations and there is no reason to think it'll ever change.

One day in August, the mission boat arrives. It's been here before and has always left. But today, something is different. The missionary says something in the language and everyone goes silent. They look at the children and slowly nod their heads. Their father tells them they're going to school to learn to read and write. He doesn't tell them where or for how long, and they don't ask.

The missionary leads them to the boat as their father tells them to listen and do as they're told. These are the last words he'll say to them for nine years, maybe longer. As they board the boat, they see other children from other camps. They are quiet and show no emotion. The missionary tells them to sit and they do it without thinking. The boat starts to move and they have the urge to stand and look for their parents, but they don't. They wonder if this is real. Maybe it's a dream. A few miles downriver, the boy sees his parents and grandparents. They are far away and motionless. They look like statues.

Their parents and grandparents don't know it, but someone or something has ripped out their hearts. They watch as their hearts slowly stop beating, then look up to see the boat disappear. They don't know it, but they're going to think about their children every minute of every hour of every day until they return. If they don't return — and some of them won't — they'll remember them forever. They'll wonder if they could've prevented it. They could've, but by then, it'll be too late.

A few weeks later, the boat arrives at the mission school and the children are herded into a building and separated: boys on one side, girls on the other. The young girl tries to go with her brother, but she's grabbed by a woman in a long black robe and pushed into another room. The last thing he hears is her cries followed by a slap, then silence.

The boys are herded into a large room where a missionary takes a pair of scissors and cuts their hair. No one says anything. They just watch. After everyone's hair is cut, they're told to remove their clothing and put them in a pile. They don't know it, but the missionaries are going to burn their clothing along with their hair and whatever else they brought with them.

The boys are bathed in cold water, then another missionary puts some white powder on them. They don't know what it's for. Some of them wonder if the powder will make them white. After their bath they're given clothes and realize they all look alike. They look like porcupines: well-dressed porcupines.

After they've been sheared, stripped, bathed, deloused and clothed, they are lined up and herded into the dorm, where they're assigned beds. Another missionary comes in and speaks in the language. He hasn't mastered it, but he gets the message across. They are to do as they're told and are not to talk back. They are not to talk to the girls or to anyone outside the yard. They are not to leave the yard and are not to speak the language.

A few minutes later, they are lined up and herded into the dining room. The young boy looks for his sister, but he can't recognize her. The girls all have the same dresses and the same haircut. Years from now he'll realize they looked like china dolls.

A missionary leads them in prayer. They have no idea what he's saying, but that doesn't matter. In a few weeks, they'll learn the words. They won't understand them, but they'll learn them. Their survival depends on it — literally.

Supper is soup made from fish. It's full of bones, scales and guts, and it smells and tastes different from the fish their parents have caught all summer. One by one they suck the broth out, then put whatever is left in their pockets. They'll find a way to get rid of it later.

After supper, the girls clean up the dining room and kitchen while the boys are told to haul water, cut wood or do other chores. If they don't do it right the first time, they'll do it a second time. If they don't do it right the second time, they'll do it a third. No one does it a fourth.

Later that night, they are told to wash and change into these other clothes called pyjamas. They are herded back to the dorm, where they are told to kneel beside their beds, fold their arms and get ready to pray. It's in English, and the new boys don't understand, but they watch the others and follow their example. The missionary once again leads them in prayer. They don't know it, but they'll pray seven times a day, every day for the next nine years. They'll learn the words to the prayers long before they know what they mean. But by then, they won't care.

After prayers, they are told to get into bed and the lights are turned off and everything disappears into the night. The young boy wonders if he'll go home tomorrow. He wonders if his parents are going to visit him. He wonders how his sister is doing.

The young boy doesn't know it, but his sister is crying silently. She's wondering why she has to be here. Did she do something wrong? Is she being punished? Will her parents come for them? How long will they stay here? Why can't she go to her brother?

Late that night, someone starts to cry. It is low and muffled. It is heart-wrenching. It sounds awful. It sounds like a million porcupines crying in the dark.

They feel the vibrations long before they can hear the footsteps. Even before the door opens the crying has stopped and so has their breathing. The missionary looks around, then mutters something that sounds like "dirty Indians," but they can't be sure. No one says anything for a few million years, then the breathing resumes. But the cries are silent. They'll always be silent.

The children wake up in the morning, get dressed, wash, then eat. They don't know what the food is and they don't care. They just hope it doesn't smell bad. After breakfast, there are chores. After chores, there is school. After school, there are more chores. After chores, it's prayer time. After prayer time comes the darkness. After the darkness, the silent cries once again emerge from the walls.

Sometime during his first week, the young boy will have no alternative but to speak his language and he will be hit, slapped or tweaked. Sometime during his first month, he'll watch his sister speak the language and she will be hit, slapped or tweaked. He'll remember that moment for the rest of his life and will never forgive himself for not going to her rescue. It will haunt him, and each time he remembers it, he will silently promise to kill anyone who has ever laid a hand on him or his sister. It will be a silent promise and no one will ever know it.

One day, when no one is looking, she'll come to him and will speak the language. "When are Mom and Dad coming to pick us up? When are we going home? Why don't they come for us? Are they dead?"

He'll smile and tell her not to worry. "We'll be home soon." He's lying and she knows it, but there's nothing he can do.

Sometime in the next nine years, they'll see things they don't understand and will not question. Strange things will happen to them and they'll try not to remember. They'll block out everything bad that happens to them and others in these hallowed halls. They'll remember only the good things, and those will be few.

Sometime in the next few years, the young boy will go to the dining room and look for his sister but he won't see her. Later that afternoon, the missionaries will tell him she has died, but they won't tell him how. A few days later, they'll bury her where so many others have been buried over the past few years. He'll show no emotion as they put her body in the cold, dark ground forever. He'll promise to return someday and take her back to the Old People. He'll promise someday to return and kill them all.

Sometime in the next nine years, he'll learn to read and write the English language. He'll learn to say the Lord's Prayer and a million other prayers, hymns and psalms. He'll learn to sweep and mop. He'll learn to haul water and clean up. He'll learn to plant, hoe and harvest potatoes. He'll learn to fish, but not hunt. He'll learn to cut, haul, split and pack wood. He'll make friends with other boys he'll never see again. He'll watch other children leave and will envy them. He'll watch other children die and will pity them. He'll get used to the fish soup, but not the smell. He'll learn how not to get hit, slapped or tweaked but will never forget how it felt. He'll learn how to hide his emotions and will rarely smile. He'll never laugh.

Years from now, the young boy will turn sixteen and will be planting potatoes. He tries to remember his parents, but he hasn't seen them for nine years. They are strangers. He can't remember his grandparents. Someone calls his name. He looks at the missionary with no emotion.

"Come," the missionary shouts. "You're going home."

He's heard, but he doesn't believe it. They've lied to him, yelled at him, screamed at him, hit him, slapped him, strapped him and tweaked him a million times over the years, and he is confused. The missionary smiles, then puts an arm around his shoulder and the young man cringes. The fear, the anger and the rage are just below the surface, but he forces them down.

The missionary leads him into the dorm and the young man does not resist. The missionary smiles again. The young man doesn't know what to make of it. The missionaries rarely smile.

"Pack up," he says. "You're going home."

The young man almost smiles, but doesn't. He packs his few belongings, then walks down to the mission boat and sees other children on board. They are all silent, but the smiles and anticipation are just below the surface.

The boat departs, and as it rounds the bend, they watch as the school disappears into their memory. They'll never see it again. They may return years later, but it will be gone. Destroyed, like evidence in the great trial of life.

A few days later, he'll be sleeping and something will wake him. Something will smell familiar. He'll walk to the front of the boat and the first thing he sees will be the Blue Mountains. His eyes will light up and his heart will beat faster.

He'll watch as his community gets closer and he'll see his People coming to meet the boat. He'll go ashore and will look for his parents and grandparents, but they're not here. He wonders if they're still coming.

Someone will call his name and he'll look at a woman he doesn't remember. She'll tell him something in a language he doesn't understand. It slowly dawns on him: he's forgotten the language. Or has he? The language is still there, but he's now thinking in English and has to translate it. It's a long and difficult process.

A few seconds later, he understands. This woman is his aunt and she's telling him his parents and grandparents are not coming. They've died. He says nothing. He's waited nine years and now he has to wait forever. His aunt asks him another question. He doesn't fully understand, but he knows she's asking about his sister. He searches his mind for the words, but they are not there. At least not yet.

Some of the other parents are asking about their children. He watches as the missionary reads the names of the children who have died. There is a great silence as the names are read one by one. Heads drop and a low moan starts. Soon, twenty or more People are moaning. They are not crying, they are moaning and it is awful. They sound like a million porcupines crying in the hills.

The young man hears his sister's name. He promised her they'd be home soon, but he was lying and she knew it. He'll remember the look on her face for the rest of his life, but he doesn't know it.

He looks at the mountains and a million questions flood his mind. Why was he taken away? Why did they take his language? Why did they take his parents and grandparents? Why did they take his sister? Why did he leave her? Why didn't he bring her home? Who is going to look after him and teach him the language? Who is going to teach him the Old Ways?

He watches the mission boat leave for as long as he can, then turns to find his aunt looking at him. She asks if he's okay in the language and he nods his head. They walk up the bank and he keeps turning to look for the boat, but it's gone. He wonders if it was a dream. It wasn't and he knows it.

For the rest of his life, the young man is going to remember the day they picked him up and the day they brought him home. He'll remember the fear, the hunger, the hits, the slaps, the straps, the tweaks, the work and the loneliness. He'll remember a lot of what went on in that place, but he'll talk only about the good things. He'll forget, or try to forget, the not-so-good things. He'll never do it.

For as long as he lives, he's never going to forgive his parents for sending him away. He's never going to forgive his grandparents for allowing his parents to send him away. He's never going to forgive the church for putting him through hell. He's never going to forgive those who lied to him and those who abused him. He won't say it out loud. He can't. They cut his tongue out and he can't talk about it.

Next year, he'll relearn his language and the survival skills he lost and will cling to them for the rest of his life. Next year, he'll relearn the customs, traditions and values of his People but will rarely talk about them. When he does, he'll look to see if any missionaries are standing behind him.

In three years, he'll marry a woman who has also been to mission school. They'll have a child and will promise never send her to that hellhole. In ten years, despite what they promised, they'll watch as she leaves for mission school, knowing they might never see her again. At that moment, someone or something is going to rip out their hearts and they will slowly die. Soon after, they'll promise never to have another child, but they will.

In twenty years, they'll watch the mission boat arrive and will pray their daughter is on board. If she is, they'll never let her go again. If she isn't, they'll wish they were dead.

But all that is someday and far away. Today he has returned home and he is a stranger in his own land. He doesn't have any parents or grandparents and he doesn't understand his language. For nine years he wished he was out of that hellhole. He finally got his wish. But today, for some strange reason, he wishes he were back. He is confused by these feelings, but doesn't dwell on it. He has to relearn his language and the ways of his People. His survival depends on it — literally.

Three

A Time of Change

By the early 1930s, every Blue Indian born in or after 1915 had been herded out of the Blue Mountains and dragged off to mission school. Most would remain there until the age of sixteen, when they would be sent home with the ability to read and write and not much else.

This first generation of mission school children relearned their language, ways and customs, and then began raising their own families; they began raising the second generation.

What they didn't know is, because they were taken away from their parents when they were five or six and returned when they were sixteen, they lacked one of the most important and fundamental skills needed to preserve the family unit. This skill cannot be taught, it can only be learned. This skill was parenting. A recipe for disaster was in the making, but no one knew it at the time.

And why did the People subject themselves to this? To send their children to mission school knowing the pain they would go through?

It was two things. First, it was government legislation and therefore against the law to keep their children from being sent to mission school. And that meant jail, or the threat of jail. Secondly, the church operated the mission schools. And at the time, the church had a firm hold on the People and their beliefs. Going against the church meant going to hell, which was a lot worse than going to jail.

The mid-1950s were a time of change. Aberdeen had two stores, a nursing station, a small government office, a three-man RCMP detachment, a power-generating plant and not much else. Tugs and barges still plied the Mackenzie and Teal Rivers each spring and summer, bringing in the annual supply of goods. Air travel was still a novelty, and the mail took a few weeks to get to and from Edmonton. Some say it still does.

There were fifty white people living in Aberdeen, and more and more were arriving every year. They lived in stick-built houses with running water, washing machines and electric lights. They had their own parties where they talked about their life in the south before being posted to this godforsaken town in the middle of nowhere. They associated with the People, but only when it was absolutely necessary.

There were between four and five hundred People living in the Blue Mountains hunting, fishing and trapping and making a half-decent life for themselves and their children. The epidemics had passed and the population was rebounding. The People still looked after their parents and grandparents and stayed in extended family units and came to town only during Christmas, Easter and for part of the summer. They lived in log houses with woodstoves and had no running water and no electric lights. They did not associate with the whites and were never invited to.

Helena had a population of fifteen hundred and boasted a new hospital, a radio station, two hotels, two bars and two retail stores. The government was also building a high school and two hostels: one for the Catholics and one for the Anglicans. Hostels. That's what the government decided to call the residential schools, which used to be called mission schools. The People still called them hellholes. Others called them shitholes. Some called them a dream. To others they were a nightmare.

In 1956, Chief Francis asked the government to build a school in Aberdeen since they had one hundred "said children" attending mission schools in other communities. That July the government informed Chief Francis that they would be building a school that would go up to grade eight and a one-hundred-bed hostel in Aberdeen. The Chief wondered why the hostel. He hadn't asked for this.

In any event, the school and the hostel were completed in September of 1959. The school was now separate from the hostel and was operated and administered by the government, who brought in white teachers from the south. It would be another ten years before the first Blue Indian became a teacher. But in Indian Time, that's a million years.

In any event, the hostel was similar to the mission schools and residential schools: it was funded by the government and administered by the church, which still brought in white people from the south to supervise the boys and girls. No one thought about hiring one of the People to look after their own children. They hired them to work in the kitchen and clean up the building.

The People still brought their "said children" to the hostel in September, but they now took them out at Christmas, Easter and for the summer. The children were still herded into dorms, their hair was still cut, they were still deloused, they were still given the same clothes to wear, they still lined up for meals, they still said a million prayers, some things still went bump in the night and they still looked like porcupines and china dolls.

It should be noted that most of the children spoke only one language: English. Their parents had done this to ensure they would never be hit, slapped, strapped or tweaked in any mission school, hostel or hellhole, no matter what they called it.

In 1960, the status Indians of Canada, including most of the Blue People, were bestowed the honour of becoming Canadian citizens.

This meant that the Government of Canada gave them the right to vote, hold public office, own property, own a business, serve in the army and consume alcohol without losing their "status." The government was right. It would not take away their status. It would take away their identity.

Four

The Hostel

The year is 1962 and the sweltering heat of July has long since gone and the bugs are slowly disappearing. The People have spent the summer drying and storing fish for the winter. They are tired of fish and hope the caribou will soon come.

The children have spent the summer running and playing with very few rules. They get up when they get up, eat when they're hungry and go to sleep when they're tired. The dark, dreary days of residential school are far behind them. They're also right in front of them, but they don't think about it.

One day in late August, the parents load up their boats and prepare to travel to town for supplies and to do other things they don't want to think about. It is a long, quiet ride. That night, the children are given a bath in a galvanized tub next to the woodstove. They are quiet and know what's coming.

The next day, they are dressed in new clothes and new shoes. There is no joy in the new clothes because it's happening and there is nothing they can do about it. They are being taken to the hostel.

A young Indian couple, Joseph and May Nathan, slowly walk out of their house with their six-year-old son, James. He is quiet and has never been to the hostel in his life, but he's heard about it. They see another couple, Matthew and Elizabeth Noland, coming out of their house with their son, Jacob. Elizabeth is carrying her baby, Esther, on her back in a shawl with a beautifully beaded baby strap. They wonder what would happen if they left town with their sons and never came back. Would the Powers That Be come after them and remove their children and take them to jail? They think about it, but that's all they do.

May and Elizabeth are each carrying paper bags containing a new pair of canvas moccasins and some extra clothing. Hidden among the clothes are a few bags of candy, some chocolate bars and packs of chewing gum. They walk behind their husbands while their sons walk between them. James and Jake have spent the last six years growing up together and have formed a bond. They look like twins and are quiet.

The four adults and two boys walk up the steps of the hostel and through the large double doors of the front entrance. It's the only time the children will enter these doors until Christmas. Then their parents will lead them out. In between, they'll use the boys' door. They walk into the foyer that is so clean it has no smell. It is also quiet, and the lights reflect off the dark green linoleum floor.

Joseph and Matthew walk into the hostel administrator's office and close the door. The administrator sits while they stand as if they are in a principal's office being reprimanded for something or another. The three men emerge from the office and Joseph looks at May and forces a smile, but she doesn't return it. Matthew does not look at his wife. He looks at his son and forces a small smile as if to say "I'm sorry."

The administrator returns with the boys' supervisor. The supervisor is in his mid-fifties and is a kind and gentle man. The boys like him and he gets along with the parents. Joseph and Matthew smile and shake his hand. He looks at May and Elizabeth, but they do not look at him.

James and Jake look at their fathers who are looking right through them into another dimension. They don't want to be here. They look at their mothers who are looking at their husbands, willing them to take their sons and walk out of this institution and never return. It doesn't work.

The boys' supervisor puts his hands on James's and Jake's shoulders and starts them off. After a few steps, they are on their own. Jake reaches the end of the hall before he turns and he can't believe what he's seeing. His father is screaming and his mother is on her knees. She is sobbing and moaning. He watches as their hearts mysteriously appear in front of them. They beat once, twice, then stop. His parents are silent, then they look up at him and smile. He blinks and looks at them again. They are now standing and are looking at him with no emotion whatsoever.

Meanwhile, halfway down the hall, James is walking. He doesn't know it but he will never run again. He will always take long, slow, deliberate steps. His eyes are on the large double doors at the end of the hall. He looks back at his parents, but they've turned to stone. No unseen force is going to rip their hearts out. They've made sure of that. James looks at the stairs, then back at his parents, but they've disappeared. He and Jake turn and walk up the stairs into a whole new world.

As they enter this whole new world, they see a familiar face: David William. He's a year older and has been here before.

"You first," the supervisor says to David.

David smiles, then puts down his paper bag and removes his shirt. He sits on a chair in the hall and the supervisor puts a sheet around him. It's over in a few minutes. His hair is cut, or rather sheared.

"You next," David says to Jake.

Jake sits and it's over in a few minutes.

"Now you're a real porcupine!" David says and laughs.

James removes his shirt and watches his hair fall and says nothing. David and Jake are smiling at him. They do look like porcupines.

After their hair is cut, they are told to get undressed and their clothes are taken away. David leads the way into a room and for the first time in their lives, James and Jake take a shower. All their lives they've had baths: a big tub in the cabin in the winter and the Teal River in the summer. After their shower, they're given new clothes. James and Jake look at David, then at each other. They look alike. They have the same porcupine haircuts, the same shirts, pants, socks and running shoes.

They are led to the dorm and are given beds and a number. Jake takes a bed between David and James and feels safe. They're glad David is here. He knows what's going to happen and he's going to be their friend for the next million years, but they don't know that. And neither do you, but how could you?

They see other boys but don't know who they are. One is standing near the window. His name is Michael Lazarus and he is seven. His parents managed to keep him out of school for an extra year, but they lied to him. They told him they'd be back, but he can see them getting ready to leave town. He will not trust them again.

James and Jake know their parents aren't coming back until Christmas. They've been told. What they don't know is that their parents are dying a slow, painful death.

Joseph and May Nathan are at home. She's screaming, but no one can hear her. She takes a pair of scissors and cuts her hair, then looks at it then at her husband.

Joseph is not watching. He's looking at the ceiling and is screaming and demanding answers. None come. He looks at his wife and smiles, then they prepare to leave town and their son with the Powers That Be.

Matthew and Elizabeth Noland are also at home. Matthew is holding Esther and is looking at the hostel. He promises he'll never take his daughter to that hellhole even if they throw him in jail. He looks at his wife sitting on their bed in their one-room house and is amazed at what he sees.

Elizabeth is cutting her wrists, but no blood comes out. She cuts harder, but still there is no blood. She looks at him and the emotion bursts forth from his soul. He looks to the ceiling and screams. After a million years, he looks at his wife and she is looking at him. They smile, then get on with life.

Half an hour before James and Jake were admitted to the hostel, Edward William had brought his three children in. His wife, Rachel, chose to stay home this time. His sons, Abraham and David, were there before and knew what to expect. His daughter, Louise, was there for the first time.

Edward talked to the hostel administrator behind closed doors while Abraham leaned against the wall and David mimicked him. Louise watched her dad through the window and said nothing. She had on a new dress and a new pair of running shoes. Her hair was braided and her beauty was evident even at this early age.

After a few minutes, the two men emerged and Abraham automatically started walking down the long hall to the boys' end. David followed.

Edward looked at Louise and handed her a paper bag that contained the usual extra clothing and goodies. He'd already told her she has to stay and go to school and he explained why. But at that moment, all the reasons he gave don't mean a thing. She's scared and he's dying.

Click! Click! Click!

It was the sound of new shoes on linoleum. Edward knows who it is. It's the girls' supervisor and she's dressed in a white dress and looks like a nurse. She isn't. She's in her early sixties and is a widow from down south with no children. Her hair is as white as her skin and she looks like she hasn't smiled in her life.

Louise stands beside her father. He puts a hand on her shoulder as if to hold her one last time, or to protect her. She doesn't know which and neither does he. He wishes he could take her out of there and the thought is on his mind. He won't.

The old lady speaks to the administrator, then looks at Louise. There are liver spots on her pure white hands and a hint of blue in her hair. She takes Louise's hand. Her father's hand is still on her shoulder and he gives her one last squeeze, then lets go. It is at this moment that some unknown force thrusts itself into his chest, seizes his heart, and rips it out. He looks at the ceiling for an answer, but none will come and he knows it. He looks down at his heart and watches as it slowly stops beating. He looks up to see his only daughter being led down the long hall that never seems to end.

Louise follows the old white woman up the stairs and sees other girls standing with their backs to the wall. They turn and look at her with no emotion.

"Okay Sarah. You first," the supervisor says. "You've been here before."

Sarah is an older girl with hair past her shoulders. She's quiet and doesn't smile. She sits on the chair and the old white woman cuts Sarah's hair in front above her eyes and the rest just below her ears. Six months of hair falls. The last time her hair was cut was at Easter, and by the same old white woman. She silently promises when she has children, no one is ever going to cut her daughters' hair.

Louise wants to run, but she can't move. Her back is stuck to the wall. She wills the old woman not to cut her hair. She looks at the door, but she knows her parents are leaving town and are not coming back until Christmas.

Back at their house, Edward and Rachel William are quiet. She looks at him as though it's his fault. She knows it isn't, but she can vent her anger on no one else. Edward has no tears or sorrow. He has no heart. It's on the floor of that hellhole and it stopped beating like it has each time he took his sons there. Today it's different. Today he took his only daughter and it would break his heart, if he had one, but he doesn't. At least not today.

Louise watches Sarah's hair fall to the floor and before she knows it, it's her turn. It's over in fifteen seconds, and six years of hair lies on the floor. She's screaming, but no one can hear her. She's crying, but no one can see her tears. She's already gone Indian, only she doesn't know it. No one does.

"Take your clothes off and put them in a pile," the old woman says.

Louise keeps her head bowed. She is ashamed of what they are doing to her, but there's nothing she can do about it. She wonders if the other girls will laugh at her. She wonders if they'll tease and make fun of her. She looks up, but no one is looking at her. They are looking at the floor. The older girls have already taken off their clothes and are going to the old white woman. She puts something in their hair, then the girls march into the shower room.

Louise already feels naked without her hair as she slowly takes off her clothes and gently lays them on the pile. She keeps her head bowed and uses her peripheral vision to look at the other girls. She's darker than everyone else and wonders why. She walks to the old white woman, who puts some foul smelling oil in her hair. She's almost crying, but forces the tears down. She wants to grab her clothes, pick up her hair and run. She pushes her wants down with her tears and follows the others into the showers and watches what they do. Afterwards, she's given a towel and new clothes. They all have the same haircuts, the same blouses, dresses, socks and running shoes. They all look alike.

There's a girl standing alone in the corner. Louise knows her name is Brenda Jacobs. She's not as dark as the rest, she's whiter.

Brenda is looking at the others and wonders why she is so white. Why can't she be darker? Will they make fun of her like they make fun of white people?

The girls are herded into the dorm. Louise and Brenda wait until the others have selected their beds, then pick one. They're given numbers and commit these to memory.

A buzzer rings. They don't know it, but that buzzer will ring eight times a day for the next five-hundred million years. It will ring once at seven to get them up and again at seven-thirty to let them know it's breakfast time. It will ring at eight for school and again at twelve for lunch. It will ring at twelve-thirty for school and again at five-thirty for supper. It will ring at eight and nine to let them know it's time for bed. Eight if you're a junior, nine if you're a senior.

The new girls follow the example of the older girls. As they enter the dining room, they look for their brothers, but they all look alike.

They all look like porcupines. Boys look for their sisters, but they all look alike.

Louise sees her brother David and smiles. She looks at the boy behind him. He's not smiling. And neither is the boy behind him.

They all stand behind their chairs and look at the food and wonder what it is. It looks different and has no smell.

"Bow your head and fold your hands," someone says.

They watch and follow what the other children are doing.

"Lord, bless this food to our use and us to thy service and keep us ever mindful of the needs of others. Amen."

They'll say that prayer three times a day before each meal for the next eight years. They'll remember the prayer for the rest of their lives. They won't know what it means until years later, but by then the meaning will be meaningless.

After supper they'll stand, push their chairs in, bow their heads, fold their hands and say another prayer.

"For these and all thy many mercies . . ."

It's a different prayer, but they'll say that one three times a day too for the next eight years and will commit it to memory. And they'll never forget it. Even after they leave the hostel, they'll never forget it. And they'll never say it again. At least not out loud.

That night, they'll put on their pyjamas, line up, brush their teeth, wash their faces and then go to bed. The lights will be turned off and it will be totally dark for a few seconds. The only sound will be their breathing. It will be a long time before they close their eyes, and sleep will not come easy. They'll get up in the morning and the first thing they'll sense is the smell, or the lack of one. They'll open their eyes and realize it wasn't a dream. It was real.

"Time to get up. Dress, wash, then line up for breakfast," the supervisor shouts.

They follow his directions and no one says anything. They line up and are marched into the dining room and sit in the same place they sat yesterday. This is their place and they will keep it until the end of the year, sometimes longer.

Breakfast is lumpy oatmeal with powdered milk and toast. The milk will give them the runs for the first few weeks, but they'll get used to it. They have to.

After breakfast, there are chores, then school. In school, they will see other Indian children who are not in the hostel and will envy them. They'll never say it. Instead, they'll call them Town Kids and will call themselves Hostel Kids. They will take pride in this until such time as they become Town Kids, then they'll hate the Hostel Kids with a passion.

After school, there is time to play. There are soccer games, crab-ball, hide and seek and the ever-popular horsefight. During this time the children will get to know one another and will form friendships that will last a lifetime, and make enemies, if only for a short time.

Supper is some kind of meat that's dry and has no smell or taste. There are cold potatoes that also have no taste. There are vegetables that do not smell appetizing. They eat the meat and potatoes and hide the vegetables beneath their napkins. After supper, they go to the playroom until the supervisor tells them it's bedtime and they will once more get into their pyjamas, brush their teeth, wash their faces, then climb into bed.

Something is happening to them, but they don't know it. They are developing a routine and someone else is making decisions for them. Somewhere in the far distant future, they will be unable to make decisions for themselves and will rely on others to do it for them.

Something else has happened today. Today they will start counting the weeks until Christmas. As Christmas approaches, they will count the days. After Christmas, they will start counting the weeks, then the days, until Easter. After Easter, they will start the countdown until summer. Time has become important.

In the late hours of the night or the early hours of the morning, a sound comes from the hallway. It is a sound that they will hear for the rest of their lives.

Tick! Tock! Tick! Tock! Tick! Tock!

Part Two

The Awakening

Five

A Typical Night

Friday, September 24th, 1999
The old wolf watched as the pack moved into the hills. He'd seen it coming, but he'd given the younger male the benefit of the doubt. He shouldn't have. He was now alone and an outcast. He was also old and tired, but he didn't know that. He was just a wolf.

Click! Click! Click! Click!

His big, black cowboys boots hit the dirt road. His heels were well worn and his boots needed a shine. There was silver duct tape on the back of the left boot.

His steps were long, slow and deliberate, and he kept his eyes forward as if he were in deep thought. His black leather jacket, like his boots, had seen better days.

He had his hands in his jacket pockets. The two people he passed looked at him and smiled. He grinned and continued on.

He turned off the main road and walked to the large brown building. Only the sign over the large double doors gave any indication of what was inside: the Saloon.

He could hear George Jones singing one of his classics on the stereo as he walked up the steps. Boom! Boom! Boom! He stopped and checked his time — six o'clock. That meant seven and a half more hours until last call. He walked in through the first set of doors. Boom! Boom! Boom! Boom! Boom!

They all knew who it was, but they looked and waited nonetheless. They hoped it wasn't the Grim Reaper coming to kick ass. He entered the second set of doors. Boom! Boom! They all looked at his six-foot frame as if he owed them a living and wished the Grim Reaper would kick his ass, but only after he bought them all a beer.

James stood while his eyes adjusted to the light, then saw thirty or so people looking at him. They did that to everyone who came in. They were checking to see if it was their husband, wife, common-law, boyfriend, girlfriend, friend, foe, son, daughter or the one they laid last night. He was none of the above, so they all breathed a collective sigh of relief and went back to their drinks and their talk.

The Saloon was on Main Street and contained twenty tables, an old pool table, a bar and room for a hundred people. There was an old jukebox in the corner that hadn't worked since everyone converted to CDs. The forty-fives in it were already antiques, like most of the customers. There were no windows, and it was always dark, except for the last fifteen minutes of the day when the lights were turned on to scare the vampires and other blood-sucking critters back to their coffins. There was the unmistakable smell of cigarettes, beer, cheap perfume and some strong cleanser used to clean the bathroom. The cleanser would do its job for a few hours, then the smells would re-emerge from the walls, floors and ceiling where they'd been hiding.

The Saloon would never make the list of the ten best places to be. It was an Indian bar. People came here to drink, to look for possibilities and to bitch, whine or cry in their drinks — in that order. They also came to beg, borrow, whine, cry or demand a beer, smoke or the means from anyone and everyone. But that was normal. It was a fucking Indian bar.

A couple of people waved at James. They knew he was someone they could sit and gossip with because he'd shut up and listen. He didn't talk much, and if you told him something he didn't spread it around. He spread other things, but not gossip. Sometimes they wondered if he was listening at all. Some thought he was crazy. Others thought he was nuts. Most just left him alone unless they wanted to borrow money or bum a smoke. Or was it bum money or borrow a smoke? Either way, he wasn't going to see the smoke or money again.

"Hey, James, gimme smoke!"

He pulled out his pack and threw it on the table.

"Hey, James, len' me loonie!"

He heard but didn't listen and walked to the bar. Boom! Boom! Boom!

"Hey, James, buy me beer!"

He went deaf, then opened his black leather jacket and revealed a well-worn black shirt.

"Hi, James." *Wanna eat me?*

He looked up and saw Karen behind the bar. She was a few years older and kept herself in good shape. She was also married to an asshole and had four kids. The asshole worked here too. She smiled, then snuck a look at his crotch. He grinned and looked at her tits then at her crotch and didn't care if she saw. She wasn't wearing a bra and she was definitely not wearing panties.

"Usual?" she asked for the millionth time.

"Why not?" he answered for the millionth time and watched her pour two shots of vodka in a glass, add some water, then bend over to get his beer.

"That it?" she asked. *Wanna go in 'a back for a quickie?*

"Pack 'a smokes." *Wanna go in 'a back for a quickie?*

She reached up and pulled down his brand. The twenty he placed on the bar barely covered the cost, but she knew she'd make twenty off him tonight in tips. *Wish he'd slip his tip into me.*

"Hey, James, len' me loonie!" *You work for the Band.*

"Hey, James, gimme smoke!" *You owe us a livin'.*

"Hey, James, buy me beer!" *Weren't for us you'd have no job.*

James made it to his table without giving away shit, but it wouldn't last. A young girl wearing a dirty denim jacket and loose-fitting pants that she hadn't changed for a few days walked up. Her hair was messy and her skin was dark from walking around all summer looking for that next drink.

"Hey, brother," she slurred. "Len' me twen'y bucks." It was more like a demand.

"Ain't got none," he said.

"Doooooon' fuckin' lie."

He said nothing, hoping she'd leave.

"Come on," she begged, waited. "Gimme smoke, 'en," she demanded. She took the smoke he gave her. "Gimme light too."

He lit it for her and watched her hair fall over her face. She looked forty, though she was in her late twenties. She took a deep drag, then turned and walked away. "Asshole," she said.

James heard but didn't say anything. He lifted his glass and took a drink. The vodka burned his throat, but he didn't taste it, nor did he smell it. He chased it with some beer and settled in.

Mutt and Jeff, the town drunks, bums and lepers all rolled into one, picked that moment to walk in looking like Mutt and Jeff: right at home. No one looked at them. Everyone just wished they wouldn't sit at their table. They ordered a beer.

"Hey, James, you ol' fart," Jeff said as he walked over. "Wanna buy fish?" He and Mutt were dressed in old work clothes that had seen better and cleaner days.

"Not today," James said, and hoped they'd leave.

"Len' us some money, 'en," Mutt asked.

"Ain't got none."

"Doooooon' fuckin' lie," Jeff whined with all the self-pity he could muster.

"Come on," Mutt pleaded. After a few seconds, they knew James wasn't going to give them shit, so they left in search of other suckers.

James lifted his glass. It was empty. He wondered if they'd sucked it back when he wasn't looking, but he knew they hadn't. It still amazed him how fast he could drink when he wasn't watching. He got up and walked to the bar.

"Another?" Karen asked.

He nodded and she gave him another while he checked the time — six-thirty. He looked at her tits then at her crotch.

"Where's Brenda?" she asked.

"Home, I guess."

"She comin' tonight?"

"Not likely," he said. *She already came twice.*

He liked Karen, but she was too good for him. Or so he thought. He'd put the moves on her a few times, but they didn't do it. He looked around for some strange stuff and came to the conclusion that they were all strange and should all be stuffed. He looked at his drink and wondered if he drank it. He turned to Karen and smiled. "Whatcha doin'?" he asked. "Waterin' down 'a booze?" She laughed. "Gimme 'nother beer while you're at it," he said.

He took one more look at her ass before going back to his table and going off on one of his tangents. He could drink, smoke and carry on a half-assed conversation even when he was off on one of these tangents. He'd been off on one of these tangents for half his life. He checked his watch — seven. He checked his glass, then looked around for the culprits, but no one was sitting at his table. He got up and walked back to the bar and Karen poured him another.

"Another beer too," he said.

Back at his table, he tipped his glass back, then drifted off into the abyss. A few seconds later, he put his glass on the table and the bar was packed. He wondered where everyone had come from. He checked his watch and realized he'd time-travelled thirty minutes into the future.

He checked his glass and it was normal: empty. He walked to the bar, where Karen poured him another. He returned to his table and looked around to see if anything had changed, but nothing had. *I wish someone would shoot 'a shit with me.* Everyone looked at the door then at him. *Not her.*

Angie Lawrence floated in like she owned the place. She had on a clean pair of jeans and her own leather jacket and didn't look too bad if you didn't count her bloodshot eyes. She looked at him, then walked to the nearest man and talked to him and let loose a laugh. *See? Other men still think I'm good lookin'.* She went to the bar and ordered a beer, then joined a couple of girls who were sitting near the pool table. They were all looking for future husbands, or at least one for the night. They had come to the right place. The place was swarming with one-night stands, but no future husbands. Not unless you got knocked up, and even then it was a long shot.

James wondered how many times he'd caught the clap from her. She was ten years older and had two kids in Yellowknife. Rumour was she had two others who were lost in the system. Still, when he was high she looked good enough to eat. If she'd asked for a quickie, he might have done it. He knew there was no "might" about it. He would've. His little head had controlled him for most of his life. It still did. *Can't do it tonight. Been fucked twice 'nd got a new woman to boot.*

He looked at his glass, then made his way to the bar, where Karen had his usual ready. He checked the time — eight. *Time's flyin'.* He saw Liz Moses and Sarah James sitting at the bar and smiled. *When 'hey get here?* He wondered where Mary and Jake were. *Prob'ly takin' care 'a business. Wish somebody'd take care 'a my business.* He smiled at his sense of humour, then at Karen.

"What?" she asked.

"Nothin'," he said, then looked at her crotch.

The next thing he knew, he was walking to his table.

"Hey, James, len' me loonie!"

"Hey, James, gimme smoke!"

"Hey, James, buy me beer!"

Karen watched his ass, then turned to Liz and Sarah. "Might have to call Jake again," she said.

Meanwhile, James had returned to his table and Alfred joined him. "Hey, Al, how's it goin'?"

Alfred was his best friend, right after Jake. They'd grown up together, and often worked together. "It's goin'," he said.

James looked for a cigarette in his jacket. "Got a smoke?" he asked.

Alfred opened the pack on the table and gave him one.

"Whose smokes?" James asked.

"Yours."

"What's 'a time?"

"Eight-thirty."

"Already?" James tried to make a joke of it.

"You okay?" Al asked.

"Fuckin' A!" James lifted his glass and drained half of it.

"Need money?"

"Everybody needs money," he said, then stretched out.

Alfred pulled out five twenties and gave them to him.

"What's 'is?"

"You loan it to me las' week. Remember?"

"Thought I drank it," he said. "Wanna drink?"

"Sure, why not?"

James walked to the bar, then made his way back to his table. He put a beer in front of Alfred.

"Thanks."

"Not a prob."

James sat and time-travelled into the future. Someone was laughing. He looked across the table and saw two women. It took him a few seconds to place their names. *Lorraine 'nd Norma. Thirty-something going on fifty with three kids each and no husband in sight.*

"Did 'at really happen?" Lorraine asked.

He'd told them a story and it must've been a good one because they were laughing. Either that or they wanted to nail him.

"Yep," he said.

He checked his time — ten. He looked around and saw the same people he saw a few hours ago, a few days ago and a few years ago.

He closed his eyes and concentrated, then opened them. It didn't work. Shania wasn't sitting on his lap in her tight-fitting Spandex. He reached into his pocket and gave Norma a twenty. "Get me 'a usual 'n two beers for both 'a you," he said.

Norma walked to the bar in her tight-fitting Spandex that left nothing to the imagination. She disappeared into the fog and emerged ten times more beautiful and with a smile that just didn't quit. It was sort of lop-sided and told him she loved him and wanted him, but she knew he had another woman. She was also ten years and three kids too late, but that didn't keep her from trying. She rubbed her leg against his. *Maybe I'll get lucky tonight?*

James felt her leg and his little head came to life. *Maybe I'll get lucky.* He picked up his drink, then looked for his beer. *She forgot it. Strike one.* He went to the bar, where Karen was waiting and watching his crotch.

"Gimme beer 'n a pack 'a smokes," he said with a grin.

She opened the cooler and gave him a good look at what he was missing. She turned and he was eyeing her crotch. *Wanna sniff?*

He looked at her and smiled. *Lemme sniff.* He gave her a twenty, then turned serious. "Karen?"

"Yeah?"

"Wanna go to my place?"

"For what?"

"I've always wanted to fuck you."

"Really?"

"Really," he said, then grinned. "Wanna?"

"You sure?"

"Yeah."

She looked at her husband, Gary, who was looking at Tina. "Gary!" she shouted. Gary turned. "I know you're fuckin' Tina so me 'n James're gonna go to his place 'n fuck!" she yelled. "It's payback time!"

"Karen!"

She came back to reality and James was still standing there, but now he was looking at someone or something.

"Karen!"

She turned to her old man. *Asshole.*

"Gimme three Blues 'n two Canadian!"

Should give you a good kick to the balls.

James turned to see if Liz and Sarah were still there. They were and now they had company. *What's she doin' here?*

It was Louise. She was looking at him and not smiling. He looked away like he didn't see her. Then he saw the fog. He forgot about Louise and gathered his courage, then went on instinct and found his way back to his table, where Norma and Lorraine were waiting for him. *When did they get here?*

Lorraine took a sip of beer and looked around for possibilities. *Limited.*

Norma wished he'd ask. *I'll show you what you're missin'.*

He was about to ask but someone had put Dwight on the stereo and he was singing like he meant business. James tipped his glass back and the fog enveloped him and he time-travelled or went comatose. He didn't know which, nor did he care. All he knew was that someone was shaking him. *Maybe Norma's ridin' me again?*

"Hey, bro, wake up."

Jake. Am I gonna have to pack him out? Hope not, 'cause I'm drunk.

"Wake up," Jake said again.

"Yup."

"Where am are?" he asked as if it were a joke, but he already knew where he was.

"Same ol'."

"Knew 'at. What am doin' here?"

"Same ol', same ol'."

"Hey, bro, is 'at you?"

"Yeah. Let's go 'fore I have to carry you outta here," Jake said.

He heard some girls laughing and tried to picture Jake carrying him out. He couldn't picture it. He could only picture Jake dragging him since he was two hundred pounds and that didn't include his jacket and boots. "You 'n what forklift?" he said.

The girls laughed at that one too and he tried to collect his bearings, but they were shot to hell. "What's 'a time?" he asked.

"Twelve."

Still got hour 'n half to go. He saw three people behind Jake and tried to focus, but it was no use. He knew two were Liz and Sarah, but the other was a mystery. He stood, adjusted his jacket, then looked at the stranger. *What's she doin' here?* He put on his cool look and stretched to his full height and towered above them.

They had to look up to see him, but his face disappeared into the smoke and fog. He steadied himself, then looked around to see if anyone had seen him at his best, but no one had. No one would've cared if he was passed out, blacked out or croaked out. *Fuckers will roll me 'fore they check for vital signs.*

The Saloon was packed. It was payday for most, pension day for others and just another day for the rest. Angie was still sitting with the girls and she was looking at him. Doreen Aaron and Daniel Carson were sitting in the corner. She was looking at Daniel who was looking at his soon-to-be ex-wife.

James took a deep breath and almost choked. The smoke was thick up in the stratosphere. The smell of smoke, beer, piss, cheap perfume, mouthwash, Lysol and a million other aromas burned his nostrils. There was the faint smell of weed in the air. *Did I light one again?*

He was known to light up two or three and pass them around to see how fast they'd go. They usually made it three or four tables and Karen sold a lot of peanuts and chips after that. Karen was known to con a joint from him and light up with Liz and Sarah in the can. *Wish she'd smoke my joint.* He smiled at his sense of humour and the girls wondered if he'd finally go for broke and go nuts. He didn't.

"You ready?" Jake asked.

"No, but lead way, Kemo Sabe. Me follow," he said in his best Tonto voice, and the girls laughed at that one. *Hi ho, Silver, away!* "Where we goin'?" he asked for the hell of it.

"My place."

"What for?" he asked for the hell of it.

"Same ol'."

"Good, thought it might be for same ol'. Who's comin'?"

"The girls."

"Good, can't party 'lone. People might think we're alcoholics."

"You're not," Jake said. "You're a zombie."

"Rather be zombie 'an a drunk. Boris Karloff is my hero."

They all laughed at that one. He might be drunk, but he still had his sense of humour.

Liz and Louise each took an arm, Sarah broke trail, and Jake picked up the rear. James wanted to walk on his own. "I can walk," he said.

Liz and Louise continued to lead him to the door. He felt her hand on his arm and smelled her. She smelled the same as she did the night they sat in the theatre a million years ago. He had a boner then and was getting one now. He wondered what she'd do if he turned and kissed her. *Slap.* She was beautiful and had a smile ten times sexier than Norma's. He was getting excited, but he maintained his cool. *Cool Han' Luke.*

Louise hoped Daniel saw her, then came to the sad realization that that kind of thinking was petty and childish and she was no longer a child. She was a forty-million-year-old woman with a soon-to-be ex-husband and a child to raise. She time-travelled back to that day ten million years ago when she and James first kissed. She closed her eyes, wished and opened them. *Didn' work. Maybe later. Maybe never.*

James emerged from the fog and was on the road. *Where am I?* He saw Jake and Sarah and remembered Liz and Louise were holding him. He looked at Louise but didn't smile. He just wanted to look. Even with the scar on her lip, she was still the best-looking thing around. *Why'd I let you go?*

Louise sensed he was looking and turned. *Kiss me.* He didn't. She then put on some attitude, closed her eyes and turned to show she didn't care. *Why do I do 'at? I should tell him how I feel.*

James watched her look away, and became solemn.

When he came back from the darkness, they were walking on the back road and he had to get his bearings again. He looked around, got them focused on staying with the living.

"Hey, Liz," he said.

"What?"

"Howwwwwwww sssssick," he said, trying out that Fort McPherson accent. They laughed at his attempt.

"You gotta say it like 'is," Liz said. "Howwwwww sssssick."

"Gee iz bad," Sarah said, and they all laughed at that one.

"Maybe you got 'a little Gwich'in in you," Liz said.

"I wish I had a little Gwich'in in me," Sarah answered, and they all laughed. She looked at Jake. *Wish I had somethin' in me.*

Liz was Beth and Isaac Moses's daughter, and therefore Jake's first cousin. She and Sarah were in their late twenties, single and enjoying life. Or whatever life in Aberdeen offered. And that was not much.

James looked up at the night sky, then walked up Jake's steps. *When we get here?* He didn't worry about it. He walked in, sat on the sofa, and the fog returned. After a few seconds or minutes, it dissipated and he was back in reality.

Liz was laughing at something or another and Sarah was looking at Jake. He leaned back and his head touched someone's arm. *What's she doin' here?* "Sorry," he said. He didn't really mean it. *Wish you'd put your arms 'round me 'n kiss me.* She was looking at him with no emotion. He decided to go for broke. *What 'a hell can she do 'sides slap me?* He put his arm around her and, surprisingly, she didn't resist.

"Louise?"

"Yeah?"

"I love you."

She started crying. "I love you too," she said, then leaned over and kissed him. She stuck her tongue in his mouth and searched for his tonsils. She was going to try to rip them out like she had tried so many times in their younger days.

He came up for air and looked over at Liz and Sarah. They were looking at Jake and laughing at something he'd said. He looked at Louise and she too was looking at Jake and laughing. He'd been on one of his tangents, but he didn't worry about it right then. He had other things to worry about. Like the fog that was now coming out of the walls. A few minutes later, it dissipated and she was smiling at him. *Why she followin' me?* Before he could answer his own question, the fog returned, this time for good. *Come with me, Louise. Keep 'em away from me.* He wanted to reach out for her and was seriously thinking about it, but she was gone.

"I think he passed out," Liz said.

They picked up their cups and moved to the kitchen table while Jake stretched him out on the sofa.

Louise put a pillow under his head and smoothed his hair. She wished she could kiss him good night. She wished she could take him home. She wished she could do a lot of things. "Think he'll be okay?" she asked.

"He'll be okay," Jake said.

"Hey, Jake," Sarah called. "Got any good music 'sides Elvis?"

"There is no other good music."

"Yeah, right," she said. "Hey, Liz, where's your Vince Gill?"

Liz reached into her handbag and threw a tape to Sarah, who put it in the tape deck and Vince Gill started crooning.

"Vince can shack up with me anytime," she said. "Be skin 'n bones when I get through with him."

Louise went to the washroom and looked in the mirror. She was forty-something, dark skinned with a daughter and a worthless husband. She had scars, false teeth and lines around her eyes. *Where'd they come from? They weren't 'ere yesterday.*

She closed her eyes and time-travelled back to the day she and James first kissed in that crowded theatre in Helena. She thought it would be forever. It wasn't. She thought about Michael Lazarus and silently cursed him and hoped he was burning in hell. She remembered the many times she wanted to make things right. She would never get the chance now. She remembered the many times she hoped he'd call.

"Louise?"

James? It was Liz calling her back to reality and it still sucked. She looked in the mirror. *Twenty-seven years ago next month we went out. Was it 'at long ago?* She fixed her hair and walked into the living room.

"What was you doin' in 'ere?" Liz asked.

Thinkin' 'bout killin' myself. "Nothin'," she said, then looked at James. *He looks dead.* She looked at his crotch, then at his eyes. *He's dreamin'.*

James was not dreaming. He was having a nightmare. He was quiet on the outside, but on the inside some serious shit was starting to happen and he didn't want to be there. He wouldn't remember it tomorrow, but that was the least of his problems. He was here and now and it was as real as it could be.

He was in a room that looked familiar. Even the smell was familiar. *What is it? It smells like . . . Oh fuck, it's his room.*

He tried to turn, but he couldn't. Someone or something was keeping him there. He knew what it was. He knew who it was. He tried to move. He couldn't. He didn't want to look, but he had no choice. *Oh fuck, it's his hand!* Soft, warm, white and hairy. *Oh fuck, le' me out!* He was being led over to the bed. *Oh fuck!*

Six

Lost Souls

Saturday, September 25th, 1999
The old wolf hadn't eaten for a couple of days and then only a few mice. He was going to need more if he was to survive the winter. He thought about returning to challenge the younger male, but his wounds told him otherwise. He looked for the caribou. They would return. They always did.

The fog was so thick he could barely see. He heard the running water and bumped into something, or someone. The fog suddenly cleared. He was in the boys' shower room in the hostel.

He looked down just as the little boy looked up, and the first thing he saw was the boy's eyes: dead and empty. *Shit!* He tried to move. He couldn't. He was forced to watch as the boy took the soap and started scrubbing his body. His breathing slowed. *He's takin' a shower. That's all he's doing.* Suddenly his breathing stopped. Something was wrong.

The boy was scrubbing away his skin and blood was pouring out. *What 'a fuck!*

The blood was flowing down the drain. *The drain! That's a way out!* He tried to pull the cover off, but it was screwed into place and his hands were too big. He stopped. Someone was on the other side of the drain. *Mom?* She was covered in blood. *Oh shit!*

James opened his eyes. He was on Jake's couch. He wasn't breathing. He took a deep breath and almost choked. His head started pounding.

"Oh fuck," he said, and fought to control his breathing. *Same ol', same ol'*. He finally took a normal breath and heard Jake in the washroom. *Fuck, I need a drink.*

Jake came out and poured coffee from his old percolator that had gone out of style in the seventies along with his velvet painting of the King in his glory days that still hung on his wall. He placed two cups on the coffee table and turned on the television.

"Got any?" James asked.

"Diddly."

"I feel like shit."

"You look it."

"Thanks for your sympathy."

"Y'know where you can find sympathy."

"George 'n Angie come to mind."

Shit 'n syphilis. "Good one."

"What's 'a time?"

"After nine."

James sipped his coffee, then he lit a cigarette. "Someone shit in my mouth."

"Yeah, I know," Jake answered. "Was me."

After a few drags, James put out the cigarette and downed the rest of his coffee. He looked at the world. It sucked. When he knew he wasn't going to die, he went to the bathroom and looked at himself in the mirror. *I do look like shit.* He fixed his hair with his hands and stepped into Jake's living room.

"Whatcha gonna do?" Jake asked.

"Shave, change 'n have a cool one."

"I can live with 'at."

The sun was shining and the country was a mixture of yellow, orange and red. In a week or two, everything would be grey and dismal like their future. A few weeks after that, the snows would come and everyone would pray for spring.

As they walked, James checked his watch. In a couple of minutes most of the regulars would be going to the Saloon to quench their thirst. He needed a cool beer. He also needed a wash, shave and some major fumigation.

They saw Ernest Austin, who was working on his old truck, which like most things in this community had seen better days. Ernest was in his fifties and a heavy equipment operator and jack-of-all-trades. He was also a good hunter and a quiet man who kept to himself. That is to say, he minded his own business.

It was also Ernest who came to town with the news of the death of Jake's parents and sister thirty years before. That's when Jake, like James, became an orphan.

"Hey, Ernest," Jake called.

Ernest looked up. "Hey," he shouted. "You guys wanna go huntin'?"

"When?"

"Nex' week."

"Where?"

"Up river."

James looked at the river that made him an orphan when he was only twelve and silently cursed it.

"What for?" Jake asked.

"Elephants," Ernest answered. They smiled at that one.

"Sure, gimme call," Jake said.

"What 'bout you?" Ernest asked James.

"Why not?" he said. "Maybe you can put me outta my misery."

Ernest laughed. He didn't know if they'd go, but it didn't hurt to ask.

James's house was on the riverbank and had a good view of the river and the hills and mountains. The house was in good shape, but it needed another coat of paint. He was offered fifty for it, but was holding out for a hundred and only when he had other plans. Like a pension plan when he hit sixty. He put about as much faith in that as he put in winning the lottery.

He walked up the stairs and opened his door that he hardly ever locked. He had neighbours that would tell him who came calling and probably what they wanted. Harry and Agnes never went anywhere yet they knew everything about everyone.

His house, unlike Jake's, was a little newer, but did not have a woman's touch. Jake's house, while a lot older, was redecorated by Mary. His was a bachelor's pad and it showed.

He went into the bathroom and looked in the mirror. *I still look like shit.* He washed and shaved, then splashed on some aftershave while Jake slapped a tape into the stereo. Elvis started singing "Moody Blue." Jake worshipped the King and his music, even the last shit he did when he was fat and higher than a kite.

"Jake?" he shouted. "Look in my water container."

Jake went into the porch and came back with four beers. *Breakfast.*

James came out of the bathroom still looking like shit but feeling better. He made coffee and began cooking some bacon and eggs. He wasn't hungry, but he heard you stayed sober longer on a full stomach. *Nothin' ventured, nothin' gained.*

He took a beer and had a long drink before going to his bedroom to change his clothes. He remembered cashing his Unemployment yesterday, paying some bills then going to Brenda's. They sat around, she made supper, they fucked, and he left for the Saloon — alone. *Same ol', same ol'*. He looked out the window at the hills.

"Caribou be comin' soon," he said.

"So? You 'n me haven't gone out for . . . How long's it been?"

"Years," he said. He poured two cups of coffee and put some bacon and eggs on two plates. He put these on the table. "Dig in."

After they'd eaten, Jake washed the plates almost without thinking.

James realized they had learned that in the hostel. *Leas' we got somethin' outta 'at hellhole.*

He also realized it had been twenty-five years since they had left the hostel, and thirty years since they both became orphans, then brothers. They were rarely apart, except when Jake went to trades school to become an electrician and he went to college to get his diploma in business management. Some people actually thought they were brothers. They weren't, they were closer. Almost like father and son.

They opened the last two beers and James lit a smoke and time-travelled to the first time he and Louise kissed. He stood up, shook off the memory. It still sucked. He wondered why he thought about her. *She was drinkin' with us las' night. Wonder if I made an ass outta myself in front 'a her.* "I'm gonna take a quick shower," he said and was in and out in less than five minutes. "Whatcha gonna do today?" he asked Jake from his bedroom.

"Nothin' much. Sit around, 'en who knows?"

James knew what he was going to do. He was going to wait for Mary and they were going to do what kids do: hump. "Let's go look for strange stuff," he said, still looking like shit, but a well-washed shit.

Ten minutes later, they walked into the Saloon like they'd done a million times before. They stood and waited until their eyes adjusted to the light or lack thereof, then looked to see who was in and who wasn't. *Same fuckin' people.*

Twenty customers turned, looked them up and down, then went back to what they were doing.

Jake walked to their table while James checked the white board to see who was lucky enough to be barred out last night. The names listed were the same people he'd bar out if he had his own bar. He checked his time — quarter to eleven. *Fourteen 'n three-quarter hours till closin' time.*

Karen had on an old sweatshirt and a pair of loose-fitting jeans that didn't hide her small, compact body. She still looked good enough to eat. "What you like?" she asked and smiled. *Know what I'd like? Like you to stick your head between my legs, take a deep breath 'n go for it.*

I'd like to rip your pants off 'n eat you. "Two Blue," he said.

She took two beers from the cooler while he watched her ass. *Wonder what it be like to hold 'em while I jammed.*

She took the ten he left and watched him walk across the floor. *Wonder what it be like to wrap my legs 'round him while he jammed.*

"Hey, Karen, gimme Bud," said some inconsiderate bastard who didn't have the courtesy to allow her to finish daydreaming. *Asshole.* Gary wasn't doing his job. He was doing Tina and everyone knew it. *Fuckin' asshole. Gotta get a divorce 'n marry Crazy James 'n have crazy kids.*

"Hey, James, len' me loonie!"

"Hey, James, gimme smoke!"

"Hey, James, buy me beer!"

James made it to his table without giving away shit, then he and Jake tried to blend in with the stains on the wall. Before they could do it, John walked over with the look of hope on his face. He was hoping for enough for a beer. "Fill uncle in," he whimpered.

James didn't have any living relatives, but it was common knowledge that everyone was related to one another in Aberdeen. Or at least that's what they said. He dropped a five on the table. "Don' bother me again," he said.

"Aw c'mon, don' be like 'at," John whined as he grabbed the five and went straight to the bar.

James and Jake listened to the music without really listening. Randy did a few tunes, then Conway took over and sang about tight-fitting jeans, and Jake smiled through it all. *Hump City.*

Alfred, Greg and Kevin pulled up some chairs, then went brain dead. They were hungover and looking forward to that second beer that would make them feel a whole lot better than they did right now.

After a few minutes, Alfred asked the inevitable question. "What's up?"

"Same ol'," James answered.

They sat, guzzled and remained brain dead.

"Hey, Al, you're up!" someone yelled from the pool table.

"Good. You guys're talkin' my ears off," Al said. Kevin and Greg followed him to the pool table.

James kicked out his legs and stretched. He was getting sleepy and it was only eleven-thirty. He downed his beer. "Want 'nother?"

Jake checked his beer. "Later."

James got up and walked to the bar.

"Hey, James, len' me loonie?"

"Hey, James, gimme smoke?"

"Hey, James, buy me beer?"

Hey, James, wanna fuck?

Karen didn't say it out loud. She opened a beer, then watched his ass as he walked away.

James returned to his table and lit up a smoke. He looked at the young people playing pool and wondered if they knew there was more to life than Aberdeen. When he was their age he did nothing but drink, work and party. He was now his age and did nothing but drink, work and party. *Same shit — different decade.*

A few minutes later, Jake sat up. That could mean only one thing.

Mary Percy was wearing tight-fitting jeans with an oversized sweat-shirt and a multicoloured leather jacket that said Aberdeen First Nation on the back. Half the bar and two women looked and wished. Her hair was tied back, showing off her soft, brown, clear face. She almost brought tears to your eyes. "Hey, babe," she said to Jake then held his hand and looked at James. "Hey, James, how's it hangin'?"

"Long, hard 'n to the left."

She laughed. "Not accordin' to what Angie wrote on 'a bathroom wall."

"Angie can't write."

"Is 'at right?" she said.

"Can't even spell VD, but she can give it."

"James, that's not nice."

"The truth is not nice." He decided to shut up. *I'm goin' philosophical.*

Mary was still smiling. "I'm gonna talk to Karen," she said to Jake. "Don't leave without me."

Jake watched her walk to the bar and thought about taking her into the can and sawing one off. "Things are lookin' up," he said to no one. *And so is my pecker.*

James said nothing. *Things better start lookin' up. I gotta fin' a job before 'a snow starts flyin'. Might have to sell my house 'n move to warmer climes. Hey, an idea. Better get some booze up 'ere 'n kill 'at idea.*

He looked around and saw the same people buying the same beer talking about the same shit they were talking about last night, last week or last year. Regurgitating old stories they'd told or heard a million times. *Same ol', same ol'.*

It was only twenty after twelve and he was already on his fifth beer of the day and that was as dead as Angie's sex appeal so he went to get another.

Sometime later, half the bar looked at the door then at him. Figured it must be Dick and Ed with his big fucking cheque from Publisher's Clearing House. *The fuckers finally pulled my winnin' ticket!* He turned to look for Dick and Ed. *What she doin' here?*

Brenda's eyes adjusted to the light, or lack thereof, and she found herself being gawked at by twenty people. Some of the men were looking at her crotch. *Sickos.*

She spotted James and walked over to him, feeling safer. You *can look all you want only if you promise to eat later.* He had a grin like he knew what she was thinking and maybe he did. *Crazy people have magical powers.* She smiled at that one and sat beside him. *Wanna go nuts between my legs?*

He said nothing as he reached out to see if she was real. She was.

"Hi, Jake," she said, and held James's hand to her face.

"Hey," Jake said as if he was embarrassed to be caught in here. Or like she was going to chase his ass out of here with a switch.

She wondered if they still carded him. He was the same age as James but looked like a teenager. She was five months older. It felt like five hundred. "What's new?" she asked James.

It was a rhetorical question, so he gave a rhetorical answer. "Diddly."

"Need a favour," she whispered. "Nothin' 'portant." *Need you to look for my accent.*

"I can do 'at 'n what you mean, it's not important?"

He is *a mind reader.* "Not 'at," she said, then blushed and looked to see if Jake had heard.

He had, but he was thinking of doing Mary a "favour" and took his leave to get her home for a quickie. He smiled at the thought of getting her out of those tight-fitting jeans.

James looked at Brenda like she was a stranger. *What you see in me? A good fuck? What you see in Raymond Seele?* He time-travelled and hoped she wouldn't mind his leaving. She wouldn't, she was doing her own time-travelling.

What 'a hell do I see in you besides a good fuck? He was always quiet, like he was thinking or stoned. Even when she'd ask what was on his mind he'd say, "Nothing." Even now he was looking at her with nary a sign of recognition or emotion. *Did your mom drop you on your head?* She immediately regretted that, knowing he didn't have a mom. At least not anymore. *Orphan.*

She remembered the time she was still married and living in Yellowknife and someone asked if she'd seen him. "Who?" she'd asked.

"James Nathan."

"What's he doing here?"

"Goin' to college."

She didn't think he had the brains, but apparently he did because he was one of very few who successfully completed the program. She did see him once or twice and said hi and that was it.

After her divorce she returned to Aberdeen, and realized there was more to him than met the eye. He was intelligent and had a good sense of humour, albeit risqué. He didn't say much, but when he did, you had to listen because you never knew what the hell he was going to say next.

She time-travelled to the day she invited herself to the Band offices and then to the Saloon with him. They sat with Liz, Sarah, Louise, Jake and Alfred and she generally felt out of place.

She knew Louise and James went out in high school before Louise married Daniel. Rumour was she was getting a divorce. Louise had jet-black hair and dark brown skin and was beautiful despite the scar on her lip. *I wish I looked like that.* They were the same age but were never close friends. *Wonder if she still loves him. Wonder if he still loves her. Did they? Of course they did. Wonder if he knows about me 'n Raymond. Course he does.*

Later that evening, when she thought no one was watching, she asked James, "Wanna walk me home?"

He grinned as if he knew what she wanted. "When?"

"Now."

He finished his beer, then stood. "Gonna walk Brenda home. I'll be back."

He did not look at anyone, but the look on Louise's face told Brenda what she didn't want to know: she was still in love with him. Or was she? It was hard to tell.

As they walked out, she noticed most of the bar watching them.

They stepped out into the open air and she put her hand on his arm. "Why'd everyone look at us?" she asked. *Do they know we're gonna fuck?*

"They do 'at to everybody."

She wondered if this was a good idea. Whatever her doubts, she didn't back out. And she didn't want to. They got to her place and didn't waste any time. They got down to business and fucked.

That had been last winter and she'd made no demands on him or his time. He came around almost every day and left for the Saloon or home afterwards. She always invited him to stay the night and he always said he'd be back, but he never did.

She went to the Saloon a few more times with him, but she wasn't into drinking since it made her sick the next day. She did invite him for supper at her parents'.

"I asked James to come for supper," she told them.

"James who?"

"James," she answered. "James Nathan."

They looked at her like she was nuts.

"He's still with Angie?" her mom asked.

"Angie who?"

"Angie Lawrence. She said they were gonna get married."

"No," she said. "He's with me now."

They didn't say too much after that and greeted him with polite conversation. They ate in the living room while she and James ate in the kitchen. She was quiet, solemn.

"What's wrong?" he asked.

"My parents," she said, then tried to smile.

"I could've told you."

"I don't care, I love you." The tears came.

"Me too," he said.

He stayed that night. The next morning she watched him sleep and could tell he was dreaming. She put her head on his chest and wondered if he was going to have a heart attack, or jump up and go nuts. He opened his eyes and started coughing. He caught his breath, then looked at her.

"Brenda?"

She snapped out of her daydream. "Yeah?"

"What favour?" he asked.

Suck me, fuck me, whatever. "Nothin' much," she said. "Tell you later." *After you suck me 'n fuck me. I'm turnin' into a slut! James Nathan's slut.*

He shrugged and looked at his watch — twenty after one. He wasn't going to make it till closing time and she knew it too.

"Wanna grab a case?" she asked. *You can do me at my place.*

"Sure," he said. *I can do you at your place.*

He got up and walked to the bar while she went to the door. Half the bar looked at her then at her crotch. *Sickos.* She waved to Mary and Karen and did not see James slipping sixty bucks into Jake's shirt pocket.

"Take two to my place," he said to Jake. "Gimme case 'a Blue," he said to Karen. *And a blowjob to go.*

Karen watched them leave, knowing they were going to fuck. *Anybody wanna fuck* me?

A million eyes watched as James left with Brenda on one arm and, more importantly, a case of beer under the other. If they'd known he was going home, half a million legs complete with bodies would be over at his place faster than you could say "free beer."

James and Brenda barely got their eyes accustomed to the daylight when they bumped into Mutt and Jeff. They who were in the same clothes they were in last night. They were also in dire need of a Maury makeover.

"Hey, Brenda, wanna buy fish?" Jeff asked.

"Where?"

"Still swimmin'," Mutt answered.

"Pay you when I get 'em," she said.

"How 'bout down payment?" Mutt asked James, who gave them one each.

"Is 'at all?" Jeff whined.

"Don' have to take it," James answered.

They took the beers and disappeared.

Brenda took James's arm and they walked by the Band offices where half the town was getting their bingo cards for the afternoon game from Sarah. *Gimme my lucky cards.* There was another game tonight, but they'd come back for those cards later. Brenda bought two.

Half the people looked at James and Brenda and wondered, what the hell is this world coming to? *Crazy fucker. Stuck-up bitch.* They thought about it for all of one second, then realized they weren't in the running for no Nobel prize and got back to choosing their lucky cards.

Tonight's my lucky night. Got close yesterday. Had one number left. Me too.

When they got to her apartment, James put the beer in the fridge and opened two. He sat on the sofa and started channel surfing. He found his favourite movie then muted the sound.

"It's thirty minutes after one," Liz said on the radio. "Bingo cards can be picked up at the radio station or from Gina's on Sesame Street. We also have two hundred-'n-fifty-dollar Nevada cards at the radio station. Bingo starts in half an hour."

James pictured Liz sitting in the little radio station. She was more like a sister, but he'd never know. *Don't have a sister. Never have a sister.* She and Sarah had partied with him a million times and usually crashed at his place. They even slept with him in his bed, but nothing happened. Or so they kept telling him. He knew it didn't, but he'd usually joke about it.

"Why am I tired?" he'd ask.

"How sick!"

"How come it's so small 'is morning?"

"Sick!"

He remembered waking up last winter with the feeling that someone was watching him. He looked at his bedroom door and saw Louise. He wondered if she was a dream. She wasn't. She was real and she was beautiful.

"I'm sorry," she said. "Didn't mean to wake you."

"Not a prob." He hoped he looked better than he felt. He couldn't remember them bringing him home the night before. "Where's Liz 'n Sarah?"

"In 'a other room."

"Where's Jake?"

"On 'a couch."

He got up and washed, then went into the kitchen. She handed him a cup of coffee. She had tears in her eyes.

"What's wrong?" he asked.

"Came home 'n found Daniel in bed with Doreen."

He opened his arms and she moved into them like she belonged. She cried for a few seconds, then went silent. He wished he could've kissed her, but he didn't. He remembered the day she'd called after he'd kicked the crap out of Daniel for beating her up. She told him to stay out of her life.

"James?"

"Yeah?"

"James?"

He came back to reality and was sitting on Brenda's couch. She had her head in his lap and had that "give it to me" look. She held on to his neck and moaned as they came together, then she put her hands on his ass and kept him in her. *Wonder if we'll have crazy kids.* His hair was messy and he had a crazy grin. *He does look crazy.* "I love you," she whispered, then arched her back as if to get him deeper. "I wish we could stay like 'is forever."

"B-4," Liz said from the living room.

"Bingo!" Brenda yelled. She grabbed her pants and T-shirt, then ran into the living room and called Liz at the radio station. "How much numbers you call?"

"O-72, N-34 'n B-4," Liz said.

Brenda daubed the numbers on her cards.

"Who's 'is?" Liz asked.

"Brenda."

"What you doin'?"

"None 'a your business," she said out of breath and laughed.

"Geez, you guys. It's 'a middle afternoon, for God's sake!"

"So?"

"Sew your dirty underwear," Liz said and hung up. "Under the G-48," she said on the radio, "G-spot! Gee iz bad!"

By the time James had a quick shower, Brenda was already into her second game. "Any luck?" he asked.

"I won 'a first game with four people." She smiled.

"How much?"

"Twen'y bucks. Another hundred thousand games 'n we can retire."

We? He downed his beer, then got another and watched Dave take on Hal in the silence of space while Liz called out bingo. He laid his head on the pillow and was out. *Hello, dreams.*

Brenda wondered if he'd stay the night. She wondered if he'd make a good father. Not that she'd ever have any more kids. Besides, she knew he'd had his tubes cut. *Been there, saw it, sucked it. Brenda, you are a fuckin' slut.*

She thought about someone else, but Liz kept calling her back to reality and for that she was grateful. She'd been thinking about her far too much in the last few months. *Wonder what the hell's gettin' into me. Was it the move back to Aberdeen? Was it the water?*

"I-17," Liz said, and Brenda daubed.

It was two-thirty, and Mutt and Jeff were carrying their catch up the bank in a galvanized tub. They had a good haul and would make a hundred dollars, enough for a bottle, a pack of smokes and a few rounds at the Saloon.

Mutt gave his opinion on life by letting loose a long, wet fart. "Ouch. I think I blew myself a new arsehole," he said, then burst out laughing.

"You *are* a new arsehole," Jeff said.

An hour later, they were at their shack drinking, smoking and listening to the bingo game hoping someone they knew would win so they could hit them up for a non-repayable loan.

"Wonder how many people had one number lef'?" Jeff asked.

"Everyone 'a them," Mutt said, and they both laughed.

Around four-thirty, their bottle was as dead as their sex drive, so they decided to try their luck at the Saloon. They were both feeling good but not yet drunk, and that's what they were shooting for.

"I know where Sam's booze is," Jeff said as they walked to the Saloon.

He didn't have to say any more. They were so much alike they even thought alike. They were going to borrow Sam Hunter's booze whether he liked it or not. They were going criminal.

His mother's long black hair was blowing in the wind. She was smiling and holding out her arms, enticing him to come to her. He started running, but he couldn't run fast enough. The fog was everywhere.

He stopped and listened. Then he smelled it. *His breath!* He turned just as the hand touched his shoulder. He wanted to run, but something was holding him. He felt the other hand and jumped. *Fuck sakes!*

James almost fell off the couch. He stood and looked around for Brenda. *Did she go into the Dream World?*

When he'd calmed down, he got another beer and put the empty in the case by the garbage. He checked the time — five-thirty. *Eight hours till closin' time.* He thought about the dream. *Fuck it. Can't remember it, can't hurt you.*

A car pulled up and Brenda walked in carrying a couple of shopping bags. "How was your sleep?" she asked.

"Good," he lied.

"Want somethin' to eat?" *Wanna eat me?* She smiled. *Geez, I've gotta stop thinkin' like a slut.*

He smiled as if he knew what she was thinking. "Whatcha got?"

Me. "Moose meat," she said.

"Sounds good."

She busied herself in the kitchen, then sat beside him and laid her head on his shoulder. *Wonder what would happen if I put his head between my legs then cut off his medication. Ride 'em, cowgirl!*

"I'm goin' to Yellowknife on Monday," she said.

"Yeah?"

"Got an interview for a job," she said. *I gotta get outta here too. I'm turnin' into a whore 'n a slut.* "You should come with me," she said. "If I get it."

He shrugged.

"I love you," she added. "That's why I'm askin'."

"It's a big move. Never lived nowhere's else."

"You lived in Yellowknife when you went to college."

"That's different. I was comin' back."

She went into the kitchen and returned with two plates and they ate in silence. Afterwards, one thing led to another and they were rutting again. She looked into his eyes as if she was trying to hypnotize him into staying the night. She'd have done it too if it wasn't for a knock on the door. She pulled on some clothes and answered it.

Liz looked at her messy hair. "Geez, you guys," she said. "Is 'at all you do?"

Yeah, that's all we do. "Come in."

Liz and Sarah were having a beer when James came out and took one from the fridge. They were smiling at him, knowingly.

"Bite me," he said.

They laughed while Brenda looked for a way to disappear. She wasn't wearing any panties and her pants were now sticking to her thighs. She wondered why they never did anything else. *What 'a hell's to do 'sides drink, dab 'n fuck? Take English lessons?* She wished she were back in Yellowknife. She wished she had some panties on.

Mutt and Jeff walked out of the Saloon at eight o'clock and were in their natural environment: the dark. They'd spent most of their money and had worn out their welcome what with being in their goofy stage and all. Jeff kept enough money for two beers just in case their heist didn't pan out, but he had no reason to think it shouldn't. *Not 'a first time we did 'is.*

"How much is 'ere?" Mutt asked.

"Leas' a case."

Mutt smiled as he thought about getting drunk for the next few days without having to work for it. He didn't think about the ethics of borrowing from Sam. He was a bootlegging old fart and an asshole. *Fucker deserves it.*

Liz was getting restless. "You guys wanna go to 'a Saloon?" Liz asked.

"Not me," Brenda said. "Got things to do." *I also gotta change my pants 'n get some panties.*

"What about you?" Sarah asked James.

"Sure, why not?" he said and put on his jacket.

Brenda watched them walk into the night. She felt her pants sticking to her thighs and thought about taking them off and showering, but decided not to. She felt like a slut and wanted to enjoy that feeling for a while longer. *James Nathan's slut.*

"You okay?" Sarah asked James as they walked to the Saloon.

"Yeah, why?"

"Thought you might not have any strength lef'."

"Could go all night 'n 'en some."

"Ol' fart like you should be glad to get it up once a month," Liz said and laughed.

"Ol' fart like me can do it all day 'n still have room for Jell-O."

They laughed at that one but shut up when two figures crossed the street and disappeared into the night.

"Who's 'at?" Liz asked.

"Beats me," James said. "Go fin' out."

"Yeah, right. Might be some pervert."

"So be gentle on 'im," he said, and they laughed again.

As they walked up the steps of the Saloon they could hear the music and the steady hum of people talking, yelling or screaming. They walked in. The smell of smoke, beer, sweat and wasted dreams hit them in the face.

Karen looked at James's crotch, knowing it was already dipped, but what the hell. It didn't hurt to fantasize about him drilling her in the back while half the town cried for a beer and the other half cried in theirs and she cried for more.

"Double 'n three beers," James said, then looked at her crotch. *Num. Num this.*

Liz and Sarah took a beer and went in search of possibilities. James stood by the bar and looked around for the ten millionth time. *Same shit — same shitters.* He spotted Jake sitting with Alfred, Kevin and Greg, then took a deep breath and swam across the sea of misery holding his beer aloft in case one of the sharks took a bite out of it.

"Hey, James, len' me loonie!"

"Hey, James, gimme smoke!"

"Hey, James, buy me beer!"

Hey, James, eat me!

That was Angie and she was doing pretty good, considering. She'd woken up that morning, had a shower, then squeezed into her tightest-fitting jeans only to find she needed a coat hanger to pull up the zipper. She thought about getting a patent on her new invention, but realized there was already one in the ladies' room. *Prob'ly seen more crotches 'an James 'n Jake combined.* She looked at Jake. *Wonder if I should fuck him to make James jealous.* She shook that thought off. *He's jus' a kid.*

Jake smiled at James. "Hey, bro, what's up?" he asked.

"Clap rate," James answered, then sat up and took a shot of vodka.

"Hey, James, what's up?" Kevin asked rhetorically.

"Diddly."

"Hey, James," Greg said. He looked stoned and drunk. "Tell us a good one."

"What am I? A fuckin' Elder?"

"Well, you are older 'n you're always fuckin' somethin'."

"Well, since you put it 'at way," James said. He looked at his glass and concluded that the Saloon had gremlins: alcoholic gremlins. They'd sucked his glass dry when he wasn't looking. He looked at the foursome and wondered if they'd noticed the little fuckers. He downed half his beer, then looked at Greg. "Y'know Mutt 'n Jeff?"

"Yeah?"

"Kiss their arse."

Alfred and Jake burst out laughing, but Kevin and Greg didn't get it at all.

"Is 'at it?" Kevin asked.

"What you want?" James asked. "Richard Pryor?"

"Who's Richard Pryor?" Greg asked.

"Kids," James said with disgust, then got up to get another.

He looked for the gremlins but found nothing on Karen's tits or near her crotch, but it did look enticing. He returned to his table to count the hours then the minutes until closing time.

It was eight-thirty and Mutt and Jeff were sharing a smoke.

"Y'know where it's?" Mutt asked for the hundredth time.

"Yeah, I know," Jeff said for the millionth time as they walked down the bank to their tent. He got a small paper bag then went into the willows. "Gotta crap," he said.

"So?" Matt replied. "Wan' me to hol' your han'?"

"Fuck you."

After Jeff did his duty, they walked along the willows, keeping an eye out for Sam's house.

"Whatcha got in 'a bag?" Mutt asked as they crouched in the willows.

"Shit."

"What 'a fuck you're gonna do with it?"

Jeff giggled. "Leave it for Sam."

"You crazy?"

"Like a fox."

"Smell like one."

"Fuck you."

After all was said and done, it was easier done than said. They snuck up behind Sam's house and kept an eye on his window while they looked for telltale signs of an alarm and found the empty bottle on the boat. Mutt removed the bottle and lifted the boat, and Jeff removed four bottles and took the only case of beer. He put the soggy paper bag in the empty case, then replaced Sam's warning system, and they faded into the darkness like born criminals. Or so they thought.

They stashed four bottles of beer and two bottles of vodka at their tent and took the remaining two bottles and eight beers up the bank and hid them behind James's house.

"What now?" Mutt asked as they each guzzled a beer.

"Let's go to 'a Saloon."

"Got 'nough?" Mutt asked.

"'nough for two. Maybe we can sell one or two?"

"Why?"

"'Cause we can sit 'round longer. I might get lucky."

"Oh," Mutt replied. He didn't pick up on the "I" part.

They walked into the Saloon at nine-fifteen and the smell of beer and smoke hit them like an aphrodisiac. Mutt even managed a little hard-on before it died like so many of his dreams.

Jeff got two beers and gave one to his accomplice. He looked around the bar. *Criminals! That's what we are! Fuckin' criminals! I'm Al Pacino in* The Godfather! He saw Jake and James and nudged Mutt, then walked over to their table. "Mind I join you?" he asked and sat down before they could answer. He looked around to make sure no one was listening, then leaned towards James.

"Ain't got none," James shouted.

"You don' even know what I'm gonna say," Jeff whined. "Got two crocks 'n six beer to sell," he yelled into his ear.

"Bullshit!" James yelled back.

"I'm serious. Wanna sell two," he whined.

"Bullshit! You had it, you'd be drinkin' it."

"Need beer money," he moaned.

James looked at Jeff, then at Mutt, then at Jeff. "Bullshit."

"Hey," Jeff yelled to Mutt. "Tell 'im what we got."

"Four bottles 'n case 'a beer," Mutt shouted. *We're fuckin' criminals, man. Don't you be messin' with us. I'm James Caan in* The Godfather — Part One!

"Four?" James said. "This guy says two."

"Got two near your house," Mutt shouted. "Got two down 'a bank."

James knew they were crooks and thieves, but they'd never cheat him. "Give you eighty!" he shouted.

"Fuck 'at noise!" Jeff shouted.

"Give you sixty!"

Jeff looked confused. He held his hand out. "Eighty."

James looked at his outstretched hand. "You wan' it now?"

"Damn right," Jeff yelled. "For eighty we wan' it now." *We weren't born yesterday, ya know.*

"You guys better be straight," he said as he reached into his pocket.

"We're not lyin'," Jeff said as he took the cash. "When you goin' home?"

"Sooner or later, but not before."

"What?"

"Soon," James yelled. "Where you get it 'n why you sellin' it?"

"We borrowed it," Jeff yelled into his ear and left some spit and other shit.

Fuck, now I gotta get a tetanus shot. "Don' wanna know!" James shouted. "Put it in my water container 'fore I go home!"

"We're gonna finish our beer firs'!" Jeff shouted.

Jake's mind wasn't on the conversation he couldn't hear. He was getting high so he just nodded his head at what was being discussed and kept looking at Mary.

Half the men and Kim and Andrea, the only two lesbians in Aberdeen to come out of the proverbial closet, also watched every time she moved. Then they looked at Jake, hoping he'd crash and burn so they could make their move. They were all going to turn into movie stars and soon. *Another drink 'n we get better lookin'. Gimme a bottle 'n I'll look like Mel 'n take her home. Gimme bottle 'n I'll look like Melissa 'n take her home.*

Jake and Mary had taken two cases of beer to James's then had a quickie. He was tired, half-cut and still horny. He stood and walked to the bar to carry on his love affair. *What you see in me? I know what I see in you. Me.*

Meanwhile, Mutt looked at Jeff, who looked at Mutt, who looked at James, who despite the time still had some control of his mental faculties, but just barely. Jeff downed his beer and walked to the bar and Mutt followed.

James finished his beer, then checked the time. *Ten! Where 'a fuck it all go?* He looked for Liz and Sarah and spotted them sitting with Louise, who was looking at him. *Wonder I should join 'em. Nah, might say somethin' crazy. Crazy James might say somethin' crazy. Redundancy at its best.* He smiled and looked around and saw the same fucking people. He thought about going home or down to Brenda's. *Fuck it, need 'nother drink.* He was about to get up when Angie joined him from out of nowhere. *Holy shit, a stalker! I got my own stalker! Call Jerry! Call Jenny!* She was liquored up looking to get licked up and she looked good. That was a clear sign he was getting drunk.

"Buy me beer," she demanded, then smiled.

It worked because he was now thinking about getting laid. He reached into his pocket and found nothing but loonies, twoonies and assorted small change.

"Gimme 'at," she said and dumped it into her hand, then walked to the bar. *Cheap bastard. I'm worth more 'an 'at. I'm use to champagne 'n caviar, not fish eggs 'n beer.*

Louise looked across the crowded bar at James and promised herself she'd tell him soon, new woman or not. *Fuck it, it's now or never.* She pushed her way across the sea of human waste and came to his table. "James?"

He looked up at her like she was a dream. "Yeah?"

"I'm still in love with you!" she shouted.

He stood up, took her in his arms and kissed her. "I love you too," he said. "But why didn't you tell me sooner?"

"I have!" she said. "Can't you read my mind?"

He grinned. "My mind-readin' capabilities are shot to hell."

"Can we try one more time?" she asked as the tears started.

He kissed her tears and she closed her eyes.

"Louise?"

Louise opened her eyes and looked at Sarah. "Yeah?"

"I ask if you wan' 'nother beer."

"Sure, why not, can't dance." She looked at James and he was still looking at her. *Is he nuts 'n crazy? He didn't act nuts 'n crazy when we went out. He just fucked everythin'. Fuckin' nuts 'n fuckin' crazy? Wonder if he'll leave with me if I ask. Geez, I'm startin' to act like Angie.* She wondered what she was doing there. *I don't drink. At least not 'at much 'n I never got drunk in my life. Do I just like to hang with peeps who're havin' a good time?* She looked at Liz and Sarah. *Why do I hang with 'em? They hang with James, that's why.*

Daniel sat in the corner with Doreen looking at his ex, who was looking at James. *Bitch! Crazy fucker!* He got up and walked to the bar and pulled out a twenty as if there was more where that came from.

Louise wondered what she ever saw in him. *Tall, dark 'n handsome, like James. A drunk 'n a womanizer, like James. An abuser, not like James. Would James have hit me if we were married?* She looked at him across a million miles of space and time and willed him to walk over, pick her up and take her out of there. He didn't, and she died a little more.

Brenda was lying on her sofa watching *Dances with Wolves* and still had her bottle of beer on the coffee table right next to a cup of coffee. She wished she'd gone with James, Liz and Sarah, but she didn't care for that type of nightlife. She'd hated smelling like stale beer and cigarettes. It wasn't worth it. She picked up her beer and looked at it. *What power do you have on people?* She dumped it down the sink and put the bottle in the empty case by the garbage. *Empties. Empty heads. Empty lives.*

She wondered how many women James had been with. *A hundred? Who knows?* She'd been with only four men in her life. Well, five now. The only men she'd been with in the last twenty years were her husband, Earl, and James.

She'd asked Julie about him when she began working at the Hamlet and was told about his wild and crazy ways. *Did Julie fuck him? Wouldn't surprise me.* The stories she heard about him were proving to be more fact than fiction. So why'd she get together with him.

Something about his quiet manner and roguish charm came to mind. *A rogue. Who're you? Han Solo? Who am I? Princess Leia? Who is Jake? C3PO? Who knows? Maybe you're just a good fuck and nothin' more. Geez, I'm really startin' to think like a slut.*

She'd spent the night at his house twice and had seen some of his drawings. She especially liked one drawing of a woman's face. It was incomplete except for the eyes. When she'd asked who it was, he shrugged and said, "No idea." She later realized it looked like Louise, or at least Louise's eyes.

With a sigh, she came back to reality. She was glad she'd told him about the interview and her intention to move if she got the job. She hoped he'd leave with her.

She pulled out one of her yearbooks and looked for him. He was tall, dark and quiet, and he hardly smiled even back then. He had very few friends, except Jake and Raymond.

She looked at Raymond's picture. *Why did you do it? Did I have something to do with it? I never told you. I didn't even tell you I was leaving.*

She'd never told anyone but her parents why she had to drop out of school and move to Yellowknife. At least not yet. *Did he know? Does anyone know?* She was fifteen in November of 1973 when she got pregnant. She told her parents and they told her to marry him, but changed their mind when they found out Raymond was seventeen and still in school. They paid her way to Yellowknife so she could have the baby and give it up for adoption.

While in Yellowknife, she lived with one of her cousins, found a part-time job and waited for her baby to arrive, and when it did, she almost kept it. But good girls did not have babies out of wedlock in those days and she gave her to a good family. The last she heard they were somewhere in Ontario and her daughter was now twenty-five. *Where did all the time go?*

Her part-time job turned out to be permanent. She met Earl Borman a few years later and they were married. Michelle came along in 1980. She often wondered if she should tell Earl about her other daughter.

Why open old wounds? Does my daughter ever think about me? Does she wonder about the woman who gave birth to her then gave her up? Does she wonder if I loved her? I loved her so much that I gave her up. She'd often thought about making a couple of phone calls, but couldn't. She knew if her daughter ever called she'd gladly meet her, but she couldn't make the first move. *That move is up to you, wherever you might be.*

She turned back to her movie and prayed James would show up, but she knew she'd lost him to his other love, the bottle. *What am I gonna do? I go to Yellowknife. With or without James? Don't matter. With or without, I'm going. Do we have a future together? Will he always be a drunk like my parents say he is? What will Michelle think of him? Would he be surprised at my other daughter? What would he say if I told him Raymond was the father? How do I tell the daughter I might never see about the father she'll never know?*

"Geez, I gotta get outta here before I go crazy 'n start talkin' to myself." *I* am *talkin' to myself.* "I am goin' crazy," she said. She pushed her thighs together. *I need panties.*

Mutt and Jeff left the Saloon and put the two bottles and six beers in the empty water container on James's steps. It was eleven when they swaggered back into the Saloon. They were still half-cut and full of adrenaline and other solvents and maybe some homebrew.

The bar was louder and smokier than ever, and most of the patrons were getting to the point of being cut off for the rest of the night. Four couples were dirty dancing to an old George Jones tune. When the night had begun, they were all like Travolta and What's-her-face in *Saturday Night Fever*. Now they were better. *Get me an agent. Look out, Hollywood.*

Mutt and Jeff rejoined James and Jake at their table. James frowned at them. *Are they part of my nightmares come to life?* He looked at Mary and Jake, who were smiling at each other.

Mary was tired of the smell of beer and smoke and Jake was high and horny. "Wanna go?" he asked.

"Sure," she said, then looked at James. *Drunk or stoned? Can't tell. Both.* "Hey, James, we're gonna go. Wanna come?"

James had a good comeback for that one. *Used it a million times already.* "Not yet. Gonna go home later," he said.

Mary looked at Angie. *Wonder if they're gonna do it. Nah, he's not that drunk. Or is he?* She looked at Jake. *High, but good for a couple of rounds in the sack.* She smiled.

Jake felt hornier than a double-horned moose during rut. He looked at Mary's tight-fitting jeans and decided to buy her a pair one size smaller. He'd switch them on her one of these days and watch her squeeze into them. He realized he was high. He was going to jump her tonight and he needed his senses to do that.

Angie was hoping James would hump her. It had been a week since someone had tried and she was hornier than a horny toad in heat. She knew better than to make a scene if she was going to get lucky. *Hope he don' remind me of his broken windows or 'a clap. Hope he got some safes. Fuck it, hope he don't. Maybe he'll knock me up 'n marry me.* She had to remind herself her reproductive functions were retired. Besides, the crazy fucker had had a vasectomy. She wished he'd buy her a beer. The last time she went to the can, she didn't look half as good as she'd hoped. *A couple more 'n I'll look like Nicole Kidman.*

James knew he should head home, or down to Brenda's, but his big head and his little head were battling for control over his common sense. His big head was losing. The few million beers he'd drunk didn't help. He hoped word didn't make it back to Brenda. *I wish I had some safes. I hope she ain't got 'a clap again. I hope I nailed somethin' to my window in case she decides to air condition my house again. I wish I had a bigger dick. I wish I was sober. No, I don't. I wish I weren't as drunk. I wish I could stop talkin' to myself in my head. Wish in one hand 'n shit in the other! Fuck you!*

"What a lively bunch for Saturday night," Jeff yelled.

"What?" James said.

"It's in your water container," Jeff shouted and left some spit and God knows what in James's ear.

They are new life forms. He wiped his ear. Jeff lifted his beer and pointed to it. James nodded. He was more tired than intoxicated. *Or was it the other way around?* He watched Jake and Mary leave and wondered what they saw in each other. He could see what Jake saw in Mary, but what did Mary see in Jake? *What does Brenda see in me?*

Karen looked over at James and Angie. *Wonder if he's gonna fuck her. Fuck* me, *James.*

"Hey, Karen, gimme one." Loose change hit the bar. *Asshole.*

"Same ol', same ol'," muttered James to no one.

"Know what you mean," Jake said and zipped up his jacket. Half the men and two women envied his upcoming task of removing Mary's tight-fitting jeans from her tight-fitting ass.

James watched them leave and thought about jumping Angie right there, but he didn't have any common sense, and he sure as shit didn't have any condoms. *Gonna have to go bareback again!*

Angie watched them leave and wondered if she'd looked as good as Mary in her younger days. She had, but gravity kicked in when she wasn't looking or when she was passed out and kicked the crap out of her looks, but she still had some left and she knew it. *I'm better lookin' 'an I ever was!*

Karen watched them leave and was about to drift off into fantasyland when some asshole threw some loose change on the bar.

Sarah watched them leave and wondered why Jake never put the move on her. She looked at herself in the mirror behind the bar and figured she didn't look too bad. She had plenty of young men who were after her, but she wasn't interested. She looked at Alfred and smiled. *What would he be like?*

Liz watched them leave and wondered what this world was coming to and where were all the good men? They sure as shit weren't in this bar, and if they were, they were taken. She looked at James sitting with Angie. *What 'a hell is he doin'?*

Louise watched them leave, then looked at James and Angie. *He's gonna fuck her. Wish it was me.* She looked at Daniel. *Drop dead.* She looked at Doreen. *You don' know what you're gettin' into. Get out while you're still alive.*

Alfred looked at Sarah and smiled. *Wonder if she'd be interested.*

Kevin and Greg looked at James and Angie. *Wonder if people 'at old can still get it up?*

At one-thirty, when things were just getting started, the inevitable happened.

"Last call!" Gary yelled and fucked up everyone's plans for the night. Last call meant a mad rush to the bar to get as many as one could buy or carry. Karen was swamped with a million people asking for a million beers.

James stood and staggered. *Didn't think I was 'at drunk*. He walked to the bar and stood behind Liz.

"Got any?" she asked.

"Any what?"

"Y'know."

"Might, never know," he teased. "See me later."

She smiled, ordered four beers and disappeared into the fog.

"Two," James shouted at Karen. He counted out his loose change and was a dollar short. She took a loonie out of her tips. "Thanks, I'll owe you," he said.

I'll take it out in trade any day. "You already gimme twen'y today." *Why don't you fuck me instead?* Loose change hit the bar. *Fuckers.*

James returned to his table and pushed a beer to Angie and time-travelled into the future and it was closing time. *Already?*

"Time to go!" Gary yelled.

Everyone heard but no one listened. They'd all gone deaf a few minutes ago. They guzzled their beers and looked to see who was going to make the first move.

"C'mon, people!" Gary yelled again. "Time to go!"

This time he pulled out his marking pen and walked to the white-board. Slowly the people got to their feet.

James came to and was standing on the steps. *How the hell I get here?* He turned and saw Angie. *Where'd she come from?*

Angie smiled at him. *Take me home 'n fuck me!* She knew better than to say it out loud if she was going to get laid tonight by the man of her dreams. *Maybe Brenda might see us. Maybe I'll get him back. Maybe he might ask me to marry him.*

"Hey, James! Wait up!"

He turned to see Liz, who looked at Angie like she was a hooker, then took his arm like she was his wife. He time-travelled and this time he was walking up his steps. He pulled two bottles out of his water container. A few minutes later, he was watching the television, but he couldn't tell what was on. He was almost passing out.

"James?"

Where're you?

"You okay?" Liz asked.

"Yeah, never better."

"We're gonna go to my place. Wanna come?"

"Not really," he slurred. "Gonna crash." *'n fuck Angie.*

"I took your last bottle."

Bottle? Where did 'at come from?

"There's some beer in 'a fridge."

Where did 'at come from? "What's 'a time?"

"Three," Liz answered.

He looked at the woman behind her. *Louise. What's she doin' here? Is 'is a dream?* There was another woman behind her. *Angie. It's a nightmare!*

"We're takin' her," someone said.

He looked up at Sarah. "What?"

"Nothing, see you tomorrow," she said, then disappeared into the fog.

He picked up his cup and downed it. He smelled perfume. *Cheap perfume. Angie? Maybe she's in 'at fog?* He walked into the fog. *Hello, Dream World.*

Hello, you big fuckin' crazy Injun! Come on in 'n see your dreams!

It was three-thirty, and Mutt and Jeff had finished one bottle and were out of beer and common sense. They were normal.

"Wanna look for party?" Jeff slurred.

"Sure," Mutt slurred back. *I need a smoke.*

Jeff put the bottle in the sleeve of his jacket and stumbled into the darkness to look for a party with smokes.

Angie looked out James's window at Mutt and Jeff. *Keep walkin', you fuckin' winos.* She'd been pissed off when Liz told her to leave with them and then didn't have the courtesy to invite her to their party. *Cunt.* They'd even told her not to think about coming back to James's because they were going to check on him later. *Dirty cunt.* She had a plan and hoped Mutt and Jeff didn't fuck it up. *Assholes.*

She watched them disappear, then went into James's bedroom. "James?" she whispered.

She could see him sleeping on his stomach and shook him. "James?"

He was dead drunk, passed out or both. She tried to take off his pants, but he was too heavy, so she pulled them partway down, then checked to see if he had any money in his wallet. *No fuckin' wallet. Asshole.* She took off her clothes and began choking his chicken, but nothing happened. *C'mon, little one. Angie's got somethin' wet 'n warm for you.* She disappeared below the sheets. Still nothing. *Somebody fucked him already 'n I'm suckin' it. Fuckin' Brenda.*

She heard the phone ringing and jumped. *Shit!* She dressed quickly. *Fuck!* After a few rings, it stopped. *Sarah! Liz! They're gonna come over.* She went into the kitchen and removed the case of beer and stumbled out the door. Halfway home she felt a draft and reached down. She pulled up her zipper and touched pubic hair. *I don' have any panties.* She thought about going back. *Them cunts might be there.* She tried to pull her zipper up, but she needed the coat hanger. *Fuck it. See what you're missin', James?*

At three forty-five, Larry and Daryl Hunter were listening to Van Halen thirty minutes out of town doing a hundred and twenty. They drank from a can and were looking at getting drunk and the sooner, the better. They had two cases of vodka and some beer and were heading to Sam's. *We're not goin' home. We're goin' to Sam's. We don' have a home. Wish the fucker would croak 'n leave us his money.*

They were in their late twenties and had never left the community for any length of time. They knew their mother was in Yellowknife, but Sam referred to her as "the drunken whore" and they didn't dare question what he said or they'd feel the slap of his hand. He'd mellowed over the last few years, but he was still a prick. *Should kill 'a fucker!*

They had an uncle, but George Standing was just another cold-hearted son of a bitch. Like so many people, they were alone on a crowded planet. *Should kill 'at fucker too!*

They did not have an easy childhood. Their mom left fifteen years before to get away from a life of abuse. She wanted to take her sons, but Sam would not allow her to even talk to them. They were also reminded by other children that they were raised on bootlegs and the misery of others. In the end, they had no real friends except each other and grew up alone and quiet. Many nights they'd lay awake and talk about running away, but that's all they did: talk. They talked about killing the old man, but that's all they did: talk. On more nights than they cared to remember, they could hear each other crying. If one started, the other would follow. They never talked about that since real men didn't cry, or that's what Sam told them.

Even now they talked about taking the truck and heading south, but they knew Sam would call the RCMP and report his truck missing and they'd be back here again, or worse, in jail. And Larry had no desire to return to that hellhole. *Even when he went to jail for bootlegging, they picked on him.* They had no education and no job experience. All they knew how to do was drive and bootleg.

"Fill 'er up again," Daryl said. *Let's drink to Sam's death.*

It was ten to three when Mutt and Jeff staggered down Main Street looking for a party in progress. They found a couple, but weren't invited. In their drunken stupor they decided to go to Fred's, which was less than a mile from town out on the highway. Had they been as sober as a priest during communion, they could've walked there in fifteen minutes. Since they were not priests and not sober, it would take them much longer.

At four, Angie made it to her apartment. She opened a beer, took a long drink, then burped. "Oops, sorry," she said, even though she knew she was alone. *I'll always be alone.* She thought about going back and sleeping with James and letting the chips fall where they may when he woke up. *I love you, James. Come for me.* She waited for him to walk through the door, but he didn't. *Asshole.* "I'm sorry." *I love you 'n I'll show you.* She lay on her sofa, kicked off her shoes, unbuttoned her pants and put her hand in. *Where's my panties? Fuck it.* She slipped in two fingers and started rubbing. "Oh James," she moaned.

Slam!

She fell off the sofa and tried to stand, but fell over her coffee table. She lay there for a few seconds and then realized it was her neighbour slamming his door. *Fucker!* She heard the beer spilling on the floor. *Fuck sakes!* She lifted the bottle. *Spilt milk. Nothin' to cry over.*

She placed her mouth to the spilt beer and sucked it. She lifted her head and pushed her messy hair from her face. *What am I doin'?* Her mascara was streaking, her lipstick was smudged, her pants were down around her ankles and she had no panties. She was also sucking spilt beer off the floor. *Where's the champagne 'n caviar? Where's 'a good life?*

The tears came and they were filled with a million emotions she'd kept hidden for thirty-five years and then some. *Fuckin' assholes!* "I was only fifteen. I was a virgin."

What only three people knew was that Angie had been raped as a teenager. The two men who repeatedly took turns with her took her virginity, her dignity and her future. They left her only one thing: the first of two children she'd give up for adoption in the sixties. This didn't include the two who were taken away from her in the eighties.

They now lived in Yellowknife.

No one heard the little china doll that night, but if she were given a voice it would've sounded like a million porcupines screaming in the dark.

He was on the highway in the mountains and it was dark. *Fuckin' night.* The full moon made everything appear dark blue. *Looks like a fuckin' dream!* He heard the wind and shivered, then put his hands in his pockets. *What am I doin' here?*

He figured out which way was home and started walking. The only sound, other than the wind, was his breathing and his footsteps. A few minutes later, he heard it. The other pair of footsteps.

He turned and wasn't surprised by what he saw: another man standing a few feet from him. The man was tall, dark and had no face, or if he did, it was covered by the darkness. He too wore a black leather jacket, black jeans and big black cowboy boots.

"Who're you?"

The man sneered. "Who am I? Why do you always ask when you know who I am?"

James looked at the land. It looked like something out of a horror movie. "Why do you torment me?"

"Torment you!" the man shouted. "Why do *I* torment *you*? Why do *you* torment *me*?"

James did not answer. He kept looking at the land and the highway.

"Why?" the figure pleaded.

"Why what?" James asked.

"Why'd you do it?"

"Do what?"

In the darkness the man's eyes looked sad. It looked like he'd seen hell and then some. "Why'd you give me your dreams?"

James looked at his eyes as if hypnotized. "You are a dream," he said.

"Why'd you do it?"

The fog was moving in, and it was black. "I don't know what you're talking about," James said.

The man looked at him, then at the fog. "You know what I'm talking about," he said as he disappeared into the fog.

James prayed the fog would swallow him. But as it approached, he saw the hand. *Fuck!* It was white and hairy, and it reached for him. He turned and began falling.

He opened his eyes. Experience told him he was still drunk and on his bedroom floor. He slowly got up and took off his clothes, then went into the kitchen. He turned on the stove light and saw the bottle on the table. *Empty.* He threw it in the garbage and looked in his fridge. *Empty.* He heard the television in the living room. *People. People means booze.* He staggered into his living room. *Where'd 'ey go? Why didn' 'ey leave some booze 'n smokes? Fuckers!*

He fell into his armchair. *Who the fuck undress me?* The test pattern sounded like an air raid siren a million miles away. *It's the end of the world.* He looked for his remote but couldn't see shit, let alone find it, so he turned the TV off manually. He watched the spot of light slowly shrink and disappear into the void. *Take me with you, little light. Take me into the void. Silence. Darkness. Fuck you, 'en.*

He staggered to his feet. Then he smelled it. *Perfume. Angie.* He walked into the fog to look for her. *Sex. Wet 'n dirty sex.* He made it back to his bed without falling and lay on his stomach. A few minutes later, he was out. *Hello, Dream World. Hello, Shadow Land. Hello, Shadow People. Hello . . . Holy shit!*

He cried in his sleep. Actually, it was more like a whimper, but what the fuck. Cries, whimpers — same diff. One lost soul seeking oblivion.

At four-fifteen, Larry and Daryl were well over the legal limit and had reached the Hamlet boundary. Daryl was now doing ninety with nothing but running lights. "We should check out Neil," he said. "You think 'a cops are out?"

Larry checked the clock. "Should be okay," he said. The van almost went in the ditch. "Slow down!" he yelled.

"Hey!" Daryl yelled back. "I can drive blindfold!"

"You're gonna fuckin' kill us!"

"So?" Daryl said and picked up speed to make his point. *So what if we fuckin' die?* They were passing Fred's shack on the highway. "Fuckin' asshole," Daryl said to all the Freds in the world.

He was now doing a hundred and twenty and looked over at Larry, who looked back at him. No one looked at the road, but they felt the bump.

His first thought was that he'd hit the ditch, but the van was still moving. His second thought was that he'd hit a moose, but the van was still moving. His third thought was that he'd hit a dog, which was why the van was still moving.

"What 'a fuck I hit?" he shouted, then slowed. He turned on the lights and stopped a hundred feet down the highway.

Larry got out and checked the custom-made bumper that showed no sign of damage to his eyes that couldn't see shit in the first place. "What 'a fuck you hit?" he asked.

"How fuck I know?" Daryl whined. "Could be dog."

Larry walked behind the van, but it was too dark to see anything let alone a dog. He stumbled back to the van. "Can' see fuckin' thing!" he said. "Let's get outta here!"

Daryl had sobered up considerably in the last few minutes, or it felt that way at least. He was thankful the van wasn't damaged or there would be hell to pay from Sam. *I'll kill him he lays a hand on me.* He thought that for the millionth time and for the millionth time he wished he meant it.

It was four-thirty when Larry and Daryl cruised down the back street hoping no one saw them.

"Who's 'at?"

"Sam's boys." *Fuckin' bootleggers!*

Larry and Daryl parked the van, then took two cases of beer and two forty-pounders to Neil's. But he was passed out and they couldn't wake him. *Fuckin' drunks.*

Neil was in his late sixties. His house was small and run down with broken windows. It contained two rooms, one of which he used as a bedroom. The main room contained an old sofa and kitchen table with three rickety chairs. His bathroom was nothing more than an old pail in the corner. It was third world, but it was normal.

Larry turned on the radio and they listened to classical music from some far distant place they would never see and proceeded to get drunk.

Sometime later, Neil woke up to find two young men in his house. One of them poured him a drink and he obliged by rambling on about the good old days. He couldn't remember passing out on his floor.

"Fuckin' ol' people," Daryl said to no one.

Soon after, another guest joined the party. *The Sex Goddess.* Lisa had recently been asked to leave another party where she'd met the man of her dreams and decided to consummate their relationship by giving him a handjob. She undid his zipper and found him ready for action. *I knew it. You got 'a hots for me.* She started stroking and was totally oblivious to the others. The next thing she knew, his wife was pulling her hair out by the roots and calling her a slut. She took her leave with much ado about nothing. Or so she thought. *Assholes. I fucked him before. Shit, I sucked him.*

She walked towards Neil's house and knew Larry would be there. *Free booze!* She fixed her hair, then smelled her hand. *Fuckin' cock.* She wiped it on her pants, shape-shifted into Nicole Kidman and made her entrance. *I'm here, Tom. Eat me, fuck me, use me, but gimme drink firs'!*

Larry's face lit up. *Hump City.* He grabbed Lisa and dry-humped her in front of Daryl.

Daryl smiled. He hoped Larry would pass out so he could jump her. *He can have sloppy seconds.*

Daryl had never had a girlfriend and only fucked girls who were drunk or passed out and didn't think there was anything wrong with it. *Half the men in town do it.* Still, he did dream about a better way of life. But that's all it was: a dream. And it was Sam's fault. It was all Sam's fault. *I wish someone would kill the son bitch.* He poured another drink. *I should do it.* He drank half his cup and then passed out.

Larry took his cup and gave it to Lisa, who drank it without stopping. She wiped her mouth on her sleeve and smiled. *Hi, Tom, I'm Nicole.*

Hi, Nicole, wanna fuck?

Sure, why not? Got nothin' else to do.

Your enthusiasm is admirable.

Fuck you 'n kiss me. Better yet, let me kiss you. You can fuck me. She kissed him and the odour of vodka, cigarettes and cheap perfume was like an aphrodisiac. *I knew it. He's got the hots for me.*

Larry took her into Neil's bedroom that contained nothing more than an old bed with an older mattress. The door was a dirty blanket that was nailed to the upper corners of where the door was before someone kicked it down.

He laid her on the old sleeping bag that hadn't been washed since Neil bought it a few years ago and it contained countless stains from many other loveless encounters and who knows what else. He removed her pants and panties and threw them on the floor. *God, Nicole, you're beautiful.*

I know, Tom. I'm fuckin' ravishin'. Eat me.

Fuck 'at noise. I'm goin' for the gusto.

Whatever!

He took off his boots and pants and climbed between her legs. *Ready?*

Ready.

Enough foreplay. He thrust, she gasped and he was done in less than a minute. *Hope she ain't got 'a clap again.* He rolled off and picked up his cup. *Too fuckin' late to worry 'bout 'at now.* With that, he passed out.

Tom, you done? Lisa opened her eyes. *That's 'a best fuck I had tonight.* She took his cup and walked into the other room. She poured herself a drink and guzzled, spilling most of it down her chin. She wiped it off, then put her hands between her legs and looked down. *I got no pants 'n I been fucked. By who?* She saw Daryl on the sofa. *Oh, him again.* She refilled her cup, then went back to the honeymoon suite and looked at Larry. *Wonder if he'll fuck me. Hey, Tom! You wanna fuck me? You don' fuck me, I'm gonna get a fuckin' divorce!*

Seven

Jake's Disclosure

Sunday, September 26th, 1999
The old wolf shivered, then looked north. Still no caribou. He walked along the hill hoping to surprise a ground squirrel. They were fat this time of the year and would provide him with the energy he needed until the caribou came, but they were too fast and he no longer had the speed of youth. He did not think about it. He was now going on nothing more than instinct.

It was eight o'clock when Chief David William looked out his window. *Wonder what sort 'a shit my People created for me last night.* He dreaded waking up to more assaults, break and enters, child neglect, child abuse, sexual abuse, spousal abuse, Elder abuse and more abuse than he cared to think of.

He drove up to Sal's Coffee Shop. The only vehicle parked there was the RCMP Suburban. That meant the Sarge was having coffee.

"Morning, Sarge," he said, then sat down.

"Morning, Chief."

Sergeant Herbert Johnson was in his late forties and had joined the force right out of high school. This was his first posting North of Sixty, and he had expected it to be the best time of his career, but it wasn't. He thought he'd come to a land where the People still lived off the land and the troubles of the outside world were far and away. They weren't. The troubles were here long before he arrived.

Sally poured Chief David a cup of coffee. David then asked the Sarge, "Did my People cause you any grief las' night?"

"Not really. Couple people in the drunk tank. Same ol', same ol'."

"So, I hear tell you're on 'a move. Any truth to those rumours?"

"True and Grande Prairie."

A short while later, they walked out into reality and it still sucked.

Fred woke up in his shack on the highway and was still drunk, or close to it. He decided to walk into town and look for breakfast, or a party, whichever came first. He was shaking the cobwebs and dreams from his booze-soaked brain when he came upon Mutt and Jeff in the ditch. *Fuckin' drunks.*

He slid down into the ditch and tried to wake Mutt up. "Mutt, you son 'a bitch, get up!"

He walked over to Jeff and shook him. "Jeff, get 'a fuck up!"

He felt the broken bottle and saw the blood, and his confused mind slowly digested what he was seeing. He ran back to Mutt and checked to see if he was breathing. *Holy fuckin' shit!* He walked towards town, where he ran into the Sarge and waved him down.

The shower room was a mile long and he could see the little boy in the distance. *Good! The farther, the better.* Suddenly the little boy was right in front of him. He started to hyperventilate. The little boy was crying. It sounded like a porcupine crying. He'd heard one crying once and he never forgot the sound.

The tears were flowing out of the little boy's eyes. They looked like blood. *What 'a hell's goin' on?* He had to get out of here. He saw someone in the distance. *Mom?*

He walked towards her. She smiled. *It is.* He ran and held her. After what seemed like forever, he looked up. It wasn't her. It was . . . *Oh fuck!*

James fell off his bed and hit the floor for the millionth time and lay there. He tried to clear his mind, but couldn't. It started pounding from the booze and now the bump. Slowly, he got up, pulled on his pants and looked for a T-shirt. He stumbled into his kitchen to look for booze. He found diddly. He did smell something. *Angie. Was she a dream or a nightmare? A nightmare.*

He went to the washroom to see if he diddled last night, but he couldn't tell. It looked dead so he choked it, and it slowly came to life. Had he been in a better frame of mind, he might've smiled. But he wasn't so he didn't. *It is small.*

He made coffee, then stripped the sheets off his bed and threw them in the washing machine. He pulled off his clothes and jumped in the shower. As he dried himself, he contemplated his next move. *Fuck it.*

He remembered the beer in his water container and to his pleasure it was still there. He opened one and downed it without stopping, then opened another. He sat and contemplated his next move. *Fuck it, fuck it 'n fuck it again.* He looked for the remote, turned on the television and searched for something that wouldn't make his head pound.

Chief David was at the construction site when the Sarge pulled up looking like he'd seen a ghost. Fred was sitting in the passenger seat looking *like* a ghost.

Five minutes later, he was driving Fred to Martin Lazarus's and the Sarge was driving to the health centre to inform Stella Madsen, the nurse in charge. Martin's wife, Jane, was cooking breakfast when David arrived. Before long, he and Martin were on their way to the scene of the accident and Fred was about to eat Martin's breakfast. Dreams were coming true for some. For others a nightmare was about to begin.

Chief David was grateful for Martin at times like this. He took charge when others couldn't or wouldn't, and that included him. He was an

Elder in the true sense of the word and a leader even though he was never a Chief or a councillor. His leadership came from his abilities and no one questioned his authority. That's the way it had been for the last forty years and that's the way it was going to be until the day he died.

It was ten o'clock when they arrived at the scene of the accident in time to see Const. Adrienne Taylor taking photos and the Sarge looking around for anything out of the ordinary. It was all so out of the ordinary it was normal. Stella stood on the other side of the road next to Mutt's body.

"Hi, Herb," Martin said. "What's it look like?"

"Hit 'n run. Early this mornin'."

"What else you gotta do?"

"Not much else we can do. I'll see if we can take 'em down today or early tomorrow so they can be shipped to Edmonton."

"We can have the funeral Friday," Martin said to Chief David.

"Yeah," David answered. "Now we have to tell Old Pierre."

"Did Mutt have any family?" the Sarge asked.

"Couple cousins," Martin said. "No immediate family."

"Was Mutt his real name?" Stella asked.

"Real name's Leon," David said. "They called him Mutt on account 'a Jeff." *Fuckin' cartoon characters, that's what we are. Roadrunners 'n coyotes. Only we don't get up after we hit the fuckin' wall. We stay down for the long count.*

The Sarge laid body bags next to Mutt and Jeff, then they bagged them and put them in the back of the suburban. Things were normal.

Old Pierre was Jeff's uncle and the only close family Jeff had. Old Pierre and Dora were in their mid-seventies and still fairly independent. When Chief David pulled up in front of their house at eleven-thirty, Old Pierre knew something was wrong. He and Dora listened and said nothing. It was as though it was inevitable.

Andy Farmer, the local minister, arrived a little while later. *Good news travels fast — bad news faster.* Martin's wife, Jane, walked in with some bannock just as the Sarge pulled up. Martin and the Chief went out to meet him.

"I already told them," Martin said.

"Thanks, I've always had trouble notifying the next of kin."

"It's not easy for anyone," Martin said.

"What's next?" David asked.

"All I have to know is who was on the highway early this morning. That shouldn't be too hard to find out."

The three men stood on the steps and said nothing. Nothing had to be said. It was a small town. Sooner or later, someone was going to come forward and confess. Or someone was going to come forward and tell what they heard or saw.

He was walking along the shore waiting for his mom and dad to pick him up and take him home. *Home: the Redstone River.*

He heard the low hum of the outboard motor and saw the boat in the middle of the river.

He could see his mom sitting with a little boy and his dad driving. He smiled and waved. Suddenly the river turned dark and the motor stopped. His mom began shouting. The wind drowned out her words. He watched as his dad began paddling for shore. *Hurry!* The waves were getting bigger and the boat was sinking. *Hurry!* He tried to run to them, but he stopped. *I can't swim.* He put his foot on the water and it held. He put his other foot on and it still held. He ran and grabbed his mom's hand and tried to pull her up, but she was too heavy. *Help me.* The young boy clung to her and disappeared beneath the water. He looked at his mom, but she too was disappearing. Far away he heard the bell calling him back to school.

"Shut 'a fuck up," he mumbled. He let the phone ring, hoping whoever was calling would read his mind and leave him the fuck alone. They didn't. He picked it up and hoped it wasn't Brenda.

"Hello," she said.

I'm guilty. I did it. "Mornin'," he answered.

"You just get up?"

He sensed the anger in her voice. "No. What's 'a time?"

"Noon."

He drank some of his beer and almost puked, but forced it down. *Can't waste good beer. It's Sunday and at a premium.* "Whatcha doin'?" he asked.

"Not much, you?"

"Nothin'."

"You heard?"

Yeah, I heard. I was there. I participated. At leas' I think I did. "Heard what?"

"About Mutt 'n Jeff?"

What? Did they poke her too? "What 'ey do now?" he asked, waiting for a good one.

"They were killed las' night," she answered. "On 'a highway."

"How?"

"Hit 'n run." After a few seconds, she asked, "You still gonna drive me to Helena?"

"Yeah," he answered. *Maybe she didn't know.*

"I gotta go to my parents. I'll call you later. We have to talk."

She knew. He did the only thing he could. He started thinking of a good lie or a way to deny it without really denying it. *Wish I was a fuckin' politician or a fuckin' lawyer.* He could still smell Angie's perfume and he had to get rid of it and his guilty conscience.

It took him two hours, but he did his laundry and swept and mopped his bedroom, bathroom, kitchen and living room. He found Angie's panties on the bedroom floor. *Must've done it.* He threw them in the garbage. *Outta sight, outta mind.*

Afterwards, he sat and opened another beer and looked at his house. *Looks like someone's tryin' to get rid of the stench of infidelity.* He opened another beer just as Jake and Mary walked in holding hands.

"Smells like Angie was here," Jake said.

James's face dropped.

"Jake!" Mary said and smiled.

Jake noticed James wasn't smiling. "I'm jus' kiddin'," he said.

James couldn't tell if he was or not, but it was too late to lie to them. They already knew by the look on his face.

"What's new?" Mary asked.

"Nothin' a good kick to the head won't cure." *Or a bullet.* "You hear?" he asked.

"What?" Mary asked, hoping for a good one.

"Mutt 'n Jeff were killed last night."

"What?" Jake said. "How?"

"Hit 'n run."

They were silent for a few seconds.

"I'm gonna go home," Mary said.

"I'll be here or at home," Jake said.

"Any idea who done it?" Jake asked when she was gone.

"No idea. Brenda tol' me. That's all I know."

The phone rang.

"When can you pick me up?" Brenda asked. It sounded more like a demand than a request. She sounded like Angie on a bad day.

"Gimme an hour," he said. "Me 'n Jake are talkin'." *Excuses. Delay the inevitable.*

"Okay," she said. "I'll see you at three."

Maybe she didn't know. Maybe the earth is flat. He made a fresh pot of coffee, then jumped in the shower again. He felt a little better. *Maybe she didn't know. Maybe it didn't happen.* He couldn't remember leaving the bar. He remembered Liz and Sarah, but not much else. *Fuck it.*

"Where you goin'?" Jake asked as he poured two cups of coffee.

"Gotta drive her to Helena. She's goin' to Yellowknife for 'n interview."

They sat and said nothing as they drank their coffee. He thought about the two bottles and six beers he bought from Mutt and Jeff. *Wonder if they'd still be here if I hadn't. Not likely.* He wondered what happened to the booze. *Liz 'n Sarah must 'a taken it. Louise was with them. When did they leave? Did they take Angie? Was she really here, or was she part 'a my nightmare?* He shook off the thought and got ready for his trip. He had some music to face and he had an excuse. *Nothing happened.*

Five minutes later, he arrived at Brenda's apartment and went in. "You set?" he asked from her living room.

She came out of her bedroom carrying a small suitcase. He looked as guilty as sin and it showed. "All set," she said.

"Can we stop at Sal's?" she asked. "I wanna get some pop 'n cigarettes."

"Not a prob. You're drivin'."

There were four trucks and a car in front of Sal's. As they entered they came face to face with Angie, who still looked half-cut. They said nothing and went in. Brenda picked up some cigarettes and pop and he picked up a cup of coffee. As they drove up the main road, they passed Angie on the sidewalk. She lifted her arms in the air, wiggled her ass and screamed, "Yahoooo!"

James wished he could disappear. He did the only thing he could: nothing. Brenda drove out of Aberdeen and headed north and went silent.

Larry woke up at four-thirty feeling and looking like shit. He was still drunk, but he knew where he was. He looked in his sock and was relieved to find his money still there, but Lisa was gone. He wondered why his shorts felt so tight. *I'm wearin' fuckin' panties!* He threw Lisa's panties in the corner. *Maybe Neil'll think he got lucky.* He dressed, then walked into the other room to find Neil and Daryl passed out and three cigarettes in the pack on the table. He lit one and wished he had more to drink. His wish materialized when he saw a familiar truck coming down the road. He ran out to meet Uncle George.

"Got any?" he asked.

George reached under his seat and pulled out a bottle and Larry gave him a hundred-dollar bill. George pulled out another. "You hear 'bout Mutt 'n Jeff?" he asked.

"What about 'em?"

"They're dead."

"No shit! What happen?"

"Fred found 'em on 'a highway 'is mornin'."

"How?"

"Run over."

"No shit!"

"When you get in las' night?"

"Why?"

"Jus' askin'."

"Don' know. Three," he lied.

"See anybody else?"

"No."

"Well, gotta go," George said.

"Hey, got any smokes?"

George threw him his pack, then drove off. *Family ties — family lies.*

Larry poured himself a drink. *Wonder if we hit 'em? The time was right 'n we did hit somethin'.* He looked at his drink. *Wonder what would happen if I drank the whole bottle myself?* He'd heard of people drinking themselves to death and had tried it many times, but he always passed out. He thought about his mom and the tears came. He pushed them back. *Men don't cry. Slap!*

He drank what was in his cup, then poured himself another and tried to shut his system down.

The Sarge had driven around the community and looked at vehicles for telltale signs of damage and found none. He knew Larry and Daryl had returned from Helena late the previous evening and had gone to Sam's house to see them. No one answered the door. He checked at Neil's, but there too no one answered the door. *Probably passed out.*

He returned home and had some tea. *What the hell is happening with this community? Can't they see it?* He was glad he was moving and hoped nothing else would happen before he got the hell out of here.

Jake woke up around nine that evening and called Mary. "I'm at James's," he said. "I'm alone."

"So?" she teased.

"So get your tight-fittin' jeans over here."

"What're we gonna do?"

"Sit 'n talk 'n ya know."

"Tell me," she prompted.

"I'm gonna jump you."

"I'm gonna hold you to that."

"Was hopin' you'd hold more 'n 'at."

She laughed. "How sick! I'll be right over."

Jake turned on the TV and began looking for something to take his mind off the events of today and his uncertain future. He'd come to the conclusion that he'd have to leave Aberdeen to find a steady job. He had hoped to spend the rest of his life here, but now he wasn't so sure. He had other things to think about now, like Mary.

He came to a show on trapping. Or was it the news? In any case, it was about trappers who had to seek other employment to make ends meet given the price of furs was still at an all-time low. The reporter took his audience into an auction house and talked to one of the employees about the upcoming season.

"Dismal," the man said. *Looks familiar.* Jake couldn't place his face. He had sparse white hair and a full beard. *Santa Claus.* His name flashed on the screen and Jake time-travelled thirty years back. *It's him.* He sat motionless until the face returned to the Dream World.

"Hi," Mary said and smiled seductively.

He came back to reality and smiled. He thought about the face on the small screen. *Wasn't real. Or was it?* He was no longer horny. *It was.*

Mary kissed him. "What's wrong?" she asked. "Change your mind?"

He looked at her.

"Hello?" she said. "You're not gettin' weird on me, are you?"

"No, jus' somethin' I seen."

"Yeah, what?"

"Nothin' important," he said. "I love you," he said after a few seconds.

"I love you too," she said. "What's on your mind?"

"Lots."

"Tell me."

Shame, sorrow, sadness, terror, fear, hurt, anger, rage. Take your pick. Lots to go around.

"You gonna tell me?" she asked.

"Sorry, I was jus' thinkin'."

"Think words."

"You really wanna hear it?" he asked. *It's over with. Done.*

"Yeah."

Jake thought about what happened in that dark room a million years ago when he was just a boy. *Or did it happen? Maybe it was a dream.* He'd pushed it so far back in his memory that it was nothing more than a dream. But it was real and he knew it.

"Jake?"

He looked at Mary. "Yeah?" His mind was reliving the memories of yesterday and he couldn't stop it. *Why can't I forget?*

"Are you gonna tell me?"

The face! The memories! Time-travel is alive 'n well 'n living on the small screen! Take a trip back in time 'n relive your Glory Days, Sorry Days! Santa Claus is coming to town! Run! Hide! Get outta here!

"Jake?"

"Yeah?"

"Tell me," she said.

He tried to smile but couldn't. What came was something neither of them expected. It started off as a low wail, then ripped a hole in his chest.

Mary did the only thing she could: nothing.

It was as if he was letting out a million years of tears at once. He was starting to hyperventilate, so he pushed the tears down and took fast, shallow breaths. *Nothin' to it.* He tried to smile as if to make it all look okay. He couldn't. She looked so beautiful and vulnerable, just like his sister had when she walked down that long fucking hallway. *Fuckers.* More memories returned and more tears followed. He tried to force them down, but couldn't. He hung his head to hide his shame. It must've been a hundred years before he finally opened his eyes.

"Are you okay?" Mary asked.

"Sorry," he said. "I'll be okay."

He walked to the bathroom and washed his face, then came back. *Nothin' to it.*

"What was it?" Mary asked.

"Nothin'," he said. "Just emotional, 'at's all."

"Why?"

"Nothin'."

"Tell me."

"It's nothin'," he said. "Happen long time ago."

"Tell me."

"It's okay." He shrugged. "It's over."

"Tell me."

Jake Noland had kept a secret for thirty years, but on this night something made him blurt it out. He didn't know what or why. "I was sexually abused in the hostel," he said.

Mary heard but it was like a dream. She'd heard of it at other places, but not in Aberdeen. She never went to that hostel, but she remembered it being a friendly place.

"Happen long time ago," Jake said. "It's over."

"Wanna talk about it?" Mary asked.

"Not really."

"You should talk to someone."

"I will," he said, and tried to smile, but the tears returned. *Dark rooms, hairy hands, shower rooms.* After another eternity, he stopped and she was still there. He thought she'd run, but she was still there.

"I don' know what to say," she said. She remembered her training and how she was not to counsel anyone she was involved with. "I'm gonna call your aunt."

"Don't," he said.

He didn't really mean it and she knew it. "I have to," she said and dialled the number. She talked briefly to Bertha Moses, then hung up. "She's comin' over."

What am I doin'? He'd heard about disclosing and knew enough. Or so he thought. *What 'a hell is 'ere to be scared of? All I have to do is talk about it.*

Bertha was there in ten minutes and that was time enough for Mary to make a pot of tea and time enough for Jake to weigh his options. *Two. Tell or not tell. Sink or swim. Run or hide. Live or die.*

Bertha walked in with a worried look on her face. "Hi, nephew," she said, using the language. *It's finally come. The time has finally come.*

"Hi."

"How are you?"

He shrugged. "Not bad."

Bertha sat in the armchair and took a deep breath. "Jake," she said. "Sit down 'n let me tell you somethin'."

Jake sat next to Mary on the sofa.

"Jake, I think I know what's goin' on," Bertha continued. "I'm gonna tell you somethin', then you can tell me what you want, okay?"

"Okay." *No problem.*

"I know 'bout it," she said. "I know 'bout Tom Kinney."

At that moment, Jake couldn't control his tears and he slowly slid off the sofa. It was as if there was a ton of them and they all wanted out at the same time.

"Let it go," Bertha whispered. "Don't hold it back."

He wanted to stop but he couldn't. Mary and Bertha sat and watched and wondered if he was ever going to stop. He did, but only after a hundred years and only after he pushed the tears and a million other emotions back down where they belonged. He sat up but kept his head bowed. It was as if he was praying.

"Jake," Bertha said. "I know 'bout it 'cause Michael Lazarus lef' me a letter before he . . ."

The sobs still came, but they were silent.

"He told me 'bout Tom Kinney. He told me what 'at man did to him 'n you."

"He did it to him too?" Jake asked.

"Yes." After a few seconds, she said, "Tell me."

"I don' know if I can."

"Start anyway. What brought 'is on?"

"I saw him."

"Who?"

"Tom Kinney."

"Where?"

"On TV."

"Where?" she asked again.

"Don' know."

"Tell us," she said.

Straight to the point. No beatin' 'round the bush. "Don' know what to say," he said. "It happened."

Bertha kept her gaze on him. "What?" she asked.

He started crying again.

"It's okay." Bertha said. After he'd cried another million years, she asked, "Did you know about Michael?"

"No."

"You okay, Mary?" Bertha asked.

Jake looked at Mary and she was crying.

"I'm okay," she said.

Bertha turned to Jake. "He gave me a letter the day he left," she said, then recalled the day Michael had come to see her.

He was in a good mood and handed her the envelope and told her to keep it for him. At the time, she thought nothing of it. A few days later, Martin found him in the hills. She remembered the envelope and opened it that night. She read it and cried.

Dear Bertha. If your reading this then I've done it. I'm sorry. This is the only way. Tom Kinney sexually abused me in the hostel in 1968. I know he did this to others. I know he did it to Jake. I'm sorry. Michael

She read the letter many times and shared the secret with only two other people: Martin and Jane. They didn't know what to do, so they kept it a secret. Nothing could be done to help Michael and nothing could bring Tom Kinney to justice. Until now. Or could it? That was up to Jake.

"Enough," Bertha said in the language. "How do you feel?" she asked Mary.

"Tired 'n helpless."

"You're not helpless. You did good."

Mary smiled and the tears came.

"Let them come," Bertha said.

Mary pictured Jake and a man in a dark room. She tried to block the picture. She couldn't. She had no choice.

Jake felt his own tears returning. There were so many that they began to hurt his eyes. His head pounded like it had never pounded before. He held Mary and cried. He reached for the china doll that he would never reach. He reached for a mom and dad he would never hold again.

After what seemed like an eternity, he got up and went to the bathroom to wash his face. He felt exhausted and light. It was as if a million tons had been lifted from his soul.

"You okay?" Bertha asked when he returned.

"Yeah."

"You sure? You don't have anythin' else to say?"

"No."

"It's not gonna be easy," she said. "Once you've disclosed you have to follow through. Talk about it to anyone who'll listen 'n understand. It's gettin' rid of it through talkin' 'n cryin' that's gonna help you. If you don't get rid of it, it'll kill you . . . like it's done to so many of our People. You understan'?"

"Yeah, I think so."

Bertha put on her jacket. "I'm goin' home. You sure you'll be okay?"

Jake looked at Mary. She nodded. "Yeah," he said. "We'll be okay."

"You might dream tonight," she said to Jake. "They're just dreams."

Meanwhile, in a hotel room in Helena, James looked at the time — three o'clock in the morning. He and Brenda had checked into the hotel, showered, got into bed, watched a movie and nothing happened. She fell asleep around twelve. He watched her. *You're lucky. You don't carry the dreams I carry. Want some 'a mine? Big fuckin' Indian dreams. Guaranteed to keep you in apathy 'n self-pity the rest 'a your life. Or in booze. Or both, if you're lucky.*

When he went to sleep, he didn't know. He did know it was after three in the morning and he was sober, and that was not good. He knew his dreams waited for him on the other side and he held off for as long as he could. He dreamed of a shower room and a little boy with empty eyes. He dreamed of mists and fog. He dreamed of big fucking monsters coming out of shower-room walls. He dreamed of a woman covered in blood. But he wouldn't remember it. Or would he?

Eight

Honour Thy Father

Monday, September 27th, 1999
The old wolf's fur wasn't as thick as it used to be. The day before, he scavenged on the highway and found nothing. He didn't realize it, but he was sleeping more and more to conserve energy. He dreamed as he slept and in his dreams he was young.

Chief David woke at seven-thirty and sat by his window with a cup of coffee. *Wonder what other shit my People caused for me las' night. What else can they do?*

He knew the Sarge was going to send the bodies to Helena this morning and he shivered at the thought, then remembered the two bodies belonged to Mutt and Jeff. *The same Mutt 'n Jeff who worked for the Band a few weeks ago. The same Mutt 'n Jeff who cut wood for me last winter. The same Mutt 'n Jeff who sold me fish a few days ago. The same Mutt 'n Jeff who didn't hesitate to go huntin' for the community when I asked them.*

He wondered what else had to be done. The boys at the shop were going to make the coffins and Martin would see to it that the grave got dug. *What 'a fuck else can go wrong?*

The little china doll was standing in the double doors at the end of the long hallway. *Esther.* He started running, but the doors kept getting farther and farther away. The old white woman was closing them. She was grinning. It was a grin that said he'd never make it.

He tried to run faster, but he couldn't. Suddenly the bars appeared out of nowhere and he stopped. He looked at the doors closing in on his sister. He pulled at the bars. *I'll kill you! Someday I'll kill all you fuckers!* He turned and saw the fog. He closed his eyes and began to breathe faster. *Nothin' to it.*

Jake opened his eyes and there was the china doll staring at him.

"Mornin'," she said, then smiled.

He wondered if it was a dream. He looked around and was still in his room at James's house.

Mary leaned over and kissed him, then she held him and the tears came. She put her head on his chest, then wiped her eyes. "I'm sorry," she said.

"It's okay," he answered. "What's 'a time?"

"Eight," she said. "I'm gonna take you home."

"Your parents know where you are?"

"I told 'em I was gonna spend the night."

"What 'ey say?" he asked.

"They told me long as they know where I am then it's okay."

"They know about us?"

"I told 'em I was seein' you long ago."

"What 'ey say?"

"As long as I'm happy, they said."

"Are you?"

She took his hand. "I am."

"Me too."

After Jake had washed they left. As they walked down the stairs, she took his hand and turned left and he turned right. They turned to face each other.

"My home is this way," she said.

"My home is 'at way."

"I meant I was takin' you to my home," she said.

"What'll your parents say?"

"My dad's gonna blast your skinny ass to kingdom come."

He looked to see if she was serious.

"Jake," she said, "I told them about us."

"What you say?" he asked.

"I told them I was gonna spend the rest 'a my life with you."

He grinned. "Is 'at a proposal?"

"That's a hint," she said.

As they walked to her parents', he thought about running, but he'd run too much in his life. He decided to let the chips fall where they may. *What could they do to me I haven't done to myself?*

He expected her dad to take the shotgun to his ass and her mom, Bella, to be cold and uninviting. But they invited him in and her mom made them breakfast while her dad, Simon, talked about the weather and the caribou. "I hope they come soon," he said. "I'm tired 'a fish."

Jake couldn't remember what it was like to have a home. Or could he? He remembered his mom and dad in their old log house in the community. He remembered the warmth of the fire and the smell of caribou cooking and hot bannock and laughter. He felt the tears returning and forced them down where they belonged. *Nothin' to it.*

Mary came into the kitchen. "I called in sick," she said.

He smiled. It was going to be a good day despite the sad occasion.

As Chief David drove into the RCMP compound, Adrienne was leaving in the Suburban for her trip into Helena with the remains of Mutt and Jeff. Adrienne was in her early thirties and single. She was five-eleven, a redhead and awesome. Or so the men thought.

David walked into the detachment. The Sarge was at his desk.

"Mornin', Sarge."

"Mornin'."

"Whatcha got?"

"Got a call this morning."

"And?"

"Someone seen Sam's van that morning."

"I knew the boys were in Helena Saturday night," David said. "I was hoping they'd stay 'n give us a rest."

"I looked for them yesterday," the Sarge said. "Just wanted to ask them a few questions. Anyhow, I got the call this morning. They came into town around four-thirty on Saturday morning." He waited for David to ask who the anonymous caller was, but he didn't. "Anyhow, I'm gonna bring them in and take a good look at the van."

"Well, you gotta do what you gotta do," David said. "You need help, let me know."

"I don't have much. The best I can hope for is a confession, or an acknowledgement that they might've had something to do with it."

"It's a start."

There were hundreds of Indians on the horizon, like shadows. *Who're they? Do other People see 'em?* Before he could answer his own questions, he saw the boat. *Mom 'n Dad.* His smile disappeared when the boat started sinking. He ran to the shore but suddenly he was running down the long hall that never ended. He slowed, then came to a complete stop. *Fuck!* His breathing was now coming faster and he wondered if he should go on or turn back. *Someone's watchin' me.*

Brenda was propped up on one arm looking at him. She watched him awhile longer, then walked into the bathroom. She had wanted him to make love to her last night, but at the same time she didn't want him. She looked in the mirror. *Why me?*

She had a shower then dressed. James was still sleeping, but now there were beads of sweat on his forehead. She took the bath towel and wiped them, and he opened his eyes.

"Mornin'," she said. He looked at her, then realized where he was. "The shower's free," she said. "I'm gonna get some coffee."

Larry woke up at nine and felt like shit. He needed a shower and a shave and another drink. He needed someone or something to put him out of his misery. He got off Neil's bed and his head started pounding. He was normal.

It was Monday morning and time to put in another week of bootlegging and taxi driving. He woke Daryl up, and they walked to their father's house, knowing they were going to get shit for one reason or another, but what the hell, they were used to it. *Maybe the old fart will finally up 'n do the world a favour.* They found Sam sitting in the living room pissed off at the world for not giving him a living. *Fat fuck.*

As he walked to the bathroom, Daryl thought about scaring the fat fuck into a massive heart attack. *Prob'ly choke me while he's dyin'.*

Larry went to the coffeepot, then looked at his father. *Loser.*

"You guys get on 'a road right away," Sam said like they were the scum of the earth. "Losin' customers." *Useless fucks.*

Fuck you 'n drop dead. Larry waited for him to clutch his chest.

"You hear me?" he asked.

Kiss my arse. "Yeah."

There was a knock. Sam waddled to the door, hoping it was a customer.

"Mornin', Sam," the Sarge said.

"What you want?" *Why don' you look for the assholes took my booze?*

"I need to talk to Larry and Daryl," the Sarge said. "Are they in?"

Larry and Daryl came to the door.

"I need to talk to you two outside for a couple of minutes."

They got their jackets and followed the Sarge outside.

"You heard about Mutt 'n Jeff?" he asked.

"No, what about 'em?" Daryl said.

"They were hit by a vehicle on Saturday morning. They're both dead."

"You're shittin' me?" Daryl said.

"I wish I were."

"What's 'at gotta do with us?" Larry asked.

"You're the only vehicle that was on the road at the time. Just wanna know if you saw anything."

"We didn' see nothin' or nobody," Larry said too quickly.

"I've got a witness that saw your van coming in about the time they were hit."

"We didn' hit nothin'. Check our van if you want."

"I will," the Sarge said. He walked around the parked van.

Sam watched from the window, then came out. "What 'a hell's goin' on?" he asked.

"Just checking out your front end and tires," the Sarge answered.

"What for?" Sam asked.

"You heard Mutt 'n Jeff were killed yesterday?"

"Yeah, so?" *Maybe they stole my booze. Assholes.*

"So I got a witness that seen your van coming in around the time they were hit."

"Bullshit!"

"You gonna give me a hard time?" the Sarge asked, hoping he would so he could make him do the fucking chicken in front of his sons.

Sam did nothing.

The Sarge took out some Polaroids and checked the tires against the photos, but he couldn't tell for sure. The grille was slightly bent, but not much. "I'm gonna ask you to come with me to the detachment."

"Why?" Larry asked. "We didn't do nothin'."

"I'm not saying you did," the Sarge said. "At least not yet, but I'm gonna need statements from both of you."

"I wanna lawyer," Daryl said too quickly.

"You can call one from the detachment. Now get in."

They got into the back of the suburban and sat on the wooden floor. Daryl was scared. He looked at Larry, who seemed calm. "What're we gonna do?" he asked.

"Nothin'. We're gonna tell him nothin'."

"What're you two talking about?" the Sarge asked as he got in the front.

"Nothin'," replied Larry.

The Sarge took them to the detachment and put them in one of the smaller offices. He offered them coffee and left. *Let them think it over.*

An hour later, he took their statements. They both said they left Helena around midnight on Saturday and drove back soberer than ten judges going to church on Sunday. They arrived around three and proceeded to get drunk at Neil's. They didn't remember seeing anyone else on the road and they sure as shit didn't hit anything or anyone. They were lying and he knew it and they knew he knew it.

"Someone seen you guys comin' in around four-thirty," the Sarge said. "And they weren't drunk."

"They're liars," Larry answered. *They're all liars.*

"I also know Mutt 'n Jeff came up the bank around three-thirty Sunday morning. That would put them on the highway about four-fifteen or four-thirty."

"So?"

"So that's the time you drove in," the Sarge said, looking squarely at Larry.

"We drove in at three."

"Not according to my eyewitness."

"Your eyewitness is wrong."

"I'm sure they're gonna do some tests on Mutt 'n Jeff's jackets. They might even ask for some paint from the van for comparison. If they match, then we have a smoking gun. You ever hear that term?"

They both sat in silence. Brief moments of that night were coming back to Daryl and he remembered hitting something, but it couldn't have been larger than a dog.

"We wanna lawyer," Larry said.

"I told you before, you're not under arrest. At least not yet."

"I still wanna lawyer."

"Why? Do you have something to hide?"

"No, I just wanna lawyer. It's my right."

"You seen too many cop shows. Let's go back to your statements. You tell me you came in at three in the morning and didn't see anything or anyone?"

"That's what we're tellin' you," Larry said.

"Okay, I've got what I need for now. I need your signature."

"Why?" Larry asked.

"To show that you've given me these statements of your own free will and to show it's what you've told me."

"What if we don' sign 'em?"

"Then I'll have to hold you."

"We didn't do nothin'," Daryl almost yelled.

"Then sign the statements and you can leave."

James carried Brenda's suitcase into the terminal. He went back outside for a smoke while she checked in. Then they sat in his truck and listened to the radio. The silence was drowning out George Strait.

"Did you fuck her?" she asked.

He hadn't expected it that way and said the only thing he could: nothing. *Maybe she'll disappear.*

"Did you?" she asked again.

"No," he said and didn't know if that was a lie or not. He saw her tears and reached for her.

"Don't touch me," she snapped.

After a few seconds, or minutes, she asked, "You know who I'm talkin' about?"

He said nothing.

"She called 'n said she spent the night with you."

"She came to my place with Liz 'n Sarah," he said. "She left with 'em."

"You sure?"

No. "Yes," he answered and hoped it sounded final.

She said nothing for a long time, looking out the window. Then she said, "I've never had to deal with this before." *If you'd only leave that booze alone.*

"I'm sorry," he said. *Did I fuck her?* "Where does 'at leave us?" he asked.

You with the clap and me outta here. "I don' know. I'll have to think about it."

"Fair enough," he said, not knowing why. Usually, he'd just laugh it off, but it wasn't going to work this time. Not with her. "Nothin' happened," he said.

"You told me," she said. "I have to believe you."

The walk to the terminal was one of the longest he'd ever taken and also one of the shortest. "Still want me to pick you up?" he asked.

"If you want."

"I'm askin'."

"Pick me up," she said and walked to the departure doors.

Larry and Daryl left the detachment at noon and walked home.

"You think they know it's us?" Daryl asked.

"Don' know," Larry said.

When they got home, they had to explain the whole thing to their dad.

"You fuckin' assholes," Sam said. "Y'know what you did?" He didn't wait for them to answer. "You lied. You signed statements sayin' you came in at three 'n they have a witness say you came in at four-thirty. Who the fuck you think they're gonna believe? You?"

They sat in silence.

"What time you get in?"

"I don' know," Larry lied.

"Well, you better fuckin' find out. You hit anythin'?"

"No," said Daryl.

"That fuckin' grille wasn't like 'at when you lef'."

"We didn' hit nothin'," Daryl said.

"You assholes are in deep shit. I want you outta here!"

"What?" Daryl said.

"Get outta here!" he screamed.

"Where we gonna go?" Daryl asked, almost in tears.

"I don' give a fuck! Jus' get outta here!"

"We got no place to go!" He was now in tears.

"I don' give a fuck! Get out!" Sam screamed. He grabbed Daryl and pushed him out the door.

Larry followed and the door slammed behind them.

"What're we gonna do?" Daryl cried.

"I'll take care of it," Larry said calmly.

"How?"

Larry walked to the storage shed next to the house. He took the axe and smashed the lock open, then went inside and found it. *Fucker.*

Sam heard the noise and swung the door open. *Assholes.* "What 'a fuck you doin'?" he screamed.

Larry came out of the shed. *Gonna blow your ass away.*

"Put 'at fuckin' gun down!" Sam screamed as he walked down the steps. *What 'a hell he think he's doin'? Tryin' scare me?*

Larry fired the first shot at Sam's feet. *Run, you old fuck.*

Sam stopped and looked down at his feet, then up at Larry. *What 'a fuck? He shot at me! My own son shot at me! My own flesh 'n blood!* He waddled back up the steps as fast as his short, stubby legs could carry his three hundred pounds. *Run.*

The second bullet entered his back and he fell forward. The steps were covered with flesh and blood. *My flesh 'n blood!* He rolled over and the last thing he saw was Larry. *My gun. My son. Asshole.*

Larry just stood there. *Die, you fat fuck.* He said the only thing he could. "You fuckin' asshole!"

Daryl watched this movie and wished it would end. *This is not happenin'.*

Larry turned to him. "It's gonna be okay," he said.

Larry then did something he'd thought about many times. He pushed and pulled the lever action then turned the gun on himself. He put the barrel in his mouth and put his thumb on the trigger. He closed his eyes and pushed the trigger.

He waited for one millionth of a second that lasted a million years. Then he heard it: the sound of metal hitting metal. It was like the sound of the Big Bang that created the universe and eventually all living things therein. Boom!

He waited for the bullet to enter his mouth and scatter his brains to the four winds and into oblivion. He waited for his inevitable journey to hell right behind his fat fuck of a father. He waited and waited.

He opened his eyes. At that moment, he gave up all hope and sat on the steps. He looked at his dad and almost felt sorry for the son of a bitch. "You fuckin' asshole."

Ernest Austin was working in his truck when he heard the shots and was the first person on the scene. He would later say it was like a bad dream. He saw Larry sitting on the steps next to his dad, who was lying face up with his eyes still open. Daryl was sitting on the ground rocking back and forth.

He went up to Larry, took the gun and patted him on the shoulder as if to say everything would be all right. He then went into the house and called the Sarge and the Chief. *What 'a fuck's goin' on? Is 'is a dream?* He knew something would happen to Sam sooner or later, but not this.

The Sarge and Chief David pulled up at the same time. The Sarge surveyed the situation, put the handcuffs on Larry and led him to the suburban.

"Daryl didn' have nothin' to do with 'is," Larry said.

"What?"

"Daryl didn' have nothin' to do with 'is."

Chief David walked over to Daryl and stood by him. *This is not real.* Daryl looked up, and for one of very few times in his life, Chief David didn't know what to do or say.

Martin arrived, looked around and then went into the house. He came out and covered Sam with a blanket. *Fuck sakes.*

Men, women and children were gathering on the side of the road watching this saga unfold. *Is Clint Eastwood actin' 'n directin' this shoot-'em up?*

Stella pulled up in the health centre's minivan and checked Sam's body. "Ernest, take him to the van," she said, nodding at Daryl.

Ernest helped Daryl off the ground then walked him to the minivan.

"Does he have any family that could look after him for the next few days?" Stella asked.

"Their mother's in Yellowknife," Ernest said.

They have a mother? "Anyone in town?"

"Only George," Chief David said.

"George who?" the Sarge asked.

"George Standing. Their uncle."

George is their uncle? Does bootlegging run in the family?

"I'll take him," Ernest said. "My wife 'n his mom are good friends. They're also cousins or somethin'."

"You got Clara's number?" David asked.

"Margaret does."

"Good. I'll see if I can get her on tomorrow's plane."

"Who's Clara?" Stella asked.

"His mom."

"Didn't know they had a mother," the Sarge said.

"Lef' ten or fifteen years ago," David said. "Moved to Yellowknife and remarried."

Ernest got into the minivan and Stella drove them to the health centre.

"I'm gonna take Larry to the cells," the Sarge said. "Be right back."

"I'll go with you," Martin said.

"I'll see if I can get Bertha to come down later," David told them. "I'll wait here." *Got fuck all else to do.* He realized that despite no formal plan, a well-oiled machine of caring, compassion and kindness had kicked into overdrive. *Too little, too late.*

They pulled out and he was alone with Sam. *I wouldn't be surprised if I woke up 'n this was all a nightmare.* He looked at the thirty or so people who had since gathered on the road. *Get back to your bingo games.* George Standing was parked on the side of the road. *Get back to your bootleggin'.* Neil was standing a little farther down. *What're you lookin' at?* A couple of people came over to see if there was anything they could do. *What else is there to do? We're killin' each other 'n ourselves. It would be easier if we all moved to the South American jungle and drank some fuckin' grape juice!*

At two o'clock, James was returning to Aberdeen and was thinking about Brenda. In the past, he'd leave a girl without so much as an adios, but he knew he couldn't do that to her. She'd treated him with respect and gave him his space and she was always there for him. *Maybe I should tell her it's over, beat her to the punch. But I don't want it to end. Or do I? I thought she'd just throw me out after one week, but she didn't. Louise. Fuckin' Louise. I should've stayed with her. Fuck sakes. I'm starting to sound like them old people. I should have done this, I should have done that. Angie. Fuckin' Angie. All I wanted was a quick 'n dirty fuck. Why didn't I go to Brenda? She was waiting.*

He thought about Jake and Mary and wondered if Jake had the same questions. He thought of Mutt and Jeff. *I don' wanna end up like 'em, at leas' not yet 'n not like 'at. I wanna go out in a blaze 'a glory. I wanna be remembered. How will 'ey remember me? James Friggin' Nathan: the drunk 'n slut. What 'ave I done with my life? Diddly. Don't even have a kid to carry on the tradition. More questions 'n what tradition? Mutt 'n Jeff? Jake 'n James? Not anymore. Jake is slowin' down. Mutt 'n Jeff are dead.*

He remembered the time Mutt and Jeff walked by his house a few years ago during Christmas looking like two orphans about to ask for more porridge. He felt sorry for them and invited them in and pulled out a couple of bottles. *Did I feel sorry for 'em, or did I feel sorry for myself? I was alone 'at day. Jake was at Bertha's 'n Brenda wasn't in 'a picture. It wasn' 'a first time I spent Christmas alone.*

He'd fried up some caribou meat and they had some potato juice as a side dish. They started telling stories and tried to outdo one another. They stayed with him that Christmas and all got drunk. The next day Jeff cut some wood for him and Mutt went to look at his rabbit snares. That afternoon, James pulled out three more bottles. *We didn't have fun 'at time. We just drank, got drunk 'n passed out. That's all I ever do: drink to pass out. Where's 'a fun? I drink to get drunk. No, I drink to pass out. To get rid 'a my dreams. Maybe I should move to Yellowknife with Brenda 'n paint. Get outta here 'n start new. I need a fuckin' drink. I wonder if other people talk to themselves in their heads. I wonder if I'm really nuts like they say I am. I wonder if I have all my marbles. I wonder if I have a full deck. I wonder if my lights are on but no one's home. I wonder —*

"I'm goin' fuckin' nuts!" he said out loud.

It was five o'clock when he got home. He could still smell the cleaning solution he'd used to hide the smell of Angie's perfume. *Hidin' the stench of infidelity.* The phone was ringing and he hoped it wasn't her.

"You heard?" Jake asked.

"What?"

"Sam's dead."

"Sam the Sham?" James asked and waited for the joke.

"Yeah," Jake said solemnly. "Larry shot him."

"What?"

"They got into an argument 'n Larry shot him."

"Where're you?" James asked after a few seconds.

"Mary's."

"Whatcha doin'?"

"Gonna have supper. Mary wants to know you wanna come over?"

"What's for supper?"

"Roas' fish."

I'm sick 'a fish. "I'll be over." *Boy, leave town for a day 'n 'a shit really hits the fan. First Mutt 'n Jeff, now Larry, Sam 'n Daryl. What's next? James Friggin' Nathan? Right after Brenda takes a shotgun to his ass?*

Jake and Mary were outside roasting fish on an open fire when he pulled up. Jake was as happy as he'd ever seen him. "What's with you two?" he asked. "Get engage or somethin'?"

"Not yet," Jake said.

Mary smiled.

"You diggin' in my stash?" James asked.

Mary laughed, then looked at James. "You don' do that, do you?"

James grinned. "Only for medicinal purposes."

After supper, they sat outside on the steps. James would always remember the exact time, since he'd just checked his watch looking for an excuse to leave.

"You remember Tom Kinney?" Jake asked out of the blue.

James heard but didn't answer. His head dropped and he travelled to another time and another place. He tried to shut out the memory, but he couldn't. He took a deep breath and came back to reality. *Nothin' to it! I'm gettin' better at 'is!* He looked at Jake and wondered what the fuck he was talking about.

"Tom Kinney?" Jake repeated. "You remember him? Our old supervisor."

"Yeah, why?"

"Seen him on TV las' night."

So? James looked at Mary and wondered what she was doing in his dream. "Yeah?" he said. "What's he doin'?" *Fuckin' little boys?*

"Was on a show 'bout trappin'," Jake answered, then looked at Mary.

Mary smiled and patted him on the shoulder.

James knew what was coming. He wanted to get up. He wanted to tell Jake to shut the fuck up. But he just looked at the sky and wished he could disappear into oblivion.

"He abused me," Jake said, looking at the steps. After a long silence, Jake added, "I never tol' anyone before." He looked up at James. "I tol' Mary 'n Bertha yesterday."

James continued to look at nothing.

Jake took a deep breath, then said, "Bertha said it happen to Michael too."

James suddenly felt dizzy. This all seemed so far away, like in a dream. He didn't know what to say or do. He wanted to get up and walk away, but his legs didn't work. *Fuck sakes.*

Jake took another deep breath, looked to the sky and for the first time in his life said it out loud. "I was sexually abused by Tom Kinney." He looked at James. "I didn' know things like 'at happen. I didn' know what he was doin'. I thought he was jus' playin'." He wiped the tears from his eyes, and Mary put an arm around him.

James wanted to stand but he didn't know if he could. *Why didn' I stay home?* He forced himself to look up and hoped the tears wouldn't show. *Why the fuck they bring me here? Why they bring back the fuckin' memories? Do they know?* He looked at them, but they weren't looking at him. Jake was looking at the floor and Mary was looking at Jake. *They don't know. Good, they'll never know — ever. It didn' happen. It's a dream 'n nothin' more.* He stood up, stretched and looked for a reason to leave.

"I jus' thought you should know," Jake said.

James nodded. He felt the tears and pushed them down. *Nothin' to it.*

When he got home he made a fire in his woodstove. He turned on the television and thought about what just happened. *What did happen? What 'a fuck's goin' on? Mutt 'n Jeff. Sam. Who's next?* The phone rang. *Let it be Angie. Need a fuck.* It was Jake. *Jake 'n Tom Kinney. Michael 'n Tom Kinney. Tom Kinney 'n a little boy.*

"Was gonna ask what you gonna do tomorrow?" Jake asked.

"Don' know," he answered. "Why?"

"Need some water."

"Can do that."

"When?"

"Bright 'n early."

"Sounds good to me."

James hung up. He wished Brenda would phone. *She's prob'ly still pissed off 'n wonderin' how to end it.* The phone rang. *Angie. Gonna get fucked.*

"Hi," Brenda said.

"Hi."

"I been callin' for the last few hours."

Was 'at suspicion? "I was havin' supper at Mary's," he answered.

"I heard what happened."

Did you now? Did you hear about Jake? Did you hear about Michael? Did you hear about . . .

"About Larry," she said.

"Oh."

"What happened?"

Tom Kinney fucked Jake 'n Michael 'n . . . "Larry shot Sam. Short version."

"Whatcha gonna do tomorrow?" she asked.

"Nothin' much. Get some water." *If I can, maybe I'll eat a bullet.*

"I could use some water too," she said. "My containers are on my steps."

Get your own fuckin' water, bitch. This is a one-way trip. "I'll pick 'em up tomorrow."

"I love you," she said and waited for his response. "Well, I should go," she said. "Gotta get up early for my interview."

"Yeah, same here."

"Just called to see how you're doing," she said.

And check up on me?

And check up on you.

"Brenda?"

"Yeah?"

"Nothin' happened."

She was quiet for a few seconds. "I know," she said.

Then why put me through this shit? He heard her hang up. He turned down the TV and turned on the radio to hear Liz and Sarah playing some country tunes, making an already miserable community feel more miserable. *Misery loves company.*

He went into his spare bedroom and opened the old trunk. He pulled out the gun case and some photo albums and took these into the living room. He took out the gun and looked at it. He pulled the hammer back and aimed at the wall. *I wonder.* He worked the lever action and watched the shell fall to the floor. *Could 'a blowed a hole right through my wall, or my head. They'd be scrapin' me off the walls tomorrow.* He put the gun back in its case and put it under his sofa. He looked at some old photos. *They're just photos.*

He put the albums back in the trunk and thought about Myra, then thought about going to George and blowing the useless fuck away and doing the whole world a favour. *Myra.* The tears came. *I love you.* He remembered the first time he made love to her and the smell of her body and the look in her eyes. He remembered what she'd told him about her husband, George. He didn't believe her then, but he came to the conclusion that she wouldn't lie about a thing like that. She was one of very few people on this planet he could say he truly loved. Sure, she was older, but he did love her. He tried to count the others. *Mom, Dad, Jake, Louise, Brenda.* At that moment he'd never felt so alone in all his life. *I'll always be alone.* He'd loved six people in this life and three of them were no longer on this plane of existence. He let the tears come for all of five seconds before he forced them down. *Nothin' to it.*

He thought about Louise and Brenda. He loved them both, no doubt about that. *It's too late for Louise. Or is it?* He thought about Michael and what he'd said about Louise and wondered if it was true. *Did he break her in?* It was and he knew it, but it didn't matter. He was not a virgin when he and Louise first did it and he shouldn't expect her to be one either. He thought about telling her he loved her, but one thing stopped him. *Brenda.* He loved her too. *Or do I?* He shook off the thought, then lay on his sofa and watched whatever was on the television. He fell asleep and dreamed of the young boy in the shower and wished he'd brought the gun to shoot his fucking dreams. He wished he could shoot all his dreams.

You can.

How?

Just put the gun in your mouth 'n pull 'a fuckin' trigger.

Who're you? Silence. *Are you the devil?* Silence. *Are you my dreams?* Silence. *Oh well, c'mon. Let's get it over with! Do your best!*

They did and they came smelling of hopelessness, despair and death. They came with big, fat hairy hands and false promises.

Nine

Famous Last Words

Tuesday, September 28th, 1999
The old wolf opened his eyes and stared at the horizon hoping the sun would rise so he could bask in its warmth. He was still tired and sleepy, but he was also hungry. He shook himself, then walked along the ridge. He could no longer wait for the caribou. He would have to meet them. His survival depended on it.

It was eight o'clock and Daryl was sitting at the kitchen table in Ernest and Margaret Austin's house. He'd been up early, having slept all of the previous evening and most of the night. He sipped his coffee and kept looking at the door wondering when the cops were going to arrest him. He watched Ernest cooking breakfast and wondered if he knew what had happened on the highway. He'd never known Ernest that well and was still unsure what was happening. He was also still very tired and everything was going too fast for him to comprehend. "So, what's going to happen to Larry?" he asked Ernest.

"They're gonna take him to Helena for his arraignment. The Chief 'n Martin are gonna see if they can keep him outta jail till his trial."

"Can they do 'at?"

"They can try, but the Sarge said it's not likely."

"Why?" *He only shot an asshole.*

"He's bein' charged with three counts."

After a few seconds, it slowly dawned on him: Mutt and Jeff. "Can I go see him?" he asked.

"The Sarge is takin' him to Helena now. We can see him down there."

He was walking down the long hallway that never seemed to end. *Again?* There were doors every ten feet and each one contained the same shower room. He must have opened a million of them and still the same thing. *What 'a fuck's goin' on?* He finally went into one and the door slammed shut behind him. *Shit.* He turned and there was the little boy in the pyjamas with the empty eyes. *Fuck sakes.* He looked for the door but it had disappeared. His heart was beating faster. He began looking for a way out but he couldn't see through the humidity. He felt a hand on his shoulder. Big, fat and hairy. *Oh shit!*

James fell off his sofa and put his hand out just in time to catch himself. He stood and looked around to see where he was and who was with him. He was home and alone. He started breathing again. *Same ol', same ol'.*

He made some coffee and prepared for his trip into the hills. He looked in his freezer and found two half-dried fish that he'd bought from Mutt and Jeff a few weeks ago and put these in a plastic bag.

Chief David was going through his mail and messages, but his mind wasn't on his task. He was going to Helena in a few minutes to see if he could keep Larry out of jail, but he didn't have much hope in achieving that. He was also going to pick up Larry and Daryl's mom, Clara. He wondered why she never visited. She had a brother, George Standing, who she could've stayed with despite the fact he was a bootlegger. He thought about Mutt and Jeff and Sam. They'd be burying them in the next few days and that meant a feast and no one in the community had any caribou or moose meat. He was about to leave when James and Jake walked into his office.

"Hey, Chief, what's new?" Jake asked.

"Same ol'."

"Yeah, know whatcha mean."

"What're you two up to?"

"Gonna get some water 'n check for caribou," James said. *Might eat a couple bullets too. Wanna come?* "Need my Treaty shells."

"Good, everybody's sick 'a fish," he said. "How much?"

"Five or six million rounds," Jake said.

David smiled. "How long since you two been huntin'?"

"Five or six million years."

David pulled out four boxes of shells. "Might be early," he said.

"Yeah, but what 'a hell," James said. *Can always blow my brains out as a sacrifice to the Creator.*

"Ernest said he's goin' up river," Jake said.

"Yeah?"

"I'm gonna head up with him."

"Me too," James said and surprised himself.

"Lots 'a moose up 'at way," David said.

"What you got planned for the day?" James asked.

"Gonna pick up Clara in Helena."

Clara, Myra, George, secrets. "Well," James shrugged. "Gotta go."

Chief David thought about their fathers. They were best friends right up until the end and they'd died a few months apart. These two were more like brothers. He tried to keep away from them, even in high school. They brought back too many memories. *Late-night visits. Shower rooms. Hostels and other shitholes.*

At eleven-thirty, James and Jake were driving up to the mountains. Jake had fallen asleep. The sun was shining, but James could see some black clouds on the horizon far to the west and hoped it wouldn't snow. He loved this time of the year. There were no bugs and little to no traffic, and this gave him the time to think, or go brain dead.

Jake woke up, looked around to see where they were, then sipped his coffee. "Me 'n Mary are talkin' about gettin' outta here," he said.

"Yeah?" James said. "Where?"

"Yellowknife. Need a change 'n a life."

"Me too."

"You goin'?" Jake asked.

"No idea. Need a change 'n a life, I mean."

They came to the creek where most of the community got their water, and they filled their containers. Even though the community had treated water, most of the People preferred the water from the mountains. It made the best tea and coffee in the civilized world and was the best tasting since Evian. Some say it was better.

After they'd loaded the last of the water into the truck, they looked for any sign of caribou in the hills. They saw diddly. James lit a cigarette, then hacked his lungs out and gave it to Jake, who threw it away.

"Gotta quit 'at shit," Jake said. "No good for your health."

"Too fuckin' late to worry about 'at now," James said. "Think we should go further?"

"Sure. Ain't got nothin' better to do."

"Wanna walk up on 'a hills. Might see somethin'."

"Sure, why not."

"Your enthusiasm is encouragin'," James said.

Five miles and an hour from the highway, Jake wished he'd said no. They were standing on a ridge looking north and were both wheezing and coughing.

James looked back at his truck on the highway. It looked as if it were a million miles away. "Think you'll survive?" he asked.

"If I don't, jus' leave me," Jake answered.

They both laughed, then started walking. Had they taken the time to look, they would've seen the old wolf on the ridge to the west of where they stood.

It took them an hour and a half to walk back to the truck. They were sweating, coughing, wheezing and ready to croak. It was two-thirty and not such a bad day if you were in shape and liked hiking in the mountains with cowboy boots.

"If you put me outta my misery I wouldn't hold it agin you," Jake wheezed, leaning against the truck.

James brought out a bottle of water and had a drink. "Bottled in 'a Swiss Alps," he read to Jake and handed him the bottle.

"And drunk by a couple 'a Injuns right next to a stream full 'a mountain water," Jake answered.

"We could bottle 'is here 'n sell it for half the cost 'a this shit."

"Why don't you?"

"Would you buy water from an Injun?"

"Only firewater."

"Exactly," James said. After a few minutes, he asked, "You ready?"

"Yeah." Jake stretched. "I think I'm gonna survive. Today is not a good day to die."

"What're you, some sort 'a Injun outta *Dances*?"

"No, heard a Klingon say 'at in a movie once."

"Injuns in space. What next?"

Jake was about to put his tired carcass in the truck when he spotted a movement in the open area between the ridge and the highway. He took out his binoculars and came face to face with the old wolf. "Speakin' 'a wolves. There's one out there."

"Yeah, where?"

"Look like he's alone. Scraggly lookin'," Jake said. "Wanna shoot him?"

"What for?"

"We're hunters. We shoot critters."

"Prob'ly not worth nothin' 'ese days," James said. He thought about the fish. "Wanna be Kevin Costner? Got some fish in 'a back."

Jake laughed. "No, thanks. He might eat my carcass."

James looked at the wolf. It was skinny and its fur wasn't in the best of shape and it was the fall. *Old.* He took the two fish and laid them on the side of the road. *Mutt 'n Jeff's fish.*

"Think he'll eat it?" Jake asked.

"Don' know. Wanna go little further?"

"Sure, why not?"

They drove farther, then went traditional and had some pop and chips. *Real fuckin' Injuns.* James was about to throw his pop can into the ditch when he remembered the trip he'd taken with Martin a few years ago. Martin kept getting out of the truck to pick up cans and beer bottles. *He's never gonna do that again.* He rubbed his eyes and wondered what the hell was going on with him these last few days. He looked at Jake, who looked like a damned schoolboy on an outing. He looked at his cowboy boots. *Real fuckin' Indians.* He could picture them carrying caribou over the flats with friggin' cowboy boots. *We're prepared, all right. We're prepared for a night in the Saloon.*

Daryl was in the Helena detachment of the RCMP looking at Larry through the glass that separated them. They'd just returned from the courthouse, where Larry had pleaded no contest to two counts of manslaughter and one count of second-degree murder. Despite Chief David and Martin's request, Larry was ordered held in custody until his trial in December. Now he looked around the small room and wondered if they had hidden microphones in here. He wondered what to say to Daryl. They'd hardly talked about much of anything in the past. They only told each other what they'd heard or what they'd seen: gossip. He didn't have to say anything. Daryl did.

"How'd they fin' out?" he asked.

"Find out what?"

"About Mutt 'n Jeff."

"I tol' 'em."

"Nobody know it was us."

"They got an eyewitness."

"Why?" Daryl asked.

"Why what?"

"Why you take it?"

Larry shrugged. "I'm gonna go to jail for Sam," he said. "Might as well go for Mutt 'n Jeff too."

"Wasn't you."

Larry looked around for any sign of a camera or hidden microphones. "It was," he answered, and his voice told Daryl that it was final.

It was after six when James and Jake pulled into town and spotted Martin sitting outside his house. They decided to stop.

"Hi, Martin, what's up?" James asked.

"Not much."

"I mean with Larry?"

"Oh, they're gonna keep him in jail till his trial."

"Too bad."

"Yeah," Martin said.

"Where they keepin' him?"

"Yellowknife."

"When's 'a trial?" Jake asked.

"December."

"What you think he'll get?" James asked.

"No idea," Martin said. "Three counts."

"Three?" Jake said.

"Yeah, he's the one was drivin' when Mutt 'n Jeff were killed."

James and Jake said nothing.

"His mom should be in soon," Martin added.

"Me 'n Jake were up in 'a hills," James said quickly. "Didn't see nothin'."

Martin looked to the hills. "Caribou'll be here soon."

"Saw one scrawny wolf," Jake said.

"Me 'n Jake are gonna go up river with Ernest," James said.

"Yeah, when?" Martin asked.

"Don' know. Maybe in a couple days."

"I wouldn't mind gettin' outta town for while," Martin said.

"Ask Ernest," James said. "More the merrier."

As they left Martin wondered if he'd been just as crazy as those two in his younger days. *Yes, I was.* He smiled at the thought of getting back on the land one last time.

Chief David and Bertha were sitting around the fire outside Old Pierre's house. Most of the People had come around all day and visited. They cooked and ate, all the while talking about Mutt and Jeff and what good men they were and wondered why these things happened.

Bertha Moses was telling Chief David about Michael and Jake and Tom Kinney. The Chief listened to the secrets others imparted to her and generally he too kept them a secret. But this one was different. This one was very different.

"I've known about it for years," she was saying. "I told Martin 'n Jane about Michael 'cause they should know. I told nobody about Jake 'cause I didn't know if it was true. Only had Michael's word for that." She looked at the fire and sighed. "Guess it was true."

David looked from her to the night sky and wondered if she knew. He looked and she was crying. After a few minutes, he asked, "So what happens now?"

She shrugged. "Don' know," she said. "We'll take it one day at a time. Up to Jake, I guess." After a few minutes of silence, she sighed again. "Well, thanks for listening. Can't keep 'ese things to myself. Drive me crazy if I do."

"No problem," David said.

Bertha looked at him sitting in the dark next to the fire. "You'll be okay?"

"Yeah."

"I'm gonna go home now," she said. "Been a long day. Good night."

Chief David sat by the fire for a long time wondering if this was real. He looked around and it was. *Was it only me, Jake 'n Michael? Or were there more? Was James one of them? Of course he was. I was there. Or was it a dream?*

He stood, looked to the sky and screamed, and it sounded like a million porcupines crying in the dark. It felt good to finally get that shit out of his system. *Should 'a done 'is years ago.*

"David?" Wanda and his two children were watching him from the steps of Old Pierre's house. "You ready?" she asked.

He looked at the fire and realized he hadn't screamed. The shit was buried so deep in his soul that it was nothing more than a dream. *Maybe it is.*

Jake checked the time. *Ten o'clock.* He was in his shorts and in Mary's bed. A week ago this would've never happened. He lay back and looked at the ceiling. *I spent 'a las' twenty-five years workin' 'n partyin'.*

Except for his house, he had no real assets. He did have his trade, but he didn't pursue it with any great conviction. The events of the last few days had forced him to re-evaluate his life and his commitment to a better future.

Mary came in, wearing an oversized Mickey Mouse T-shirt and nothing else. She crawled in next to him. "Hey, hon, whatcha thinkin'?" she asked and poked him with her tits.

"You, me 'n Yellowknife."

"Think we should?"

He thought about it for a few seconds. "Think we should," he answered. "Nothin' here for me 'n I need a full-time job. I can get on with one 'a the companies."

"You could. There're few jobs in my profession, but I'll take anything."

"What're your parents gonna think? You runnin' away with a semi-old man."

"Already told you what I told 'em. It's me 'n you all the way," she said. "I'm gonna spend the rest 'a my life with you."

"You sure?" he asked.

"I'm sure," she said, almost in tears.

"I mean about me?"

"Yes." She hugged him.

A few minutes later, they were making love. She arched her back and moaned as she came and held him. He was the best lover she'd ever had. Not that there had been many. He stopped and she looked up at him

"Mary?" he whispered.

"Yeah?"

"I jus' wanna thank you for comin' into my life," he said and the tears started. He did not hold them back. He raised himself on his arms. He was still hard and was still in her. "Mary," he said, "I know you've been waitin' for me to ask and I can't think of a better time."

She put her arms around his neck. She knew what was coming, or at least she hoped she knew what was coming. She felt him deep inside her and moaned.

"Mary," he said. "Will you marry me?"

She closed her eyes and started crying. She arched her back, took a deep breath and said, "Yes, I will."

They lay there for a few seconds, then she began moving.

After they'd come together, he looked at her and smiled. He was still in her and she was smiling. "You know," he said, "someday, someone is gonna ask what you were doin' when he proposed."

She laughed and wrapped her legs around him and said, "Havin' the best sex of my life."

"You don't mind I wasn't on bended knee?" he asked.

"Well," she said, "you were on your knees. Sort 'a."

A few minutes later, she lay in his arms and he had his head buried in her hair. He loved the way she smelled.

"Jake?"

"Yeah?"

"Can I tell James?"

"Sure."

"Right now?"

"Whatever."

She picked up the phone and dialled James's number.

"Hello?" he answered.

"Hey, James," she said.

"Hi, who's 'is?"

"Angie. Who you think?"

"Hi, Angie, wanna come over?"

"You would too, you shit-heel."

James laughed. "What's up?"

"I'm gonna get married!"

"To who?"

"To *who?* To Jake!"

James laughed again. "Congrats."

"Thanks. Wanna talk to him?"

"Sure."

She handed the phone to Jake.

"Hey," Jake said.

"Hey. You did it."

"Sure did."

"When?"

"No idea."

Mary grabbed the phone. "James, you'll be the best man, won't you?"

"Can you think of a better man?"

"Only one." She grinned at Jake. "James?"

"Yeah?"

She felt the tears. "I just wanna say thanks."

"For what?"

"For being there for him."

"Worked both ways."

"I know," she said. "But thanks anyways."

"My pleasure."

"Good night, James."

James hung up his phone and looked at his television. He wasn't watching. He was thinking of his future and other things. Things were happening too fast and he felt uneasy. He wished he could slow things down. The phone rang again and he knew it had to be Brenda checking up on him.

"Hi, Brenda," he said into the phone.

"Fuck Brenda, you asshole," Angie slurred.

He hung up and it rang again. He picked it up.

"You're mad or what?" she said.

"I really wish you wouldn't call," he said.

"Why? You don't like me anymore?"

"Why am I talkin' to you?" he asked, then hung up.

It rang a few more times. Half an hour later, it started ringing again. This time it was Brenda.

"What's the latest on the home front?" she asked. "Any more bad news?"

"Just one."

"What happen now?"

"Jake 'n Mary are gettin' hitched."

"You're kiddin'!"

"No."

"Good for them."

"How'd the interview go?" he asked.

"Good. They're gonna send me an offer. I'm the only one they interviewed."

"Congratulations."

"Thanks. I'm checking some places down here," she said, then went silent for a few seconds. "You gonna come down with me?"

"You want me to?"

"Yes."

"Consider it done."

"Really?"

"Really."

"When are you gonna pop the question?" she asked, and then said, "Sorry, I shouldn't 'a said that."

"No, that's okay. I'll ask when I ask 'n not a moment before or after."

"I'm gonna hold you to that."

"You do that."

"Just thought I'd call to let you know I have a new job," she said.

"Me 'n Jake are goin' up river with Ernest," he said. He then realized he hadn't been up river since he was eleven.

"When?"

"Couple days. I'll know tomorrow," he said. "Think I should sell my house?"

"I can't make 'at decision for you," she said. "It's a big move."

"I can rent, I guess, but I'd rather sell than become a landlord."

"What about Jake 'n Mary?"

"They're thinkin' of leavin' too."

"Really? Where?"

"Yellowknife," he answered. "Nothin' here for a young couple." *Young couple. Why do I feel old all of a sudden?* "I'll pick you up tomorrow," he said, having nothing else to say.

"James?"

"Yeah?" He knew what was coming.

"I love you," she said, then waited for him to say it. Instead, he said the same thing she'd heard a million times before.

"Me too."

Why can't you say it? Tell me. "See you tomorrow," she said.

"Yeah," he said and hung up.

From out of nowhere the tears came. Great big sobs were being forced from the depths of his being and there wasn't a fucking thing he could do about it.

He slowly dropped to the floor and willed himself to stop. He couldn't. He willed himself to disappear. He prayed to the Powers That Be to help him. He lay there for what seemed like hours, but no help came. *Fuck you, 'en.* After a few minutes or hours, he looked to see if anyone had seen. He was alone. *I'll always be alone.*

He got to his feet and wiped his eyes and thought about going for a drink. *Jus' one.*

No such thing as one.

Fuck off!

A picture flashed through his mind.

It's time.

He reached under the sofa and pulled out the gun case his mom had made in another time and another place. He smelled it and the memories returned. *Tanned moose skin! Mom! Dad! The Redstone! Home!* He didn't fight the tears this time. *Mission schools! Residential schools! Hostels! Hellholes! Shitholes!* He closed his eyes and hung his head. *Dark rooms! Hairy hands! False promises! Little boys! Shower rooms!*

Once again he dropped to his knees. *The pain! The foul stench of his breath! His hairy hands!* The scream that came had been bottled up for a thousand years and then some. *Why?*

You know why.

Fuck off! He wiped the tears from his eyes and took out the gun. *Why not?*

Why not?

Nothin' to it.

'Course not.

Put it in my mouth 'n pull 'a fuckin' trigger.

Do it.

Fuck off!

He thought about it. *Will I burn in hell?*

Anywhere is better 'an 'is fuckin' place!

Fuck off! He sat on the floor and put his head against the wall. He loaded one shell. Click! *Nothin' to it.* He put the barrel under his chin and put his thumb on the trigger. He closed his eyes and tried to think of what to say. *Famous last words.*

Tick! Tock! Tick! Tock! *Why is 'at clock so loud?* He opened his eyes. *What 'a hell is 'is?* He was in a long hallway that somehow looked familiar. *What 'a fuck is 'is? Where is 'is?* It smelled like an institution: sterile. The walls were barren and painted an ugly green made uglier by the fluorescent lights that gave off a low, steady hum.

Tick! Tock! Tick! Tock! He looked up at the clock like he'd done a million times in a former life. *Four o'clock. Why always four?*

You know why.

Fuck off!

Not now 'n not ever.

He started walking down the hall to the stairway, but something was not right. The end of the hall kept getting farther and farther away. *What's goin' on?*

It suddenly came to him. *It's a dream! I'm in my fuckin' dream!* He closed his eyes and willed himself to wake up, but before he could do it he got a feeling he was not alone. *Someone is . . .*

He opened his eyes and stopped moving. He stopped breathing. He waited. *Where're you?*

The young Indian boy emerged from the wall as if pushed. James jumped. *Shit!*

The boy was dressed in a pair of nondescript pyjamas and his hair was cut very short. *I'm in 'a hostel 'n it's thirty years ago! It's 'a day I was —*

The day you were what?

Fuck off!

The little boy's head was bowed for one second, then he looked up at him. What James saw made him take one step back. His eyes were empty. *Fuck sakes!* He wanted to run, but he couldn't. Something was keeping him here. *What? Who're you?* He received no answer. He continued looking at the little boy. The little boy was looking at him. Or was he? It was as if he was looking right through him. *Move! Run! Get outta here!*

As if he'd heard, the little boy started walking down the hall. He disappeared into the wall and re-emerged in the shower room. James looked around. *How'd I get here? Why am I here?*

A picture of the room and bed flashed through his mind. *That didn't happen!* He turned on one of the showers and the cold water hit him as though he'd been slapped. He gasped and held his breath. He put his face in the water and tried to push the pictures from his mind. He couldn't. They were too disgusting. *The pain! The foul stench of his breath! His hairy hands!*

He kicked off his pyjama bottoms. He pulled off his top and threw it to the floor. He hoped the water would wash away the stench. It wouldn't and somehow he knew this, but that didn't stop him from trying. He reached for the soap and began scrubbing. He prayed. *Please, help me.* His breathing came faster, his actions more urgent. He could still smell his breath. He could still feel his hairy hands. He scrubbed harder. *It's not comin' out.*

He stopped. *Someone is watchin' me.* He turned and saw another boy. *What's he doin' here?* He dropped the soap and immersed his face in the water. He willed the other boy to disappear. *He can't be here. This is not real.*

After what seemed like an eternity, he slowly opened his eyes and the other boy had disappeared. *It's a dream.* He looked up at the ceiling and the tears returned, this time accompanied by a scream. *This is real! It's not a dream!* He tried to hold them in. He couldn't. He closed his eyes. *Why is 'is happenin' to me? Is 'is right? Am I bein' punished?* He wished his parents were there. He wondered if they knew what was going on, but how could they? His body trembled. *This is wrong!*

After his tears had flowed down the drain and after his cries had dissipated, he reached for his pyjamas and wrung them out. Then an idea formed in his young mind. It was a horrible one, but it was the only one he could think of. He looked around, but he was alone. *I'll always be alone.*

He put the pyjamas around his neck and slowly tightened them. But he couldn't do it. Something or someone was stopping him. He looked around. *Who're you?* He received no answer, so he tried again. But again something would not let him.

He was now sobbing. The memory of what had gone on in that room dragged his young body to the floor. *Why?* The scream that followed came from the depths of his being and echoed off the shower-room walls. It was a silent scream, but if it were given a voice, it would've sounded like a million porcupines crying in the dark.

After another eternity had come and gone, he sat up and dried himself with his pyjamas, then wrung them out again. He put them on then walked into the hall and turned towards the dorm. He thought about the other boy. *Was he really there?*

He looked up at the ceiling. *I'm in 'a dorm. I'm in my bed. How'd I get here? Maybe it was a dream.* He looked at the boy in the next bed. *Is he up?* He looked like he was staring at the ceiling, but James couldn't tell and he really didn't care.

He closed his eyes and tried to drive the memory into the Dream World. *Things like 'is don' happen. Or do they?* He thought about the other boy. *Was he real or part 'a my dream? Does he know what happen?*

James opened his eyes and he was still sitting on the floor of his house. He still had the gun in his hand. *Was 'at real or a dream? Who's 'a little boy? Why's he in 'a shower?* He knew who and why. *They're part 'a the Dream World 'n not real. Or are they?* He thought about it and for one of the very few times in his life everything became clear and his mind was made up. *This time. This time it's for good.*

He put the barrel under his chin and put his thumb on the trigger. He closed his eyes and said the only two words he could think up. "Fuck it."

Ten

Deep Dark Secrets

Wednesday, September 29th, 1999
The old wolf stood on the highway where he had found the fish and searched for more. He looked in the direction the truck had gone and hoped they'd return. They didn't. After a few seconds, he turned north to meet the caribou.

Jake and Mary got up at eight and told her mom and dad about their plans. Her mom hugged them both, but her dad was more cautious. "Take care of her," he told Jake.

"I will," he said.

Mary went to work and wrote up her letter of resignation that morning and gave them three months' notice. *We could head to Yellowknife right after Christmas.* She was walking on air.

Meanwhile, Jake had walked over to James's house and found it locked. He could see the television still on and banged on the door. *Did he do it?* He looked through the window and saw James coming out of his bedroom looking like shit.

"You look like shit," he said when James let him in.

"Feel like it. Didn' know I was so outta shape."

"Same here."

"I gotta take a wash," James said and went into the bathroom.

Jake looked in the spare bedroom and was surprised to see the gun on the bed. He worked the lever and out popped a shell. He put it in his pocket and returned the gun to the trunk.

"You had breakfast?" James asked from the bathroom.

"Jus' coffee."

"Wanna go to Sal's? My treat."

"Sure. You need company to Helena?"

"Sure," James answered as he came out of the bathroom. He grabbed his jacket and followed Jake out the door.

Sarah smiled when they walked in to Sal's. "Mornin'," she said. "Whatcha gonna have?"

"Gimme two bacon 'n eggers to go 'n couple cups of coffee," James said.

She returned with their coffees. "What's new?"

"Diddly," James answered. "Jake popped the big one."

It took her a few seconds to get that one. "He did?" She looked at Jake. "You did?"

"Yep."

"When?"

"Las' night."

"When's 'a big day?"

"No idea."

"What about you?" she asked James.

"What about me?"

"When're you gonna pop the question?"

"Geez, Sarah. I thought we were jus' good friends?"

"Not me!" she said. "I meant you know."

James shrugged. "Who knows."

When they left the coffee shop, James said, "There, you don' have to send out invites now. Be all over town by time we get back."

Jake laughed at that one and knew it would be.

The highway was covered with yellow leaves and they were halfway to Helena when Jake asked, "What you remember 'bout Tom Kinney?"

Asshole. "Not a hell of a lot. Big, fat 'n a beard." *Smelly 'n hairy.*

"Not 'at tall. He was short. We were small."

"So what happens now?" James asked.

"No idea."

They drove in silence for a while before Jake finally said something that made James tense for a few seconds. "So far it's just me 'n Michael 'n he's dead. I wonder if there were others."

James kept his eyes on the highway. "I'm sure there were."

"No doubt."

Little do you know.

Brenda was waiting for them in the terminal. She held James like she hadn't seen him in years and that, he figured, was a good sign. She also gave Jake a hug and he looked like a kid again.

"Congratulations," she said.

"Thanks."

"There's a message for you at the airline counter," Brenda told James.

James went to the counter. A few minutes later, he was back. "David wants me to pick up Mutt and Jeff," he said.

Half an hour later, they were on the highway heading home. One live body, two dead and two walking dead.

Daryl walked down the blood-splattered steps and looked at the shed. He carried a small bag with most of his clothes and wondered if he'd ever be back. *Not likely.* He'd made up his mind to return to Yellowknife with his mom and get on with life, or what was left of it.

He walked to the van and looked at the bush guard and thought about Mutt and Jeff and knew he was the one who killed them. It was an accident, but he'd killed them nonetheless.

He thought back to yesterday and his tearful reunion with his mom at the Helena airport. He thought he'd hate her for abandoning him and Larry, but he didn't. He'd cried a million tears and today he felt better. They'd gone to see Larry, and his mom cried for what seemed like forever. Larry would be leaving for Yellowknife today and would return in December for his trial. He would probably get five to ten if he was lucky.

"You okay?" Grace asked.

He looked up at Grace and Bertha, who'd come with him to help clean the house. "Yeah," he answered.

His mom wouldn't go into the house. She ran out a million years ago and had promised never to return.

Around four o'clock James and Jake dropped Brenda off at her apartment. "Wanna come for supper?" she asked James. *You can do me afterwards, or before, or both.*

"Long as it's not fish," he said. *Don' mind if it smells like fish.*

She laughed.

They drove to the church and unloaded the bodies of Mutt and Jeff. James then drove Jake to his house.

"Gonna hang a For Sale sign on my door," Jake said as he got out.

James looked at the house. "Lots 'a memories."

"Any good?"

He thought for a while. "Can't think 'a one."

"It's jus' a house."

"Got 'at right."

"Gonna change," Jake said. "See you in a bit."

James drove home. He needed a shave and a shower and some major fumigation, but for now he washed, shaved and changed his shirt.

When Jake came in, James said, "Ya know, if you were gonna stay, I'd give you my house."

"Does 'at mean you're leavin'?"

"She asked 'n I did promise."

"Well, I been doin' a lot 'a thinkin' 'n we're outta here."

James said nothing.

"You gotta get outta here too," Jake said.

"I know."

Jake took the bullet from his pocket and tossed it to James. James caught it, looked at it, then put it on his table. He said nothing.

With that, they walked out into the cool autumn evening and headed for the main road and came out across from the Saloon. They both stood and looked at it as if it were a dream or a nightmare. Jake had promised he'd never go in there again. James wondered if one more wouldn't hurt.

Jake then headed north and James headed south. After a few steps, Jake turned. "James?"

"Yeah?"

"I tried it."

James didn't have to ask.

"It ain't worth it," Jake said.

James didn't know what to say.

After what seemed like an eternity, Jake said, "You're my brother."

In the thirty years since they'd become brothers, this was the first time one of them had ever said it to the other. James said the only thing he could. "I know."

"See you tomorrow."

Around four-thirty, Jane, Clara, Bertha and Margaret were catching up on stories and gossip at Martin and Jane's house. Martin was sleeping and Daryl was in one of the bedrooms watching television and thinking. He'd asked Larry about the house, vehicles and other things that they'd now inherited. Larry had told him to give it away since they were never coming back. Daryl had already given the van to Martin, who took it without a word. He still had to decide what to do with the house and the other truck. He walked into the living room and told the women he was going to see Ernest. *Time to get rid of the past.*

Ernest was tinkering with his old Ford. He was ready to drive it into the river and drown it when Daryl drove up in Sam's new truck.

"What's wrong?" Daryl asked.

"Beats me."

He looked at Ernest's truck, then at Sam's. He looked at the keys in his hands then held them up to the sun setting in the west. "I wanna say thanks for takin' me in other night," he said and felt the tears coming. *Push 'em back where they belong. Men don't cry.*

"No problem."

"Here." He handed Ernest the keys. "You can have the truck."

Ernest stood there with the keys to a brand-new truck in one hand and a wrench in the other. "You sure?"

"Yeah. Larry tol' me give it away."

"I don' know what to say."

"Don' have to say nothin'," Daryl said. "It's me has to say thanks."

It was after six and Brenda and James were sitting on her sofa watching television. "I seen couple good places in Yellowknife," she said, then looked up to see if he was listening, but she couldn't tell. "I also got enough for a down payment."

"I'm gonna sell my house," he said.

"You sure?"

"I think so."

"James, you have to be sure. Once you sell, there's no turnin' back."

"I know, but what's here for me?"

"What is here for you?" she asked.

Nothin' but memories 'n not good ones at that. There's Louise, but she's married 'n she don't care 'bout me anyways.

"Is 'ere anythin' here for you?" she asked again.

"There's nothin' here for me," he said, and it sounded final.

"We'll have 'nough for a down payment," she said. "And you can get into paintin'. I've always wanted to marry an artist."

"Is 'at a proposal?" he asked.

"No, that's a hint."

"Keep hintin'."

"I will," she said.

They sat around and one thing led to another and they were in bed. Afterwards they lay in each other's arms and looked at the ceiling. James was thinking about Jake and what he'd told him about Tom Kinney and the hostel and dark rooms and shower rooms and . . . *He didn' tell me 'bout shower rooms! Where 'at come from?*

"James?"

"Yeah?"

"Whatcha thinkin' 'bout?"

"Oh, nothin'."

She rolled over to face him. "You know we never talk?"

"Whatcha wanna talk 'bout?"

"I don't know. Tell me your secrets." *Tell me you love me. Say it.*

"You don' wanna hear 'ose."

"Why not?"

"Too dismal," he said.

She laid her head on his chest. "James?" *I've got a secret for you.*

"Yeah?"

"Tell me yours 'n I'll tell you mine." *My one 'n only secret.*

"What you wanna know?" *Wanna hear a real good one?*

"Tell me your darkes' secret."

"Which one?" he asked and gave a small laugh.

"Ha! You got lots?"

"Not really," he said.

"Tell me somethin'," she asked. "An' promise you won't get mad."

"What?" he asked.

"How come you 'n Louise broke up after high school?"

Gave her the clap too many times. "Don' know," he said. "Jus' happened."

"She's a beautiful woman."

She is.

"You still think about her?"

"No," he said. "Why all 'ese questions?"

"Jus' wanna know more about you."

"Nothin' to know about," he said. "Lived 'n worked here all my life. Ain't got no secrets."

"So you don't have any deep dark secrets?" she asked.

He thought about Jake and Michael and Tom Kinney, then he thought about his dream last night. *Or was it a dream?* "No."

Eleven

The Confession

Thursday, September 30th, 1999
The old wolf followed the instincts given to him by his ancestors thousands of years ago and walked north to the caribou. The clouds were low and the wind chilled him to the bone, which was all he was at this point. He stopped in the middle of the valley, lifted his head and howled his displeasure at the fact that at that moment he was alone and very lonely. He waited for an answer. None came. None would ever come.

Chief David woke up and followed his routine. He made coffee, then sat by his window and wondered what other shit his People created or conjured up for him last night. When he became the Chief, Chief Alfred had come to his house and talked to him. He told David that he'd be getting up every morning and sitting by his window worrying about his people. He did.

He made breakfast, then woke up his wife and left. He stopped by the cemetery on his way to the office to see if the graves were completed. They were. *One big grave for Mutt 'n Jeff. Lived together, died together, buried together.*

He looked at Sam's grave in the corner of the cemetery and had trouble being sympathetic. *The booze Mutt 'n Jeff drank prob'ly came from him. If he didn't sell it to 'em, they would still be alive lookin' for money to buy another one from him. Nothin' would change. I'm gettin' tired 'a this shit.*

Brenda woke up at eight and wondered if she should go into work now that she had a new job. She'd have to tell the mayor and he would not be happy. She looked at James sleeping, then kissed him on the cheek. *He's dreamin'.*

James woke up and looked at Brenda, then let the dream slip back into the Dream World. It took him a few seconds to realize where he was. "Mornin'," he said.

He got up and made coffee, then looked out the window at the fall colours and the leaves that were starting to fall. *God, I hate this time 'a year. Gotta look for a job. Can't wait for one to come knockin'. Too many people doin' 'at.*

"Whatcha gonna do today?" Brenda asked.

"Look for a job, sell my house, look for caribou, see when Ernest is goin' up. Lots," he said. "What about you?"

"I'm gonna go in for half a day then hand in my resignation. I'll give 'em two, maybe three weeks' notice."

"When you start?"

"November."

"I wonder if Ian 'n Bella would be interested," he said.

"In what?"

"My house."

"You should ask."

Later, James made plans to sell his house. *The only thing keepin' me in 'is hellhole is Louise 'n she don't care.* He thought about the few times they'd talked in the last twenty years and she always seemed to be in a hurry to get away from him. *Why am I wastin' my time?*

He called Ian and Bella and asked if they were interested in his house. Ian and Bella owned the Saloon and were looking for a new house. They asked for a ballpark figure and he told them a hundred and they damn near croaked. He laughed and told them eighty, and that was more reasonable. He didn't tell them about the dreams and nightmares it contained, but if they didn't want them he'd take them along. Like he had a choice. In the end, they offered him seventy and he told them he'd get back to them.

He called Jake and said he'd meet him at the Band office in a few minutes, then picked up his jacket and walked out into the morning air. He passed Louise on her way to work and smiled at her and said nothing. *What do I say? She was yesterday. Brenda is tomorrow 'n forever. Can't fix the past, but I can plan the future. Ain't got nothin' else.*

He watched her walk down the gravel road. She was still tall, dark and beautiful, and she still had her long, black hair. He time-travelled back to the first time they stood outside the hostel. Then he turned and got on with life, or what was left of it. *That's the past.*

Had he turned again, he would've seen Louise looking at him. *Wonder if it's too late. It is. He's the past 'n I have no future.* She turned and got on with life, or what was left of it. *Nothin' left.*

James was getting some coffee in the Band office just as Jake walked in looking like he was in love or smoking something. They sat in the boardroom and James told him about Ian and Bella's offer.

"Sounds good to me," Jake said.

"What about you?"

"Talked to John Harley 'is mornin'. The bugger talk me down to forty. Said he can get a mortgage."

"You gonna take it?"

"Have to. It's not like there's a big market in town. Besides, the land's worth ten 'n the house is only worth about thirty, if that."

James thought about that, then called Bella and dropped his price to seventy-five on the condition they pay for the legal work and such. She jumped and he took.

"Done deal," he told Jake.

"You know what you're doin'?"

"I haven't the foggiest. If it don't work out I can always cut my ear off 'n move to Tahiti. Certainly be cheaper."

Ernest came by looking for Chief David.

"Hey, Ernest, when you leavin'?" James asked.

"Prob'ly this afternoon."

"Who's goin' with you?"

"Got Ken 'n Rick to come with me," he said. "Gonna need meat for feast tomorrow."

"Think you'll get one?" Jake asked.

"Millions 'a moose up 'at way," Ernest said. "Wanna help me load? You can drive my truck back."

"You still gonna go up Saturday?"

"Yep, Martin's comin' with me."

"I'm goin' up too," Chief David said. He turned to Jake. "You wanna tag along?"

"Sure," Jake answered.

"You?" David asked James.

"Yeah," he said. "Why not?"

Jake went to Bertha's office and talked with her and James went with him, having nothing else to do.

"The more you talk about it, the easier it becomes," she said. "Don't expect changes overnight." She also told him she had a two-day healing workshop starting on Wednesday and it would be good if he attended just to take it in. She also said he might want to go the legal route, but that would mean going public and that wasn't going to be easy.

Jake agreed he'd let it be for now. *Maybe forever.*

James spent most of the rest of the day cleaning up his house and wondering what he should take, what he should leave and what he should burn. He didn't have that many clothes and most of them were black. *Who am I? Johnny Fuckin' Cash?* He didn't have a hell of a lot of mementos except for an old trunk full of dreams and an older gun full of nightmares. *Is 'at all I accumulated in my short 'n colourful life?*

He wondered if Liz or Sarah would like to take some of his furniture. He checked the clock on the wall. Mary had invited him and Brenda for supper and it was quitting time.

Five minutes later, he was parked in front of the Hamlet office. "You do it?" he asked as Brenda sat in the truck.

She smiled. "Done it."

"How'd he take it?"

"Didn't like it, but what 'a hell."

"Sol' my house."

She was going to ask if he was sure. She didn't.

Jake drove to the health centre in Ernest's truck and picked up Mary at five o'clock and they went shopping. He told her about John Harley's offer and she thought it was fair but was sad. It was the house that Jake had always known. *It was the house where we first made love.*

At home they made their plans about Yellowknife known to her mom and dad. They weren't excited, but were glad since Aberdeen was no place to raise a family right now. Or so they said.

That was something Jake never thought about: kids. He looked at Mary and she read his mind.

"Not right now," she whispered, and he breathed a sigh of relief.

Jake had sent his resumé to the employment office in Yellowknife and had checked the papers and found a couple of jobs in Hay River and Fort Simpson, but nothing in Yellowknife. He sent it to some of the larger companies in the city and made a few phone calls, but it was too early to tell. *Jus' wait till the Band got their phone bill next month.*

Mary had given her notice to the health centre and faxed her resumé to a bunch of agencies and departments in Yellowknife. It would be a month or so before she got a response. Her last day was the end of December and they would leave after New Year's Day. *Things are movin' so fast.*

Brenda and James showed up and everyone sat around talking in the kitchen.

Mary was peeling potatoes and Jake was cutting up some meat for stew. Her mom had some bannock cooking in the oven and the whole house smelled like home.

"How does December 21st sound to you?" Mary asked.

"For what?"

"Our weddin'."

"Whatever turns your crank."

"You do," she said. "I want somethin' simple, not fancy."

"I can live with that."

"Guess that means I'm gonna have to practise my jiggin'," James said.

"You ever jig?" Brenda asked.

"Not sober."

"I saw you once," Jake said. "You were not bad. 'Course don' take my word for it. I was drunk too."

James and Brenda drove to his house at nine-thirty and he picked up some clothes and his shaving gear.

It was a big step for him and Jake to be taking in such a short time, and Brenda wondered if they were up to it. Mary was just back from college and the adjustment wasn't going to be difficult for her. *I lived there for twenty years. It's home. This was never home.*

She watched James pack and wondered once again what was the attraction. He was temporarily unemployed, but a person with his knowledge and intelligence shouldn't have a difficult time getting a job. He might be crazy, but he had a brain in that mixed-up head of his. She hoped he'd get into painting and drawing again. He was good and she knew it, but he still had doubts and needed something to boost his confidence.

James was thinking about the future and wondering if he was doing the right thing. *Things are movin' so fast.* But he knew it was for the best. *What are my options?* He could stay and continue to look for work here and there and live on Unemployment in between and wait for his Old Age Pension. He could stay drunk and womanize for the rest of his life and maybe get run over by some drunk driver on the highway in the middle of the night. *Stay 'n die. Go 'n live. Sounds easy, but it ain't.*

He'd told Bella to get her lawyer to draw up the papers. Soon after he signed on the dotted line, he and Brenda would leave with nothing but their personal belongings in the back of his truck and their future in front of them. It still hadn't dawned on him that it was forever, since nothing in his life was forever. *Only temporary.* He looked at Brenda. *Wonder if I can live with her forever.* He then realized he had no other options. *None whatsoever.*

"Brenda?"

"Yeah?"

"How much you payin' for your apartment?"

"Lots."

"Wanna move in here for a month?"

She looked at him to see if he was joking. "Are you sure?"

"Havin' doubts?" he asked and smiled.

"No." *Not really.* "You really want me to move in?"

"Yeah, be only for a month, then we're outta here."

"Together?"

"Together."

"What will people think?" she asked.

"It's not like we're the first ones to shack up, ya know."

"I know, but . . ."

"You havin' second thoughts?"

"No." *Not really.*

"Tell you what. We'll go to your place 'n you can think about movin' in later. How's 'at?"

"I'll get outta my lease tomorrow 'n I can move in on the weekend."

"Me 'n Jake are gonna head up river with Ernest on Saturday."

"Oh," she said and thought. "Well, Saturday is a good day to have a sale at my place. All I need is my personal stuff. The rest I can sell."

They took the scenic route: Main Street. They saw a couple of people staggering to a party or the hopes of a party. They also saw Angie walking down the road looking like she was finally sobering up.

"I won't mention her again," Brenda said.

"Thanks."

Chief David and his wife, Wanda, were sitting in their living room watching the news and not really paying attention. She laid her head on his shoulder. "What's on your mind?" she asked.

"Lots."

"Like?"

"Mutt 'n Jeff, Sam, Larry 'n Daryl, Martin, Michael."

"Michael?"

"Lazarus."

"Why him?"

"Bertha talked to me 'bout him," he said. "She knows why he did it."

Wanda said nothing. *If he wants to talk about, he'll talk about it.*

"He was sexually abused by Tom Kinney," David said. "So was Jake."

Wanda took this all in, then asked a rhetorical question. "How many more?"

"At least one," he said quietly.

She knew what he meant. "You okay?"

"Yeah, I talked about it when I was in treatment, but never to you or anyone else."

"You're not alone," she said. "You'll never be alone."

"Thanks. For a while I thought it was jus' me and I thought no one would believe me. Or they wouldn' understan'. Or they would jus' laugh 'n ridicule me."

"It's too serious to be ridiculed or laughed at," she said.

"I know," he said. "Bertha's puttin' on a healing workshop nex' week," he said. "That'll be a good place for people to talk about this 'n other things."

"If they do."

"They will."

"How?"

"Gonna tell 'em."

"You mean you're gonna disclose?"

"Gotta start somewhere," he said. "Why not me?" *It's time anyhow.*

"What's gonna happen?" she asked. "Afterwards, I mean."

"Don't know. Prob'ly cause one hell of a commotion. We're talkin' 'bout things that happen long time ago." *Thirty-two years next month.*

"I'll stand with you."

"Thanks," he said. "You're a good wife."

"I know," she said and smiled.

"You're takin' this well."

"I'm not. I'm jus' goin' with the flow. You're my husband 'n I love you. You're also a strong man 'n you can deal with it." *You have to.*

Chief David woke up early that morning and sat by his living-room window. *Am I makin' the right decision? Of course I am. One person is dead because of this fucker.* He thought about Jake and James. *What about 'em? They ever think about endin' it? Endin' it? I can't even say it.* After what seemed like forever, he said it. "Suicide."

He sat in absolute silence for a few minutes. *How many times have I thought about it? Too fuckin' many.* It was a long time before he made up his mind.

"Fuck it," he said. "It's time."

Twelve

A Celebration of Life and Death

Friday, October 1st, 1999
The old wolf had taken to eating dead leaves and the few berries that still clung to the plants. He travelled at a slower pace to conserve the energy he'd need for the chase that was yet to come. If it came.

Brenda phoned in sick only to find the Hamlet office was closed for the day because of the funeral. She made coffee, then started cooking breakfast while James washed and shaved. She had a big job ahead of her. She had to talk to her mom and dad, then she had to call her daughter. She wondered how Michelle would like James given that he was younger than her dad, unemployed and an alcoholic. *Just fine, thank you.* She knew her mom and dad had nothing against him. They were just not overly impressed with him and didn't like that he was sleeping with their only daughter. *Fuckin' me is more like it.*

James came out of the washroom and smiled. She was sure of it. It was her life and if she wanted to spend it with a forty-year-old alcoholic then so be it. *Nobody's business but mine.* "I'm gonna see my mom 'n dad 'is mornin'," she said. "I'll call Michelle later."

He said nothing and they had breakfast. *Why him? Why now?* Back in their high-school days, he was screwing everything in sight and was crazy. Or so they said. *Was he? Why is he so quiet? Is it me?*

They finished their breakfast in silence, then he did the dishes and drove her to her parents' house. "I'm gettin' outta shotgun range," he said.

She laughed at that one, then walked into her parents' house, praying for the best. "Mom! Dad! I'm movin' back to Yellowknife," she said. "With James."

Peter and Eliza looked to see if she was serious. She looked to see if they'd heard.

"You pregnant?" Eliza asked.

"No, but that's an idea."

"That's not funny," Peter said. "You know what you're gettin' into?"

"Yes," Brenda said.

"You love him?" Eliza asked.

"Yes."

"You think he'll settle down?" Peter asked.

"I think so."

"He love you?" Eliza asked.

"Yes," she replied. *He hasn't said it, but . . .*

"What're your plans?" her dad asked.

"He's gonna sell his house 'n move to Yellowknife with me. We're gonna look for a house 'n he's gonna look for work."

"Good," her dad said.

"You gonna be happy?" her mom asked.

"I'm happy now," she said.

"You know he's your first cousin?" her dad asked.

"What?"

"Just kiddin'," he said.

"Even so," she said, "we're not gonna have kids." *We're jus' gonna have sex 'n lots of it!*

"We talked about this," her mom said. "We're not happy, but if you love him . . ."

She did not finish. There was no need to.

"At leas' 'is time I get to give you away," her dad said, then smiled for the first time.

Brenda suddenly realized what they were thinking.

"When?" her mom asked.

"We're not gonna get married right away," she said. "We're gonna move, then we'll see what happens."

"He asked?" her mom asked.

"Not yet," she said. "But he will."

They said nothing, since living together was more or less the norm for these times.

Brenda later went to the radio station and announced her house sale and someone put two and two together. And before you could say sin, the whole town knew they were going to live together. And before you could say rumours, they were getting married.

The funeral for Mutt and Jeff was held at two o'clock, and James, Jake and ten men carried the coffins out of the church and laid them to rest in an already overcrowded cemetery. Old Pierre and Dora thanked the People for coming. Old Pierre said it was an accident and the People shouldn't hold it against Larry because these things happen and that's the way it is. He then invited them to his house for something to eat and to talk about the good old days.

James caught a glimpse of Clara and said nothing. What was there to say? It was none of his business and the person who told him about Clara and her brother, George, was no longer living. He looked at Myra's grave and promised someday to buy a headstone, then shook off the memory and got on with life, or what was left of it.

He and Jake drove up to the dock at three o'clock and met Ernest,

Ken and Rick. They loaded the moose they'd killed into Ernest's truck, and Ernest, Ken and Rick drove to Old Pierre and Dora's and unloaded most of it.

James dropped off Jake, then picked up Brenda and drove her up to Old Pierre's.

"My mom 'n dad want a ride up," she said.

"You wanna pick 'em up?"

"No, you do it."

"You know if he's got a shotgun?"

"I talk to them 'n they're okay with it," she said. "Not ecstatic, but okay."

"I'll take my chances," he said as he dropped her off.

Peter and Eliza were still in good shape and could've easily run up to Old Pierre and Dora's but saw this as an opportunity to meet James. It was not as though they hadn't met him before, just in a different mode.

Peter opened the door for Eliza and she hopped in like she was going to a bingo game. James watched the old man to make sure he wasn't packing any heat. The ride was short and uneventful and it didn't hurt as much as he thought it would. They both told him to make her happy and that was that. *Nothin' to it.*

Outside Old Pierre's house, Chief David was cutting up moose meat and placing the pieces on the grill. There was fish, ham, turkey and a million types of salads, but everyone was waiting for moose meat. They were sick of fish.

Clara and Daryl arrived with Martin and Jane and went in to see Old Pierre, where Clara attempted to apologize for her son's mistake. Old Pierre would not hear it. It was an accident and things like this happened all the time. Clara cried while Daryl stood and said nothing.

It was five-thirty when Chief David took a break and joined James and Jake at the fire. "Gonna go up with Ernest 'n Martin," he said. "You guys wanna take my boat?"

"Sure," James said. "When you gonna head up?"

"Ernest is gonna leave at nine with Martin," he said, then looked at the two men sitting next to him. *Hostels, dark rooms, hairy hands.* He looked at Jake. "Heard about your experience," he told him.

Jake looked at him. He'd told no one but Bertha and Mary.

"Bertha likes to dump on me," David said. "She has no one, so I'm the lucky one."

"That's okay," Jake said. "Gotta talk 'bout it sooner or later."

James didn't know why he said it, but he did. And by the time he was aware of it, it was too late to retract. He looked at the flames. "Happen to me too," he said.

Jake heard but did not look at him.

Chief David did look at him and nodded. *I know. I was there.* After a few rounds, he said, "I was in his room a few months earlier," he said.

James and Jake heard, but not really. They didn't hear the word "earlier," or if they did, they didn't dwell on it. Earlier meant before a specific time. The specific time was a dark, cold night in January of 1968. A few months earlier meant October of 1967.

"Wonder how many?" Jake finally asked no one and no one answered.

David stood up and looked at the crowd. "Bertha's gonna have her workshop nex' week," he said. "I'm gonna say somethin' 'bout what happened to me."

"You gonna disclose?" Jake asked.

David looked at him, then at James. "Why not?" he said. "Somebody's gotta do it sooner or later."

The three men watched the fire in silence and listened to people talking and laughing at a funeral.

David did not tell them he was awake when Tom Kinney came in and took James out of the dorm. He did not tell them he was awake when Michael and Jake snuck into the hall. He did not tell them he was awake when they returned and went to sleep. He did not tell them he was awake when James returned with his pyjamas soaking wet. He did not tell them he was glad when Tom Kinney moved on to other boys. He did not tell them he had the same demons, dreams and nightmares. He did not tell them he tried to take a one-way ride into the hills many times. He only told them they weren't alone.

It was eight o'clock when James and Brenda brought her things over to his house. He sat at the table and waited for the kettle to boil and Brenda to finish unpacking. "You call your daughter?" he asked.

"Not yet," she said. "I've been tryin' to think of what to tell her." *Hi, Michelle, guess what? I'm gonna shack up with a forty-year-old alcoholic who's outta work 'n a starvin' artist.*

"She know about us?"

"I told her last spring. She did say she was gonna break it to her dad, but I don't know if she did."

Did you tell her I was a drunk 'n a whoremonger? Makes you a whore.

"What am I worried about?" she said. "This is the happiest I been in a long time 'n I have nothin' to worry about. She don't like, she don't like it. She's a grown woman — almost." *Didn't tell her you're a drunk 'n a whoremonger. That makes me a whore.* She took the phone in the bedroom and was out in fifteen minutes. "Well, now they know," she said.

James didn't ask how they took it. *None 'a my business.* He also realized two things. First, it was Friday and his table was waiting for him at the Saloon. Second, he hadn't had a drink since Sunday.

Thirteen

The Dream World

Saturday, October 2nd, 1999
The grizzly was digging up ground squirrels with ease, using his massive forepaws. In his younger days, the old wolf might've gone to investigate, but today he was no match for the grizzly and he knew it. His instincts kept moving him north.

Saturday saw the sun shining on the land of the Blue People. Ernest, David and Martin left the community around nine and were on their way up the Teal to the Redstone. James and Jake prepared to follow in David's boat. Mary had decided to go at the last minute and was busy taking photos of James, Jake and anything that moved. They pushed out, and Brenda watched them leave for a place that James and Jake had not seen in thirty years. They caught up to Ernest about fifty miles up river and decided to make a fire and have lunch.

"Where was your dad's cabin?" David asked Jake as they sat around the fire.

"Down below 'bout five miles."

"You didn't tell me," Mary said.

"Nothin' there," he said, then looked downriver and the tears came.

"Sorry," David said.

"Not a prob." He smiled. "Gotta deal with it. I was hopin' I could jus' pass it." He was silent for a few minutes. "I gotta stop on 'a way back," he said to James.

James shrugged. "No prob."

The funeral for Sam Hunter was held at one o'clock, and thirty people showed up. There were no twenty-one-gun salutes and no tears. Clara and Daryl did not attend, but no one noticed. Or if they did, they didn't care.

Afterwards, the congregation hurried off to buy bingo cards or get a crock from George Standing, who was glad that one of the competition was out of the picture. He was even happier it was Sam, but he didn't tell anyone since he had no close friends and no family as far as he was concerned. He did have a sister and saw her only from a distance. No one noticed that he didn't talk to her and very few, if any, gave a shit.

Brenda was standing in an empty apartment that only a few hours earlier had contained all her worldly possessions. Nothing remained except for a few wall hangings she didn't want to let go. She took these and walked out of the apartment for the last time. She'd sold everything she owned and there was no turning back.

The two boats were approaching the Redstone. James could barely remember how it looked, but he knew it was there. *The place of my birth. My home.* He tried to hide the tears, but couldn't. He sat down and let them come.

Jake drove the boat and said nothing while Mary watched. She was not surprised, since Jake had told her what James and Chief David had said the previous night. She patted James on the shoulder. "It's okay."

James looked to the west and saw the same mountains his mom and dad woke up to every morning for the twelve years they were married. This was where his dad shot the moose they tanned and made into a gun case that now rested on the side of the boat. This was where he was conceived, born and raised for the first six years of his life. This was where he spent every summer after he entered the hostel until he was eleven. *I can't remember one damned thing about those years. Where are they? In the Dream World?*

They landed, and James walked up the bank and looked at the one-room cabin that looked so much bigger in his dreams. He opened the door. *Home.* Someone walked up behind him.

"I remember the year he got married 'n brought your mom here," Martin said. "You were born two years later."

Martin looked better than he had in a long time. He was in his element. He too was home.

"He asked me 'n Jane to be your godparents," he said.

"I don' think I was baptized."

"I know. They kept wantin' to do it but never found the time. Sometimes I think he didn' wanna do it."

"I'm not really into religion," James answered quietly.

Martin didn't ask. He looked at the river, hills and mountains. "Me, this is my church."

The land was beautiful and virtually untouched. No one had come up here since the seventies, when trapping was still a way to make a living. It was God's country and then some.

By six-thirty they'd set up a camp. After eating, they sat around the fire and watched the sunset. They also listened to Mary ask a million questions. "Are there any old graves around?"

"None," Martin answered. "Long ago when our People died, they brought 'em up here 'n burned the body."

"Why?"

"Our People believe the Creator created us in 'a Redstone River," he said and pointed south. "Jus' up there. They say when you burned the body, you sent 'eir soul back to the Old People 'n returned their body to the land."

"Who's 'a Old People?"

"The Old People were the first People the Creator made. They say they still live in 'a mountains." He walked to the bank. "You guys all know I'm gonna die. Not right now, but soon. Maybe in six months or a year. Be spring or fall 'en." He looked at them sitting around the fire. "I already tol' my wife I don' wanna be buried in town. I wanna be sent back to the Ol' People."

"How does it feel?" Mary asked.

Martin looked at her.

"To know?"

Martin looked to the mountains. "I've accepted it. I had a good life. Did what I wanted. Got no regrets." He sat and looked at the fire, then at James. "Sometimes you jus' gotta play the hand you're dealt."

James looked into the fire, then at the land, and a million questions came to mind. A million questions with a million possible answers.

Clara walked to the cemetery that evening and looked at the fresh mound of earth that covered the remains of the man she once loved and married. There were no flowers and only a bare wooden cross to mark his grave. She took a wedding band from her purse and looked at it for a long time. *You were never a husband or a father.* She dropped the ring on the mound, stepped on it and said the only thing she could. "I should've done it myself." She walked away.

It was ten o'clock and the stars were out in full force. "Gonna be good day tomorrow," Martin said.

"How come our People don't drum anymore?" Mary asked.

"Missionaries took 'at away in 'a 1800s."

"Why?"

"Devil's music, or so they tol' our People."

"So our People haven't drummed for a hundred years?"

"Las' time 'ey drummed was 1965 when Chief Francis died. Always liked drum dancin'. Be good if someone brought it back." He paused. "Our language will be gone in 'nother generation. Once 'at goes we'll have nothin'." *We'll be jus' 'nother bunch 'a Indians.*

David looked at Jake, then at James. They were both looking at the fire. "I'm gonna tell 'em," David said.

Everyone looked at him, but only James and Jake knew what he meant. James looked at Jake, who shrugged. "Gotta do it sooner or later," he said.

David looked at the fire, then at the sky, then at the darkness that surrounded them. He took a deep breath. "Bertha's gonna put on a healin' workshop nex' week 'n I've decided to disclose."

Ernest looked at Chief David, then at Martin, then at James and Jake. Somehow he knew what was coming and wasn't surprised.

"Go ahead," Martin said in the language.

David looked at Martin, and somehow this Elder gave him the strength to say it. "I was abused sexually in the hostel." He took another deep breath. "By Tom Kinney."

"When?" Martin asked.

"October '67," David said without hesitation.

"Who else knows?"

"Except for you, only my wife."

"You should let Bertha know."

"I will."

"How you feel?" Martin asked.

David grinned. "Not as bad as I thought I'd feel. Relieved."

"That's good. It's not your fault, you know."

"I know," David said. "I know that now."

Jake looked into the fire. As if hypnotized, he said, "Happened to me too."

No one said anything for a million years, then James heard a voice. "Me too." He looked up and everyone was looking at him. He realized it was his voice. Somehow he did not feel the shame he thought he'd feel. He felt good. He also felt like telling more, but didn't.

"Happen to Michael too," Martin said to the fire.

Again, no one said anything.

"That's why he lived the way he did. That's why he went into the hills." Martin looked at Chief David. "You're not alone."

"I know," David said. He wondered how alone he'd be at the healing workshop, but thought the hell with it. *It's time.*

"Thanks," Martin said.

The three men looked at him and nodded. Nothing was said after that. Nothing had to be said. The proverbial fan had been turned on.

Soon after, Martin and Ernest went to the cabin to sleep. Jake and Mary went to the tent, where Jake dreamed of a little china doll standing on the bank waving as they drove by. He didn't look at her and she was crying. He had some unfinished business that he needed to take care of.

James and David sat around the fire looking at the stars and listened to music on the small tape deck they'd brought. Eventually David asked, "You ever tell anyone?"

James looked at him like he was a dream. "Not a one."

"I tol' some people when I was in treatment couple years ago. Tol' my wife a few days ago." He looked into the night sky. "Gonna have to tell my parents before the workshop."

"What happens after?"

"No idea," David answered. "Leas' not yet." He looked at James sitting on his sleeping bag next to the fire. "James?"

"Yeah?"

"You ever think about it?"

James looked away. "Thought about it," he answered. "Tried it too."

"Jus' thought I'd ask," David said, "I thought I was the only one." He lay on his sleeping bag and looked at the sky. "What a fuckin' life," he said.

James did not respond. He too lay on his sleeping bag and looked at the night sky and listened to the fire, the river and the wind in the trees. He didn't know it, but he was trying to stay awake as long as possible. *Old habits die hard.*

A few minutes later, he heard laughter coming from the cabin and wondered what Ernest and Martin were doing. *Playin' poker?* He walked to the cabin and opened the door. *What is this?*

His mom was sitting at the table sewing and his dad was tickling a young boy on the bed in the corner. They were laughing, but he couldn't hear them. All he heard was the wind and the river. He closed his eyes and took a deep breath, and everything went quiet. *They're gone. The dream's over.*

He opened his eyes and they were looking at him. *How can they? This is a dream!* He looked at his mom and she smiled and the tears came. A million years of sorrow, sadness and anguish poured from his soul and he slowly sank to his knees. *I'll wake up. I always do.*

After an eternity, he looked up and they were still there. His mom walked to him in slow motion. She reached out and touched his face. Her hand felt warm. He looked into her eyes and saw the compassion. He felt a hand on his shoulder and turned to see his dad smiling. His dad and mom then slowly walked out the door and into the night. *Shadows. Is 'at what I see in my dreams?*

He expected the little boy to be gone, but he was still there. James looked at the moose-skin moccasins. *I still have 'ose at home.*

The little boy looked at him with no emotion. He held up his arms as if he expected to be picked up. James picked him up and became one with the dream. He closed his eyes and felt a peace he'd never felt in his life.

Fourteen

Intimate Conversations

Sunday, October 3rd, 1999
The old wolf came over the hill and there they were: the caribou. He tested the air to make sure he was downwind, then rested his tired body on a hill. He began looking for the old and the weak.

"What you wanna do?" Ernest asked as they arrived at Joseph Nathan's cabin. They'd spent the better part of the day up the Teal hunting and had taken three moose and were tired. Most of the meat was piled neatly on spruce boughs in David's Lund boat.

"I'd like to stay 'nother day or two," Martin said. "Do some more huntin' tomorrow 'n leave the nex'."

"Good," Ernest said. "Don' know when I'll be up here again."

"Sounds good to me," Chief David said. This trip had given him the opportunity to think about what he was going to say at the healing workshop, and he still needed more time.

"What you gonna do?" Ernest asked James, Jake and Mary.

After a few seconds, Jake said to James, "I'd like to see my dad's cabin."

He then realized that Jake had never been there since the fire. "Not a prob," James said, then turned to Chief David. "We'll head in tomorrow 'n let 'em know you'll be in day after."

James then walked over to the cabin. He opened the door and looked inside. *What did the dream mean? Is that their way of sayin' goodbye — for now? Is that their way of sayin' I'm on my own?*

"They'll always be here," Martin said.

James did not turn.

"They were always here," Martin continued. "You just have to remember they're with the Old People now."

James looked at him.

"That's why I wanna be sent back," Martin said. "I'd rather be out here than in some hole in 'a ground."

James looked across the river at the mountains. It was as if they were in another time. The problems of the real world were far away and far downriver. "This is the first time I've been here since they died," he said.

"You got lots of time to return. This is my last time," Martin said. "For a while." He smiled.

James pushed the tears down where they belonged.

"It's not their fault," Martin said. "It's not yours too. That's jus' the way things worked out 'n nothin' we can do will change that."

James wondered if Martin knew about him and Jake before last night. He knew about Michael, but did he know about them? And what of David? Did he know about him as well?

"You understan'?" Martin asked.

James felt the anger and the tears. He wanted to scream. He wanted to hit something. He walked to the bank, sank to his knees and cried. After he'd summoned the strength to push the tears back down to the depths of his fucked-up soul, he stood and screamed so loud that no one said a thing. His scream echoed out over the land and disappeared into the primordial forest.

Martin came up beside him. He folded his arms and waited. After a few minutes, he said again, "It's not your fault 'n it's not theirs."

James took a deep breath. "I know."

Martin had tears in his eyes. "They were my friends," he said. "He was my brother 'n she was my sister."

Then it dawned on James. Martin was telling him in his own roundabout way that James was his son and he was his father. Not biologically, of course, but traditionally. And sometimes that's even stronger and more lasting.

James remembered the many times Martin had talked to him like an old friend over the years. He remembered Martin coming to his house to ask him to take him into the hills to hunt, or to just kill time, or just to get out of town for a few hours. James never hesitated when he asked, nor did he ask why. He just did it. Martin had sons and sons-in-law that could've taken him, but he'd asked James. James thought nothing of it. That's just the way it was.

"Thanks," James said.

Martin grinned. "That's what I'm here for."

It was four-thirty when James, Jake and Mary reached the site where Matthew's cabin had once stood. Jake guided the boat to shore and James tied up.

"We don't have a tent," Mary said. "What kind 'a Indians are we?"

"Not prepared ones, 'at's for sure," Jake answered, and they laughed at that one.

They walked up a trail that hadn't been used for more than thirty years to a site no one had stood on for just as long. Only a few charred logs showed Jake where the cabin had once stood. Suddenly it came to him. *They're still here.* He sank to his knees.

Mary watched, and after a long time she asked, "You okay?"

"Yeah, I'm okay," he said, and slowly got to his feet. "They're still here."

James knew what he meant, but Mary didn't.

"They're still here," Jake said to Mary. "They were never buried in town."

"I'm sorry," she said.

Jake kneeled and touched the ground, then looked at the river. *Part 'a the land, part 'a the water.* "A few years ago I heard a Chief up north say that healin' was a journey 'n there is no end." He looked at Mary and smiled. "I thought he was full 'a shit. Now I understand."

They made a fire and boiled some tea and roasted some meat, then sat around and looked at the land as Jake's parents and sister must have done in another time. It was six when they set their sleeping bags around the open fire.

"I remember when my mom 'n dad came to town to pick up Esther from the hostel," Jake said. "I asked if I could go, but they told me to stay. I thought they didn't care." He felt the tears coming. "I remember Esther walkin' down thc hall." He paused. "They cut her hair 'n I wanted to kill 'em." Then he stood up and screamed. "I wanted to kill you!" He looked at Mary. "Don't ever cut your hair," he said quietly.

Mary didn't know why she said it, but she did. "I'm not Esther."

The tears returned, and Jake sank to his knees again. When it was over, he stood and looked at the mountains and the sky. *When will it end? How long do I carry the hate, the anger, the rage 'n the sorrow?* He sat and looked into the fire. "I'm sorry," he said to Mary.

"Don't be. It is not your shame 'n it's not your rage. Give it back or let it go."

He said nothing.

"Know what I mean?" she asked.

"Yeah," he said and smiled.

They sat around for an hour making small talk and generally killing time. Sometime around nine, Jake stretched out on his sleeping bag and immediately fell asleep. Mary watched. Tonight he would have to meet his dreams on his own. She covered him with his jacket, then sat beside James. "Thank you again."

"For what?"

"For bein' there. For bein' here. For lookin' after him."

"My pleasure," he said. "I'm afraid I never did a good job."

"You're his brother, not his father."

"I know, but sometimes it felt 'at way."

Mary looked at the fire. "What're we doin' here?"

James thought about that one. "I've no idea," he said. "It was jus' a huntin' trip."

"Do you feel it?"

"Yeah. I don' know how to explain it, but I feel it."

"Some things don't need explainin'."

"Things are goin' so fast I don' know what to think. Other day when we were outside your house I wanted to get outta there. I couldn't stand hearin' him talk about it. It brought back too many memories."

"I understand."

"I went home 'n took out some old photos," he said.

"And?"

"And I took out the gun Michael left me." He took a deep breath. "There was a shell in it 'n I knew what it was doin' 'ere." He paused. "I thought about it many times."

Mary said nothing.

"I tried it many times."

"Say it," she said.

"What?"

"Say it. There's a word for it. Say it."

"Suicide."

"There."

"I thought about suicide many times," he said. "I thought about it other night after you called tellin' me you was gettin' married."

"Wasn't over me, was it?" she teased.

He smiled. "No. It was over my wasted life. It was over Tom Kinney. It was over Angie. It was over Brenda. It was over Louise. It was over my mom 'n dad. It was over everythin'."

"Jake tol' me."

He looked at her, confused.

"About Tom Kinney," she said.

"Oh."

"You're not angry?"

"No, feel better about it, I think."

She said nothing for a long time, then asked, "You still in love with Louise?"

He thought about that for a few seconds. "I still care for her, but Brenda 'n me got plans."

"Are you still in love with her?" she asked again.

"I don' know," he lied.

"Are you?"

He realized she was trying to get a straight answer from him. He said the only thing that came to his mind: he told the truth. "Yes."

"Wasn' 'at hard, was it?"

"Not really," he said and smiled.

"One 'a my instructors said if you wanna move forward, you have to take care of your past issues. Know what I mean?"

"I think so."

"I don't know what you 'n Jake went through 'cause I was never in the hostel except in Helena 'n it was different. I guess I came along at the right time."

"I seen shows about mission schools. I wonder how many of our People went through what I . . . what we went through. People like Martin, Ernest, Sam, George 'n Myra." He stopped.

Mary waited. "Were you 'n Myra lovers?"

"How'd you know?"

"Seen you two in Helena a couple times when I was in 'a hostel. I never figured it out till just now."

"She was lonely 'n one thing led to another."

"Were you in love with her?" she asked.

"She was a very beautiful woman."

"Were you in love with her?" she asked again.

"Yes," he said. "I asked her to leave with me. But she said she was too old. Funny you should mention her, I thought about her the other day."

"I didn't."

"What?"

"I didn't mention her. You did."

He thought about it and she was right. "I gotta get outta here," he said. "Before it kills me." *Or before I kill myself.*

"That's just geography."

"I know, but 'at's all I got right now. Better 'an the alternative."

"Guess you're right," she said. "What other secrets you got?"

"None."

She said nothing.

"Lots," he said.

"You ever think of quittin'?"

"Quittin' what?" *Life? Lots. Just tol' you that.*

"Drinkin'."

"No," he said. *I don' have a problem.* Then he realized something and grinned at Mary. "Haven't had a drink for a week," he said.

"Miss it?" she asked.

"Not up here."

They heard Jake moving and she went over to him and slipped into his arms. A few minutes later, he fell asleep again while she listened to his heart and followed him into the Dream World, wherever that was.

James added more wood to the fire and lay on his sleeping bag. *What am I doin' here?* He looked at Jake and Mary and wondered if he loved Brenda as much as Jake loved Mary. He wondered if Brenda loved him as much as Mary loved Jake. *Why're all these questions comin' now?*

He looked into the darkness and wondered if the dream was real. He suddenly realized it *was* a dream. Or was it? *Dreams are not real. Or are they?* He thought about Tom Kinney. *You, I'm gonna kill.* He thought about Myra. *I love you. I'll always love you.* He thought about Louise. *Why am I thinkin' of you after all 'ese years?* He thought about Brenda. *Are you just 'nother stop on my way to oblivion?*

Fifteen

The River

Monday, October 4th, 1999
The old wolf could spot no weakness in the herd. He walked towards them from downwind hoping to get as close as he could before starting the chase. He could wait no longer. His hunger urged him on.

Jake opened his eyes and saw the fog above him. He wondered if it would roll in and consume him like it had in his last million dreams. He shivered, then saw the china doll lying next to him, sleeping. He touched her face and she opened her eyes.

"Mornin'," Mary said and held him. "What's the time?"

Jake looked at his watch. "Seven." He looked at the clouds, then realized this wasn't part of the dream. He tried to remember it, but it was fading fast. Would they show up again? Only time would tell, and he had lots of it. He felt better than he had in years. He felt lighter, like a million pounds had been shed from his soul. He tried again to remember the dream. He remembered holding his sister. Or did he?

Did he finally make it to her? Did he finally rescue her from the old crone in the long hallway? Was she home where she belonged? He felt she was.

"We should leave," James said. He was sitting by a small fire. "Coffee's hot. Pack 'n let's get outta here before the weather gets worse."

In ten minutes, they were heading north to Aberdeen. Half an hour later, it started raining and the wind had picked up.

Fifteen miles from Aberdeen, they had to cross the river and the waves were now huge. James steered into the wind and slowly crossed, moving with the waves. It took him a half-hour and they drifted a half-mile up river, but he did it.

He looked at the river with hatred in his eyes. *I beat you, you fucker.* Then he looked at Jake and Mary and smiled. "No sweat in 'a arctic," he shouted.

As they approached the community, they saw his truck and Chief David's truck parked by the dock. Brenda was driving his, and Abraham, David and Louise's brother, was driving the other and he had passengers: Louise and her daughter, Caroline.

James looked at Louise, but she was busy with Caroline. Or so it seemed. In any event, she didn't acknowledge him.

"Hi, Abraham," he said. *Hi, Louise.*

"Hi."

"They're gonna be down tomorrow."

"Good," Abraham said.

"Got lots 'a meat."

"Even better."

Brenda got out of his truck and hugged him. He felt uncomfortable knowing Louise was watching. He wondered if Brenda's hug was for him, or for Louise's benefit.

Louise, too, wondered if that hug was for James or for her. Then she realized that it didn't matter. She was married. Well, sort of married. And she had a daughter and he had a new woman and that's all that mattered.

That night, James told Brenda about the trip, but only in general terms. He did not tell her about his dream, nor did he tell her about his conversation with Mary. *All in good time.*

Meanwhile, at Simon and Bella's house, Jake was lying in bed and Mary was showering. He thought about his dream and wondered if he'd ever dream of them again, or of the little china doll at the end of the long hallway. Somehow he felt he wouldn't. But even if he did, what mattered was he was not to blame. Or so he tried to convince himself. He started crying uncontrollably.

Mary picked this time to walk into the bedroom with nothing but a towel wrapped around her body. She stood there and let him get it out of his system.

After a few minutes, Jake looked up at her. "Sorry," he said.

"Not a prob," she answered. "Remember what Martin tol' James? It's not your fault."

Jake nodded. "Healin' is a journey," he said. He didn't know how to put it into words: the tears, the hate, the shame, the million emotions that threatened to kill him each and every chance they had. *Will they ever end?*

He didn't have to. Mary got it. "They will," she said. "With time."

Jake said nothing.

"Who said 'at?" she asked.

"Said what?"

"Healing is a journey."

"Some chief up north. Robert somethin' or 'nother. Don't remember. Said it only once 'n I remembered it. Sort 'a stuck with me."

"I think I know who you mean."

"Yeah?"

"Never met him, jus' heard 'a him."

Jake looked at the towel wrapped around her body. She dropped it. She was smiling.

Sixteen

David's Disclosure

Tuesday, October 5th, 1999
It was snowing, and the old wolf was tired and wet. He crossed the valley and went straight for the herd, hoping they'd stay. But they spotted him and began moving. He picked up the pace, but after a mile he realized he was no match for the herd. He turned, but the pack wasn't there. He was alone.

James got up at seven and made some coffee. It was overcast with light rain and it looked like it was snowing in the hills. He wondered if he should go hunting today or . . . *Or what?* He had no job and there was nothing on the horizon. At least not yet and maybe not for a long time. He wondered if he dreamed last night. He didn't wake up hyperventilating, and that was a good sign.

Brenda woke up at eight and she poured herself some coffee and sat across from him at the kitchen table. "Whatcha gonna do today?" she asked.

"Check out the Band office. You?"

"Going in today, but might take the afternoon off," she said. She thought he seemed quieter than usual. Although how, she didn't know. He was always quiet, very quiet. "Bertha called yesterday. She needs help settin' up the hall for her workshop."

"I'll see her later," he said. Then he added, "David's gonna disclose."

She looked puzzled. "Disclose what?"

"Disclose," he said. Then he realized she didn't know. "I don' know if I should be tellin' you this, but . . ." *Why not?* "David was abused in 'a hostel."

"What?" she asked. "Which one?"

"Ours,"

"When?"

"Don' know." James shrugged. "Sixty-seven."

"Who?"

It took him a long time, but he finally got it out. "Tom Kinney."

"Shit," she whispered. "Never did like him." After a while, she added, "Wonder how many others?"

James wondered how she'd take it if he told her. "At leas' one," he said. "Or two."

She held her breath and waited for him to say it. He didn't.

"Michael Lazarus," he said quietly. "Jake too."

"I don't know what to say."

"Nothin' to say. Happened 'n 'at's all there is to it."

Later, he drove her to the Hamlet office, then he went to the Band office to see if he could find a job or a future. But like most people in the community, he couldn't and he didn't. At least not then.

James, Jake and Chief David's brother, Abraham, drove up to the community dock that afternoon and picked up Ernest, Martin and David. They looked frozen.

"I think we made it in time," Ernest said. "Might freeze in couple days."

They'd shot two more moose. They loaded them up into the three vehicles and took them into the community for the Chief and Abraham to distribute.

Later that afternoon, Chief David and Wanda went to Bertha where he recounted his days and nights in the Aberdeen Hostel. He was surprisingly calm. Later, they all went to his parents' house, where he told his mom, dad, sister and brother about his days in the hostel and things that went bump in the night. They all cried, but that was normal. They all wished they could run out of the house and back in time and kill them all. That too was normal. It wasn't easy, but it had to be done since Chief David had bigger things on his mind.

That evening, Louise thought about James and wondered if anything had happened to him. She remembered the time she went to Helena and saw him for the first time in almost two years. She remembered the first time they kissed. She remembered the first time they had sex. She wondered if he knew he was not her first. She then cursed Michael for fucking up her life. Would they still be together if he was her first? She wondered what he'd do if she told him she still loved him. She wondered about a lot of things, but one thing came up time and time again: they had no time left. He had a new woman and she was married with a child and getting a divorce. Or was she? *What 'a hell's goin' on with me? Why am I thinkin' like this after all 'ese years?*

Seventeen

The Battle for Souls

Wednesday, October 6th, 1999
The old wolf watched as the grizzly stalked the cow and her calf. In less than a half-hour, he brought down the calf, and the herd, including the cow, scattered and regrouped a mile away. The old wolf lay down and thought about giving up.

It was almost eight o'clock and Chief David was having his morning coffee and listening to the radio. Wanda came into the kitchen. "You look happy," she said.

"Feel good."

"Despite what you're gonna do today?"

"That I'm not worried about," he said. "I'd rather tell it than keep it in for the rest of my life."

"Good."

"Well, I better get going. Got a lot to do today. I'll meet you at the hall later."

She handed him a paper bag and he opened it. It was a new pair of moose-skin slippers. The tears came to his eyes. "Thanks," he said.

Wanda touched his arm.

He took her in his arms and held her. "I love you."

"I know," she said. "I'll be there."

"You always were."

He went to work feeling better than he had in years. *Maybe today wouldn't be a bad day after all.* He made his rounds and found everyone at work getting ready for Bertha's healing workshop.

That morning, Ernest drove by the Band office with Daryl and Clara and they said their goodbyes. Clara thanked the Chief for what he tried to do for Larry. She was going home with one of her sons and had one other thing to do: she had to return for the other.

Louise woke up tired and alone, and for the first time in her life, she realized she might have to spend the rest of her life alone. She never thought about other men. Just one: James.

Angie woke up alone and reached for James, but he wasn't there. She got dressed, then looked at the time and wished the damned bar would open so she could go for a stiff drink and wait for James to walk through the door with a stiff dick and carry her out of there like Richard Gere. *I'll be Debra Winger.*

At ten o'clock, one hundred people were in the community hall waiting for the workshop to start. Most looked liked they were there for some root canal work and wished it was over so they could get on to more important things like bingo or poker. Half of those in attendance were from out of town and few, if any, had a genuine interest in the healing process. But it was a chance to travel to another community, visit old friends and put in for some honoraria and meal money.

Shortly after ten, the Reverend Andy said an opening prayer and the workshop got under way. The Chief thanked the People for coming and welcomed the out-of-towners to his community. He acknowledged the presence of the government bureaucrats, who stood to polite applause and waved to the audience. The Chief thanked them for their hard work and dedication to healing and the healing process, stating for the record that if it weren't for people like them, where would they be? He thanked them for the funding, stating for the record that it was never too late for contributions, no matter how long it took in coming. His sarcasm was lost on very few. The locals nodded in agreement. Not at the contribution, but at the timing, or lack thereof.

The two reporters from Helena checked to see if their recorders caught this little bit of sarcasm. The radio reporter thought it would make a good opening to his story that would be aired later this evening.

Bertha talked about healing and the healing process, and everyone paid attention and some took it to heart. Others thought they didn't need it. *I only get drunk every other weekend. Nothin' wrong with me.*

Jake and Mary sat and listened as an Elder talked about the good old days and told the young people they should get back to those days and the land no matter what it cost or how long it took. They'd heard it a million times and everyone listened with one ear and automatically nodded their heads in agreement, but no one really heard. *We got millions of dollars an' nothin' but time on our hands. Why not?* Sarcasm reigned supreme in the minds of those whose minds still functioned on all levels.

James and Brenda listened to another Elder who said the young people should get back to the church and its teachings. "All you gotta do is pray and go to the Lord on bended knee," she said. "You don' need this healing. It's not ours."

Brenda felt James tense.

Everyone let the Elder ramble on until her rambling did her soul good, then she sat and prayed.

The Sarge and his wife sat in the crowd and he wondered if anything would come of this. Or was it all talk and no action? He was glad he was moving but he'd told no one and he never would. He'd just pack up and move. Some things are better left unsaid.

Liz sat in the back with Sarah and prepared to videotape the conference for posterity's sake.

Louise sat next to them and watched James and Brenda and died a little more. She looked at David and wondered if he was going to go through with it. She remembered the scene at her parents' house and how he'd told them what had happened to him. *Was 'at a dream? It was real.*

Her parents had cried and asked for forgiveness, but David told them it wasn't their fault. *How could they have known? How could anyone have known?* Bertha also told them about Michael Lazarus and the reason he went into the hills. Louise heard, but said nothing.

Meanwhile, Angie sat in the Saloon and waited for James to walk through that door and carry her out to a better future. He didn't, and she cried and died a little more. Alfred looked at her, then bought her a beer out of pity.

She looked up at him. "Thanks, James."

"Think nothin' of it, Cinderella," he answered.

Angie smiled. She didn't get it.

During lunch, Chief David and Bertha talked to the Reverend Andy and told them he was going to disclose. He didn't know how he was going to start, but he said he'd think of something.

At two o'clock, he put on his new moose-skin slippers and picked up the Talking Stick. It had been around the Band office for many years, but no one used it anymore. *Gone like so many of our traditions an' customs.* He remembered that the People had used it at meetings thirty years ago when he was just a kid. Anyone who held the Talking Stick could speak, and some said it gave them the power and courage to say and do things they normally wouldn't. Chief David didn't know it, but he was about to prove this to be fact.

He looked at his wife and children and made up his mind. *It's time.* He stood and grew ten feet tall then looked at his People who'd come for another workshop on healing. Or so they thought. *They look bored. They look like they're in church. They look like they're at a Hamlet meetin'. They look like they can't wait to get to a poker game.*

He was going to hit them where they lived. He was going to hold nothing back. Then he said it. "Thirty years ago I was sexually abused in the hostel."

One hundred people did a double take. They looked around to see if others had heard. *What 'a hell did he say?*

The sound of so many empty heads reverberating in the community hall woke a million, trillion, gazillion demons, dreams and nightmares from their slumber. They poked their ugly little heads out of the ceiling, walls and floor to see what the fuck was going on. They wondered who the hell had woken them up so early in the day.

"What?" someone said.

"Thirty years ago Tom Kinney sexually abused me. I was thirteen years old."

"Shit!" someone whispered.

"Thirty years ago Tom Kinney forced me to perform oral sex on him."

"Holy shit!" someone else said a little louder.

"Thirty years ago Tom Kinney sodomized me."

"Holy fuckin' shit!" everyone yelled.

"Thirty years ago I was sexually abused by this man that the Powers That Be put in charge of my welfare an' the welfare of a hundred others!"

Wanda cried and her children held her. Bertha and the Reverend Andy walked up to Chief David and stood by him.

Chief David then grew twenty feet and held himself like a Warrior of Old. He spoke of his days in the hostel and of a man named Tom Kinney. He spoke of trust, honour and respect. He spoke of distrust, dishonour and disrespect. He spoke of little boys and little girls in the hostel. He spoke of porcupines and china dolls. He spoke of late-night visits and long hallways. He spoke of dark rooms, lonely shower rooms and dark dorms. He spoke of another young man who had found peace in the Blue Hills. He broke down and started sinking into the floor.

From deep within their troubled and tormented souls, James and Jake heard a voice, then stood and walked to the front of the community hall in their big friggin' cowboy boots. Sparks flew with each step they took and their footsteps echoed like distant thunder. They lifted Chief David up through the floor and stood him on his feet, then folded their arms, looked up at the ceiling and held demons, dreams and nightmares at bay while their Chief spoke in a loud, thundering voice that vibrated the ceiling.

Chief David grew thirty feet tall and spoke of suicides, killings and death. He spoke of anger, rage and terror. He spoke of hurt, shame and sorrow. He spoke of demons, dreams and nightmares. He spoke of the future, hope and healing.

Chief David then did something very few people have ever done. He reached deep down into the very depths of his tormented and fucked-up soul, pulled out the rage, anger, hate, sorrow and sadness by their roots and threw them on the floor for the world to see. He then proceeded to choke the little fuckers like they deserved it.

James and Jake looked straight ahead and evoked nothing but grim determination and courage. They looked like Warriors of Old protecting their Chief from the enemy.

Louise watched her brother and cried for him. She thought about Michael and wondered how many else there were.

People kept looking around to see if they were hearing this shit.

Chief David spoke long and hard about his battle with alcohol, and it was dramatic to say the least. After a million years, he looked at his People like he'd just come from battle. "I'm tired," he said. "I'm tired of runnin'. This is where it ends. Right here an' right now. This is where we make the change for ourselves an' for our children. I will run no more!"

He took the Talking Stick and drew a line across the floor of the community hall. Big friggin' sparks flew like he was using a cutting torch.

His People sat in stunned silence and vibrated from his words. *Is he tellin' the truth? Is he lyin'? Is he doin' this for sympathy? Is he nuts?*

Is he under a spell? Did we drive him to insanity an' beyond with our bitchin' an' complainin'? Some looked for a way out, but the doors were a million miles away. Even if they could make a break for it, they didn't want to leave. They didn't want to miss out on what was going to happen next. Some people pulled out their cell phones and called their friends, family and acquaintances and told them to haul ass to the community hall 'cause shit was gonna fly. *Oh, an' pardon 'a French.*

Then Jake turned to Chief David, looked him right in the eye and smiled like he had a secret. "Mussi," he said in a loud voice filled with pride.

Some People would later say that Jake looked like that little Indian in *Dances* right after he put a tomahawk into the chest of his enemy and watched him join his ancestors. He stood at the front of the community hall and looked at the ceiling and dared his demons, dreams and nightmares to show themselves. You couldn't hear it, but you could see it in his face and in his manner. *How dare the demons, dreams an' nightmares fuck with his Chief!*

Jake then looked at Bertha, who smiled and gave him courage. He looked at his brother, James, standing ready to protect him from any untold horrors and terrors that may come his way. He hung his head and you could tell he was reaching deep and that it took every ounce of his strength to be standing there. He slowly raised his head, looked one hundred people right in the eyes and told of the same time, the same man and the same fucking thing.

One hundred people wondered what the hell was going on. *Is this a dream?* Some people slapped themselves to see if they were going to wake up back in their beds. It didn't work. *It's fuckin' real!*

Jake Noland did not cry. He had cried enough. He was here to confront his demons, dreams and nightmares on his own fucking terms and that was it, Jack. He let loose such a scream of utter rage and immense hatred that the whole building shook.

The demons, dreams and nightmares gave serious thought to fucking off elsewhere in search of easier prey.

Jake started sinking into the floor, but James reached down and with an arm that looked like it belonged on Hulk Hogan, lifted him up from the steps of oblivion.

Jake Noland grew forty fucking feet tall and the People looked at him with awe. They wondered if he'd stomp-kick their asses into oblivion.

Mary Percy stood up in her new loose-fitting jeans, walked to the front and stood by her soon-to-be husband. She looked at her lover with the nice ass, smiled and nodded. *Let's rock an' roll.*

Mary then looked up at the ceiling. She didn't say it, but you could see it in her eyes and in her stance. She issued a dare to the demons, dreams and nightmares. *C'mon, do your fuckin' best!*

People were almost blown off their feet. Mary Percy grew fifty feet tall and damned near split her new loose-fitting jeans. They were loose no more. Nothing was going to get by her and get to her man. *Not now and not ever!*

Jake Noland then spoke from the heart and soul in a loud, clear voice that vibrated the floor and walls. It felt like the space shuttle was taking off from the roof of the community hall. Some say Jake looked like Chief Joseph of the Nez Perce. Some say his old leather jacket changed into a war shirt right before their eyes. Some thought it was the shit they'd injected into their system over the years.

Bertha, the Reverend Andy, Mary Percy, James Nathan and Chief David stood by his side and pushed back demons, dreams and nightmares with nothing more than attitude. Somebody later said you could hear war drums if you listened real hard, but personally I think it was the thumping of their hearts.

Jake Noland then did something they still talk about today and will talk about for as long as the sun shines, the grass grows and the rivers flow and then some. He reached down and pulled out a caribou-skin rope. "Holy shit-fuck!" someone screamed. "He's gonna stake himself!"

One hundred chicken necks stretched to see. It was as if they were all looking to see who won a bingo game so they could curse them.

Jake Noland tied one end of the caribou-skin rope to a brand-new cowboy boot and the other to a stake. He then looked at the ceiling and in a calm, deliberate manner did what no one has seen in these here parts since forever: Jake Fucking Noland staked himself like he'd heard some Plains Indians did in another time. Jake Noland was telling his demons, dreams and nightmares that he was here for the long haul and then some. He was telling them he was going nowhere and they'd better know it. He was telling them he was prepared to sacrifice himself for his Chief and People, if it came to that. He was telling them he was ready to do battle and to get it over with.

It was really fucking something!

Jake Noland then spoke of the hurt, shame and anger. He spoke of the thirty years he spent running from his demons, dreams and nightmares. He spoke of his search for peace. He said the only peace he could think of came out of the barrel of a gun. He spoke of the many times he almost found peace. He spoke of his mom, dad and sister and screamed from his soul. It sounded like a million demons screaming at once.

After a few hours or a few days, he looked at the People. They could see the hurt, the pain and the anguish. He looked for all the world to have aged a million years in the last few minutes.

"I too am tired," he said. "I'm tired of runnin'. I too shall run no more."

Jake Noland then picked up the Talking Stick and drew the line even deeper. People didn't have time to close their eyes and some were blinded for a few seconds.

Jake Noland looked up at one hundred people with nothing but hatred and rage shooting from his eyes, then pivoted on one cowboy boot, pushed with the other and spun around to his brother James and said in a loud, thundering voice, "Healin' is a journey — there is no end!"

James Nathan looked his brother right between the eyes and said in no uncertain terms, "Ain't 'at 'a fuckin' truth!"

Young women fainted and grown men shivered in their rubber boots. Two young women wondered what it would be like to jump these two men and get straight. Mary Percy felt so damned proud her jeans got tighter and she grew sixty fucking feet tall and then some.

People were coming into the community hall left, right and centre. They strained their scrawny necks to see what the hell was happening. There were two hundred people in the building and they were over the maximum allowable limit according to the fire marshal, but they didn't give a shit. This shit was worth getting thrown in the slammer for.

James Nathan stood up there like some Injun cowboy right out of that song by Buffy Sainte-Marie. He looked for all the world like he was about to get on the meanest bucking bronco this side of Hades and ride him straight into hell and back just for the hell of it.

James Nathan did not smile. He had smiled enough. He had used his smile to hide the pain and the anguish. He had used his smile to get laid. He was going to do some laying today.

James Nathan looked at Louise, then at Brenda. He then looked two hundred people right in their beady little eyes and told of the same time, the same man and the same fucking thing.

Louise, Brenda and two hundred people stopped breathing.

"Holy fuckin' shit!" someone yelled. "How many were there?"

James Nathan said in a voice so loud and angry that people out in the street heard it and damned near shit their pants, "Too fuckin' many!"

His voice knocked those sitting too close off their chairs and onto their arses. The building bent under the strain of his mighty voice, but he did not cry. He had cried enough in his dreams and in the privacy of his own hellhole. Today he would make his demons, dreams and nightmares pay. He looked at his brother Jake and nodded.

Jake reached down, picked up some caribou-skin rope and threw it to his big brother, who caught that rope like some major league baseball players only dreamed they could: with no effort and no fear.

Louise, Brenda and two hundred people watched as James Nathan tied one end of the caribou-skin rope to his big cowboy boot. He tied it tighter than a banker's arse. He then tied the other end to a big stake about the size of a baseball bat, and the community hall went quiet. James Nathan kneeled and held the stake in both hands, then raised it over his head and slammed it into the floor. Big fucking sparks flew. It sounded like lightning had struck the community hall.

Jake Noland watched his big brother with nothing but fucking pride, then grew to seventy feet tall in his new cowboy boots.

James Nathan too was going nowhere, Jack. He was prepared to do battle until the very fucking end. Jake Noland's brother meant business and then some.

Liz checked to see if she had enough film in her camcorder. She slapped in a new cassette just in case.

James Nathan was still on one knee. People held their breaths. James Nathan kneeled for a few seconds like he was praying to his Creator, then he slowly stood and grew to one hundred feet tall. He had a scowl on his face and his eyes were blood red. He picked up the meanest-looking war club ever seen and slowly looked at the ceiling and in a loud, thundering voice called out to his demons, dreams and nightmares: "Come on out, you motherfuckers!"

James Nathan's voice was like the north wind just before it blew you off your arse: cold, hard, mean and loud. He stood there like Conan the fucking Barbarian and screamed something terrible for his demons to come forth and show themselves. "I'm here, you little rubber boot wearin' chicken shits! I ain't goin' nowhere!"

His voice sounded like a million nails clawing across a blackboard. It sent shivers down every spine within two miles. It was as if he didn't care if they took him into oblivion and beyond. It was as if he didn't care if they killed him. He just wanted to do battle. Win or lose, it didn't matter. "Let's get it over with!" he screamed.

Louise stood in the back and wept for the man she loved. She cried as he summoned his demons from the dark recesses of his troubled mind and tormented soul. It was too much for her to watch. She wanted to go up and help him. She wanted to protect him.

Brenda sat alone and watched James scream to the heavens. The scream sent shivers through her whole body. This was it. He was going nuts. She looked around to see if anyone was looking at her, but everyone was looking at James, or at the ceiling, or at the floor.

Liz and Sarah were standing in the back with tears running down their faces. They'd cried for Chief David and Jake and now they cried for James. They now knew why he was so silent. They now knew why he was a loner. They now knew no matter how many people he had around, he'd always be a loner.

As if summoned by some unknown force, these four women slowly stood and walked up to the front and stood with Chief David, James and Jake.

James saw these four women and grew one hundred and twenty-five fucking feet tall. His head broke through the roof just as the demons, dreams and nightmares started oozing from the walls, ceiling and floor. They were ugly, mean and pissed. They were humongous. They smelled something terrible. They smelled of hopelessness, despair and death. There must have been a bazillion of them. All shapes, sizes and colours. They were the meanest motherfuckers this side of hell. They were hell's rejects.

Two hundred people shit their fucking pants! I shit you not! I was there and I smelled the stench!

Martin stood and walked up to where James Nathan stood. He folded his arms and said, "It's time."

James Nathan looked up and stared his demons, dreams and nightmares right between their three eyes with nothing but fucking hatred. He grinned that friggin' Nathan grin, then let loose such a horrendous godawful battle cry of rage, hatred and vengeance that the roof of the community hall blew off and scattered to the four winds.

The demons, dreams and nightmares shivered in their rubber boots and looked around to make sure the others didn't fuck off. They had no intention of fighting this fucker alone.

There was no turning back. There was going to be a loser and there was going to be a winner. There was going to be no fucking truce or surrender. James Nathan was either going to win or he was going down. He didn't care which. He just wanted to get it over with.

James Nathan's demons, dreams and nightmares came seeking revenge. They were going to take him to the other side this day. They were going to show him once and for all who was the fucking boss and make the fucker pay. *How dare this mere mortal challenge us in broad daylight in front of his People!* They charged ahead and met James Nathan head on.

Two hundred people witnessed James Nathan meet his demons, dreams and nightmares with nothing but grim determination in his soul and vengeance in his heart. He waded into battle seeking nothing more than total victory and freedom.

It was really fucking something! I shit you not!

James Nathan started laying demons out left, right and centre. Demon arms, legs and heads were flying everywhere. One head fell into the lap of Old Pierre. He picked it up, poked out its beady little eyes and threw it on the floor. Dora stomped its ass into oblivion and beyond with her brand-new rubber boots.

James Nathan was slamming dreams into the floor. Dream blood was splashing everywhere. One little fucker fell in front of Margaret and Jane. They jumped on the little pecker and slammed its two heads into the floor as if they were daubing the winning number at a bingo game. The dream disappeared. Margaret and Jane looked at each other, yelled, "Bingo!" then pulled out their real daubers and looked for more of them little scumbags.

James Nathan was kicking nightmares in the balls with his big fucking cowboy boots. Nightmares were flying this way and that way and into the laps of the good folk. The good folk stomped the little peckers right on past oblivion and into China.

James Nathan was like a knight in shining armour. He was like Kevin Costner in *Dances with Wolves*. He was like Crazy Horse charging into battle. He was like Geronimo at his best.

He was a fucking sight to behold! I shit you not! You really had to be there!

Young girls dreamed of marrying him. Young boys dreamed of becoming him. Elders dreamed they were him and cried for the good old days.

James Nathan was fighting one hell of a fight, but there were too many demons, dreams and nightmares for one man to take on alone.

Jake Noland picked up a sword and waded in to help his brother.

He mowed them down faster than Arnold Schwarzenegger on a good day.

Chief David picked up a spear and waded into battle. He killed more demons than Sylvester Stallone on a bad Monday.

Martin, Bertha, the Reverend Andy, Mary, Wanda, Brenda, Liz, Sarah and Louise looked for all the world to be singing some old Indian war song. Their voices were loud, proud and mean. It sounded like it came from the mountaintops. It sounded like it came from wide-open valleys. It sounded like it came with a fucking vengeance. It sounded like the Mormon Tabernacle Choir singing *The Messiah* on acid. It sounded like a million Plains Indians all singing at once.

The three Warriors heard this war song and it gave them strength and courage. There was such a fucking commotion what with blood, guts, arms, legs and heads flying every which way that no one breathed or blinked an eye lest they miss a thing.

The skies opened up and the People could see a billion light years into the universe. They watched as a million stars suddenly went supernova and lit up the entire universe and then some. A gazillion neutrinos came slamming into the community hall and blasted demons, dreams and nightmares into smithcreens and knocked some good folk on their asses.

They watched as James Nathan, Jake Noland and Chief David slayed demons and nightmares left, right, centre and in between. They watched as James Nathan, Jake Noland and Chief David picked up big fucking scary dreams and hurled them back from whence they came. They watched as the dreams scurried off with their tails between their legs.

Demons, dreams and nightmares looked around and saw others fucking off out of there, then whipped their tails between their three hind legs and fucked off faster than a bootlegger can count money on a cold night in December. *We're not stickin' 'round here. Fuck 'is shit!*

James, Jake and Chief David stood above slain demons and nightmares like great big fucking Warriors of Old covered with blood, sweat, guts, tears and pride.

James Nathan was tired. He smiled at two hundred people and said in a voice so fucking loud and proud that people in Helena swear to God they heard it: "And that's the way it is!"

Jake Noland stood there with a nightmare still skewered to his sword kicking its last kicks. He pulled the little fucker off, threw it to the floor and stomped its ass into oblivion with his brand-new cowboy boots now covered in demon blood. He looked at James Nathan and said in a voice that sounded like someone pulling a rusty nail but magnified a hundredfold: "You got 'at fuckin' right!"

Chief David shook two demons off his lance. They scurried off with their tails between their legs. He calmly and quietly looked at James Nathan and said in a voice that some say sounded like squeaky brakes on the bus to Hades: "Fuckin' A!"

Two hundred people began to breathe again. Cool air rushed into the community hall and swept the demon stench into oblivion and it smelled like it did right after one humongous thunderstorm. It smelled clean. It smelled like new beginnings.

Two hundred people sat in stunned silence and in total admiration of these three Warriors. They quietly kneeled in humble reverence and veneration as the Reverend Andy led them in prayer for lost souls, lost youth, broken trust and forgotten promises.

It was really fucking something! You had to be there! I shit you not! I was and I still can't fuckin' believe it!

The People started slowly coming to life. They began cleaning blood, guts and other demon parts from their faces, clothes and hair.

Brenda wiped demon blood from James's hands and face. She was so fucking proud of him. He reached out and touched her face to see if she was real. He then gave her the biggest kiss since Jim Carrey sucked Lauren Holly's face off in that movie *Dumb and Dumber*.

Wanda hugged Chief David for doing so well in battle. For the first time in a long while, she gave him a kiss using as much tongue as she could muster and then some. She was going to ride this friggin' Warrior tonight to hell and back and then some.

Mary put her arms around Jake, then shape-shifted into Kathleen

Turner. "Hey, Big Man," she said, "wanna carry me home?" She kissed him and squeezed his ass and the blood rushed from his big head to his little head and he damned near fainted.

Two hundred people stood up and gave a thundering round of applause not heard in these here parts since forever and a day.

"We should compose a song to mark this great battle!" one old man said.

"Fuckin' A!" said another. They laughed at that one.

The radio reporter checked to make sure he'd got it all on tape and thought about working for CNN. The newspaper reporter started taking photos and thought about submitting them to *Life*, *Time* or *Newsweek*. The bureaucrats from the higher echelons of government looked at each other and smiled. *Where would these People be without us?*

Bertha gave them all a big hug and thanked them for battling their demons, dreams and nightmares in front of everyone.

Louise watched James and Brenda and died a little more that day, then went to her brother and congratulated him. For the first time in a long time, she gave him a hug. "I'm proud of you," she said, then looked for James and Jake, but they were gone. *I'm proud of you too.*

Later that night, after the smoke had cleared and the People returned to normal, Bertha and Isaac went to the cemetery and stood over the grave of Michael Lazarus.

Bertha said a prayer, then cried for his lost soul. After a million years, she said in the language, "It's time to send him home."

Isaac knew what she meant. *The Old People. The Old Ways.s*

Eighteen

The Return of the Drum

Thursday, October 7th, 1999
The old wolf watched the grizzly eat. Then the grizzly walked into the mountains for the winter. The old wolf walked over to the kill and chased away the crows that were already gathering. It wasn't his and it wasn't much, but it would help him regain his strength until he could bring down his own.

The sun rose on Aberdeen like any other day. Some expected things to change overnight while others went about their business as usual. They went to work. They waited for the Saloon to open. They waited for Dick and Ed to waltz in with their cheque from Publisher's Clearing House. They waited for someone to provide them with the means.

Those who went to work looked at the community hall and were amazed that the roof was still there. They wondered if it had really happened.

The events of the previous day made the news that morning and were silently discussed over coffee in most parts of the Northwest Territories. The Chief's name was mentioned, but James and Jake were described as "two others." Their anonymity would not last. Nothing does. Tom Kinney's name was not mentioned, since the radio reporter obtained a legal opinion. His anonymity would not last. Nothing does.

The newspaper reporter's dream came true. He called his office in Helena and screamed, "Hold the presses!" He spent the better part of the day working on his story and it would make tomorrow's paper. He'd taken some photographs at the workshop, but his hands were shaking so much that they were all out of focus and overexposed.

Angie too woke up that morning shaking and out of focus. She decided to get rid of the shakes at the Saloon. She squeezed into her tightest-fitting jeans, making sure she showed some crack, then went to the Saloon to wait for James. *Maybe he'll show up today. Maybe he'll slip his tongue in my crack.*

George received a few customers throughout the night, but he didn't answer his door. He'd heard the news about the workshop and wondered if they knew about him and his sister. He didn't venture out that day.

What really happened at the community hall in Aberdeen that day? Despite all the blood and gore, it was all very simple: three men disclosed. They talked honestly about a sexual abuse that occurred thirty years ago. They spoke of oral sex and sodomy. They spoke of the shame and the pain and of being alone. They thought it had happened only to them. They called Tom Kinney a fucking asshole and a cunt. They said if he ever returned they would kill him. They spoke of how they turned to drugs and alcohol to hide the shame and the pain. They told of how they became sluts to show they were men. Real men fucked their brains out, and that's what they did. They fucked anything that moved. They lied about the women they fucked and took advantage of them. They said they hurt people and hurt them big time and apologized. They said they hoped their children would never have to go through the same thing. They yelled, screamed and cried, and held nothing back that day. It was time for change.

James and Jake made the people sit up, take notice and do some serious thinking. *How many people committed suicide for the same reason?*

Chief David, James and Jake became men that day and could talk about what had happened without shame, fear and sorrow. It was not their shame, fear or sorrow. It never had been.

But would it last?

Two hundred people attended Bertha's workshop that day to see if any more Warriors were going to do battle or, at the very least, disclose more shit. The People were hesitant to speak at first lest they get their asses kicked by their demons, dreams and nightmares, but as soon as they saw Chief David, James and Jake walk through the door they were frightened no more. Some even picked up James's war club, which had changed back into the Talking Stick, and spoke from the heart and soul.

Fifty people stood that day and wrenched their demons from their souls, threw them on the floor, then stomped the shit out of them while three Warriors stood by and dared the little fuckers to fight back. The demons lay there and took the shit-kicking that was coming and liked it. They had no choice.

The workshop came to an end and Chief David and Bertha thanked the people for attending. They'd hoped to have a feast that night, but the hall had been booked months earlier for something more important: bingo.

Some People went home and did their own battles in the quiet and comfort of their own homes. They cried for long-lost parents, sons, daughters and other loved ones who had gone on to the Promised Land and not-so-Promised Land in the south. They remembered the three Warriors and gained courage and strength. They too kicked the shit out of their demons, dreams and nightmares. They were tired and they weren't going to take it anymore. *Not now and maybe not ever.*

Others sat around and waited for things to change, or waited for others to change things for them. They would wait a long time, but they don't know that. Maybe they never will.

Others went home and packed their daubers and lucky trinkets into their special bingo bags, then looked up at the Creator and demanded they win tonight. *Jus' this once an' I'll never ask again.*

The events of the workshop again made the news that afternoon. James and Jake listened and were glad their names weren't mentioned. They knew it wouldn't last. It never does. The rumour mills were already in full gear. People were calling their relatives in other parts of the territories and in other parts of Canada. In one week, Chief David, James and Jake would be known all over the NWT. In two weeks, they would be forgotten.

Bertha and Isaac visited Martin and Jane and listened to the news. They knew it wouldn't last. People would talk about it for a week or two and then it would be forgotten. Margaret and Ernest came in shortly after and they talked about taking Michael into the hills where he belonged. They all agreed, then wondered how they should go about it.

"We should talk to Chief James," Margaret said in the language. "He'll know what to do."

Bertha, Isaac, Margaret, Ernest, Martin and Jane went to see Chief James. He and his wife, Lucy, were both in their seventies. Over the last two decades the People had all but forgotten that he was the last of the Old Chiefs, and only the Elders paid him the respect he deserved. The young people had other things on their mind, or in their minds. They talked to him about their wishes, and the old Chief shed a tear for the good old days and agreed that's the way it should be.

Later, they went up to Chief David and told him what was going to happen and he agreed. *The traditions are coming home. Wonder if they'll stay.*

Jane and Martin called Michael's sister, Joanne, in Edmonton and told her about the workshop and the disclosures. They told of Michael's letter and the reason for his violent departure from this plane of existence. Joanne had never really known her brother and finally realized why he had always been alone and quiet.

"Do you want to come up?" Jane asked Joanne.

"When?"

Bertha looked at the calendar on the wall. "Sunday we can exhume his body," she said. "Monday we can take him into the hills."

"I'll be up on Sunday," Joanne said.

"I'll get James to pick you up," Jane said.

Still later that evening, they talked to the Reverend Andy and his wife about traditions, customs and legends. The Reverend Andy smiled, and they knew it would be okay. The long journey back to the Old Ways took another step out of the darkness and into the light.

Old Pierre and Dora had kept the fire going outside their house for the last few days hoping to keep the feeling that the tragedies had brought to the community. The feeling of togetherness. The feeling of family. The feeling of tradition.

They sat around the open fire in the cool autumn evening with Peter and Eliza, Simon and Bella, and Edward and Rachel. Old Pierre was humming an old chant that told of Warriors returning from battle in days long since gone. He couldn't remember when the last great battle was fought. It was a million years ago and a million miles from here. He hummed and the others joined in, and soon the chant became a song. They'd heard the song in another time and another place. They now heard it in their dreams. They started moving their feet like they were young and they sang it loud and clear.

Bertha and Isaac heard the singing and went to see where it was coming from. When they got to Old Pierre and Dora's they were joined by Martin, Jane, Ernest and Margaret. The six of them looked and listened as if it were all a dream. They had goosebumps and joined in and sang to the heavens. They remembered their parents singing this a long time ago and far away.

Brenda and James were at home looking for something to talk about when they heard the singing. They went to see what it was all about. They held hands and joined in the dancing.

Chief David and Wanda could see the flames from their house and went to investigate. What they saw were over a hundred People dancing around the fire singing a song not heard in these parts since the drums migrated west. Chief David shed a tear and joined Wanda in a dance he didn't know how to do. He didn't have to worry. It came naturally. It was genetic.

The Reverend Andy and his wife drove up to see if the Warriors were doing battle again. They came upon a dance in progress. Andy watched and started moving to the beat. His dancing didn't come naturally. It came by osmosis.

Jake and Mary were lying in bed taking a breather when they heard the singing and thought it was coming from the television. They got dressed and walked past the Saloon down to Old Pierre and Dora's and were amazed to see a scene right out of the history books. A blast from the past, so to speak. An oldie but a goodie, if you please.

Angie was sitting in the Saloon when she thought she heard the closing theme to *An Officer and a Gentleman*. She ordered a double. *James is gonna walk in 'at door any minute!*

Chief James and Lucy were sitting at home when they heard the drumming. They looked at each other, then at the door. They waited for the Old People to come walking in and take them into the hills. Instead, their son, Alfred, and his wife, Eunice, walked in and took them to a drum dance in progress.

The bingo players were sitting in the community hall daubing away when they heard the singing and thought nothing of it. They had more important things on their mind.

Liz and Sarah were sitting with Louise when they heard the commotion. They looked outside and saw the flames.

"Fire!" Liz screamed and grabbed her camcorder.

They headed down to see what the hell was going on and came upon a dance in progress. They watched in awe. Liz started rolling.

They watched as Old Pierre and Dora, Peter and Eliza, Simon and Bella, and Edward and Rachel were taken back a hundred years in time when they still lived on the land and still became part of the land, part of the water. Their voices rose and fell in unison as they praised the young Warriors who came back from battle.

Gradually, the chant died and the People looked around nervously as if they didn't know what to do. Or as if they were guilty of something.

Chief James looked at Old Pierre and nodded. "It's time," he said in the language.

Old Pierre went into his shed and returned with five drums that he'd made many years ago. He'd wanted to bring them out sooner, but didn't know how the People would react to it. He thought about the government and the church, then looked at the Reverend Andy standing with his People. *Times are changing.*

He gave one drum each to Peter, Edward and Simon, then spotted Neil trying to blend in with the darkness. But Neil's power wasn't as strong as it used to be. Old Pierre used nothing more than willpower to summon him to the fire.

From the dark recesses of his troubled mind and tormented soul, Neil heard. As he walked, he grew. By the time he reached the fire he was one hundred feet tall. Old Pierre smiled and gave him a drum and Neil shed a tear for times long since gone.

The five old men slowly started beating the drums, and the People turned to see what it was. It was like a dream in slow motion. Five old men beating drums that had appeared out of nowhere. Four old women behind them singing. They lifted their voices to the stars and heavens and it sent shivers down every spine in Aberdeen.

The five old men became young and brave like they were fifty years ago. They all grew a hundred feet tall and their store-bought flannel shirts changed to moose skin with long fringes. The four old women grew a hundred feet and stood behind the men. They wore dresses made of caribou skin and their hair became as black as the night. Their skin was brown, smooth and clear as pure mountain water. They looked like Poca-fucking-hontas.

Neil was once again a proud young Warrior and grew two hundred feet tall. No one had ever grown this tall before and the People looked with admiration and respect. He sang so loud he shook hills, mountains and trees far away in another time and another place.

Old Pierre sang for his dearly departed brother and his friend. He wished them well on their journey to the Old People. He hoped they'd find peace somewhere over the horizon.

Chief James and Lucy looked at this vision and silently thanked the Old People, and their hearts soared up to the heavens.

The bingo players were all starting to arrive. They hid their daubers and lucky trinkets and blended in with the crowd. They tried not to look at the winner and criticize her, but old habits died hard. *She don' need it. I had one number lef'.*

The People watched this epic unfolding. No one slapped themselves to see if they were dreaming. No one wanted to wake up if it was a dream.

The drums had found their way home, if only for a while, in the form of five old men and four old women singing as if they were young again. They sang of beautiful women and strong young men. They sang of little girls in caribou-skin dresses. They sang of little boys playing in their fathers' arms. They sang of great battles in days gone by. They sang of the great battle they'd witnessed yesterday. They sang of the great Warriors who did them proud. They sang of tall mountains and wide-open valleys. They sang of thousands of caribou moving to the rhythm of the seasons. They sang of the Old People moving with the caribou. They sang of hope and new beginnings. They sang their hearts out and it was a fucking sight to behold.

Late that night or early that morning, depending how you look at it, everyone went home and most dreamed of good things, hope and new beginnings. They dreamed of Jake Noland pivoting on one cowboy boot, pushing with the other and spinning around to his brother James Nathan and screaming, "Healin' is a journey — there is no end!"

They dreamed of James Nathan growing one hundred feet tall, picking up a war club and daring his dreams and nightmares to come out and do battle. They dreamed of James Nathan screaming for his demons to come forth and show themselves. They dreamed of James Nathan meeting his demons, dreams and nightmares head on with nothing but grim determination in his soul and vengeance in his heart.

They dreamed of James Nathan, Jake Noland and Chief David as they slayed demons, dreams and nightmares and sent them scurrying off with their tails between their legs. They dreamed of three Warriors standing above slain demons, dreams and nightmares like great Warriors of Old covered with blood, sweat, guts, tears and pride.

They dreamed of James Nathan as he slowly raised his head and looked at the People and said, "And that's the way it is!"

They dreamed in Technicolor, Panavision and stereo. It was in IMAX and then some.

It was really fucking something, but then I've already told you that.

Nineteen

The Caribou and the Wolf

Friday, October 8th, 1999
The old wolf finished what was left of the grizzly kill, then looked for the caribou. The main herd was still north of him, but a few were moving south to a ridge that looked familiar. A dream? He followed the smaller herd at a distance and was in no hurry.

James woke up and looked at the ceiling. *Was 'at a dream or did I tell the whole town what I went through?* He remembered he'd woken up around four that morning and felt like he had a hangover, then felt someone in bed with him. He looked at Brenda and wondered if she was a dream.

"You okay?" Brenda asked.

"Yeah," he lied. He got up and made coffee. *Snow.*

"Whatcha gonna do today?" she asked.

"Check for caribou." *Maybe blow my brains out.* "You?"

"Make some calls to Yellowknife. Gotta find a place." *Should've kept our house. Me an' Earl's.*

They sat at the kitchen table and smiled uncomfortably as if they didn't know what to talk about. And that wasn't too far from the truth.

Jake walked in and saved them from any further embarrassing silent moments. "Gotta remember I jus' can't come bargin' in anymore," he said. "Whatcha gonna do today?" he asked James.

"Check the hills."

"Good, I'll go with you."

Why not? You can bring my carcass home.

Brenda watched them leave and wondered if they were going to do it. *Does Mary worry about Jake?* She was surprised by James's disclosure, but she decided not to bring it up. If he wanted, she would talk about it. *Besides, I can't deal with it. Not now an' maybe never.*

The ride was long and silent and the roads slippery and muddy, but that was normal. James thought about his life and the events of the last few days. *The road to hell. Is that where I'm goin'?* He realized that he and Jake had never really talked about much of anything in their lives. *Booze, broads an' nothin' else.* He was the father and Jake was the son and he'd taught him almost everything he knew and protected him even when he didn't need it. *What kind 'a father would I really have been?* He shook the thought off and concentrated on driving. *Nothin' else to think about.* It started to snow as they drove into the mountains.

"Winter," Jake said.

"Yeah," James answered. "Be glad to be outta here."

As they drove James realized he and Jake didn't have to look for a reason to talk. If they didn't, they didn't. If they did, they did. *Speak only when it improves the silence. Where did I hear 'at?*

The five cows, three calves and old bull slowly made their way across the open area between the ridge and the highway. The old wolf rested his weary body and watched them.

"Caribou," James said, and pointed.

They stopped and got their guns ready and waited. "How many?" he asked.

"Five cows, three calves an' a bull."

"Bull's far."

"Too far."

"Whatcha wanna do?"

James looked at Jake, then at Jake's cowboy boots, then at his own. *Fuckin' Injuns ready for a night in the Saloon.* "Take a shot at the bull," he said. "You hit it, you hit it. You don't, you don't."

"Logical," Jake said and rested his gun on the hood of the truck.

The shot resounded over the land and the caribou disappeared up the ridge.

"Missed," Jake said.

"Didn' wanna shoot 'em anyway," James said. "Be a bugger skinnin' 'em in 'is weather an' carryin' 'em back in cowboy boots."

Jake looked at James in his black leather jacket and cowboy boots, then at himself and smiled. *Saloon attire.*

"Las' time I was up here with Martin he told me we should always let the first herd pass," James said. "The rest will follow."

The old bull ran up the ridge. He did not see the wolf until it was too late and by then he was too tired to run any farther. The old wolf was just as surprised. They faced each other for a few seconds, then their instincts took over. It was another battle of sorts, but this time it was a battle for survival. When it was over, the hunter had triumphed and the hunted would not see another winter. The old wolf was exhausted. He rested his tired body next to his kill. He was no longer hungry. He was lonely.

That evening, Jake and Mary lay on her bed and Jake talked about his family and his life. He told Mary about the good times and the not-so-good times. He told her about the women he used and discarded. She listened and said nothing. Nothing had to be said. His past was his and his alone. His future was theirs and theirs alone. Things were beginning to change.

Back at James's house, Brenda lay in his arms and they watched television. His hand went to her button and the next thing they knew, they were in bed. He was proving to her that he was still normal and that it didn't matter. She was proving too that it didn't matter. It did, but they didn't talk about it. Things were more or less normal.

What Brenda didn't know and what James didn't think about was that when he was making love to her, he was thinking about someone else.

Twenty

The Spirit

Saturday, October 9th, 1999
The old wolf had a good sleep and was content. He ate some of his kill, then went to the ridge and waited. He was no longer hungry and had time to think of other things, like how alone he was. He sat and looked for the pack, but his eyesight wasn't as good as it used to be. He fell asleep again and whimpered as he slept.

James got up at six o'clock, turned on the coffeepot and wondered if he should take another run up to the hills and this time with the proper boots. He wanted to do something — anything. He wished none of this had ever happened so he could go for a cool one at the Saloon. He'd thought about it last night and wanted to ask Brenda, or just go without asking. He knew he couldn't have just one. He'd have one and then another and then another and then another until he wouldn't remember leaving. He'd be waking up about now hungover with Lord knows who and carrying God knew what. He wondered if he'd ever drink again. *Prob'ly.* He wondered if he was making the right decision by selling his house and moving to Yellowknife with Brenda. *What if it don't work out? Can I come back an' carry on where I lef' off?*

Jake and Mary were preparing for a busy day. They were going to clean his house from top to bottom in between bouts of lovemaking. He had told her about a job offer he had from one of the more reputable companies in Yellowknife. It was only short-term, but it could very well turn into something permanent. He also told her that he was going to leave with James and Brenda as soon as they were ready. She was sad, but she knew he couldn't help it. They had to get a future and it sure as shit wasn't in Aberdeen.

Chief David made some coffee, then sat by his window. *Why all this an' why now?* He thought about the healing workshop and wondered if it was all a dream. He thought about Michael Lazarus and how silent he was. He thought about James and Jake and himself. *We're all quiet.* He wondered if James and Jake ever talked about it. He thought about what it all meant, but came up with nothing. He thought about the drum dance and wondered if that was a dream. *Will it stay? Who'll carry it on?* Then it dawned on him. *It's up to me an' everyone else.*

"What happens now?" he asked out loud.

"What?" Wanda asked as she walked into the kitchen.

"I was jus' wonderin' what happens now. What happen las' night?"

"You worry too much. Take it as it comes."

"Yeah," he said. "Guess I should."

"I'm gonna start cookin' for the feast," she said. "Gonna ask Louise to help me."

Louise was sitting at home thinking about her future. *None.* She thought about James and how he was always silent even when they were going out in high school. He'd sit and would not talk unless spoken to and had very few friends. *Jake an' Raymond and that was it. Are those the traits of the abused?* She thought about Michael and how quiet he was — almost dangerous. *He was.* She thought about Daniel and wondered what the hell was wrong with him. *He was so different. Before an' after we were married. Did somethin' happen to him? What was it they said? Abused people abuse. Was 'at why he abused me? Why did I put up with it for so long?* He'd never spoken of his real parents and only said his adopted parents were nice. *Did they do somethin' to him? What about his real parents?* She still had trouble accepting James's disclosure. *He was only eleven or twelve. A kid.*

Chief David had gone to the offices, where he called Bertha. "What do we do?" he asked.

"We exhume 'a body tomorrow," she said. "Then take him up into the hills the next."

"Where?"

"Somebody should look for a place."

"I can do that."

"Get somebody else," she said. "You gotta get on 'a radio today 'a let a' People know what's gonna happen."

"I'll call James," he said. "See if he's gonna go up again."

Bertha was about to ask him to get someone else, but didn't. *Gotta trust him.*

At three o'clock, James was two hours out of Aberdeen. He was going to ask Jake to come along but had decided to go it alone. Why, he had no idea. *I do know why. Wanna be alone.* He was glad the Chief had called. It gave him an excuse, and a valid one at that. He'd told Brenda he might stay overnight. "Get some caribou," he said. *It wasn't a lie. Not really.*

He listened to Liz and Sarah calling out bingo while George Jones sang backup. *Drinkin' songs.* Liz and Sarah weren't their usually bubbly selves and he knew why. The entire community knew why. *Shit happened an' big shit at that.* He hadn't talked to them since his disclosure. He'd only smiled like it was nothing. He needed time alone. Or so he'd convinced himself. *Wonder how they think 'a me now? Fucked up the ass an' all.* He'd seen Louise only once and wondered how she felt about him. *Did she know? How could she? No one knew.*

"Why am I still thinkin' of you?" he asked out loud.

He stopped and filled two water containers and put these in the back of his truck, then looked for a smoke. He checked his glove compartment, then his toolbox. Nothing. He did find something else and wondered where it had come from. He lifted the bottle out and tried to remember when he'd put it there. He couldn't. He cracked open the bottle and sniffed to make sure it was vodka. It was tempting. He put the lid back on, climbed into his truck and drove on.

An hour later, he stopped where he and Jake had seen the caribou. *Good a place as any.* He got out and looked north to the ridge for any sign of the caribou. He saw nothing. He did not look for the wolf. It didn't even cross his mind.

He took out the gun and walked to the south of the highway and looked over the wide-open valley. *Good place for dyin'.* He thought about it, then realized he was already dead. He looked at the land as if he was seeing it for the first time: the tall mountains, the low rolling hills, the wide-open valley to the south and the clear mountain streams. *How many times have I come up here to kill myself?* He looked at the gun and thought about Michael. *The asshole!* He looked to the clouds.

"Why'd you leave it for me?" he asked.

He listened, but all he heard was the wind. He felt tired and abandoned. *It's all a dream.* He was about to turn when the hair on the back of his neck stood. He was being watched. *Mission schools. Residential schools. Hostels. Late nights. Dark nights. Dark rooms. Hairy hands. White hands. Fat hands. Foul breath. Sweaty body. Smelly body. The promises. The pain. The confusion. The smell of semen. His semen. The long hall. The shower room. The dorm. Two boys. Little boys. Dressing. Middle of the night. Walking out into the night. Running up the river. The Teal River. The Blue Hills. The Blue Mountains. Trying to go home. Home. The Redstone. Running.*

Walking. Running. Walking. The cold. The fire in the trees. Tired. Exhausted. It was a dream. It wasn't real. It was. They rested. They fell asleep. Or did they? Something. Something was watching them. They looked up. They saw it. The wolf on the river. Black on blue. Death on ice. Fear. Silence.

He came back to reality and the feeling was still there. He slowly turned, expecting to see his demons, dreams and nightmares. He saw the old wolf standing a few hundred feet off the highway looking at him. *You're a dream too.*

Instinctively he raised the gun and pulled the hammer back in one smooth motion. He pulled it against his shoulder, aimed, got his target and squeezed the trigger. The sound was deafening. It echoed over the land.

He watched the wolf drop in slow motion. Blood was everywhere: on the highway, on his truck, on the hills and on the mountains. By the time the old wolf hit the ground, he knew it was dead. *Why? Why'd I do it?*

Slowly, deliberately, he reloaded the gun. He put the barrel under his chin and lowered his head. He'd done it a million times. It was almost natural. He positioned his thumb on the trigger and prepared for his ultimate journey to hell. *Push the trigger. Boom! One nanosecond of pain, then peace. Forever. No pain. No memories. No feelings. Nothing.* He took a deep breath, then slowly pushed his thumb against the trigger. He felt it give, moving back. He knew from experience that one more push would do it. He pulled the barrel harder under his chin. He did not want to have any second thoughts. He did not want it to move and . . . *And what? I'll be dead by the time they find me.* He took another deep breath and prepared for the final push. *Do it.* He exhaled, then stopped.

Someone was with him. He slowly opened his eyes and saw the wolf looking at him. It took him a few seconds to realize he hadn't shot it. He relaxed his thumb, then slowly dropped to his knees. He laid the gun on the ground and held out his arms outstretched as if to show he meant no harm. As if to say he was sorry. The wolf looked out across the wide-open valley while he remained kneeling with his arms outstretched. James looked to the clouds. *Why am I doin' 'is? When am I gonna stop?*

He didn't know how much time passed, but he slowly lowered his arms and hung his head. He was tired. He was exhausted. He looked up and the old wolf was gone. He'd never felt more lonely and abandoned in his life. He got to his feet, then picked up the gun, took one more look around. *Where'd he go? Maybe he was a dream.*

He turned his truck on, then turned up the heat. He tried to tune in the radio station, but he was too far away and knew it. He slipped in a tape. He liked music, but he'd never really listened to it and today was no different.

He pulled out his Thermos and poured some coffee, then looked at the bottle on the seat. He opened it and filled his cup to the top. He sniffed it, then drank it.

He immediately felt the warmth and the power. *Nothin' to it.* He wondered what would happen if he took the bottle and sat out in the open and went to sleep. He wondered what would happen if he took his gun and blew his head off. He wondered what would happen if he took a hose, hooked it up to his muffler and put the other end in his cab and closed the windows. He looked at his cup. It was empty. *I need a smoke.*

Twenty-One

The Exhumation

Sunday, October 10th, 1999
The old wolf stood on the ridge and looked out across the land. He was lonely and longed for the company of the pack, but they were gone. He looked to the heavens and howled. No one answered.

The first thing he felt was the cold, and then the ground. The first thing he saw was the darkness. He lifted his head and immediately regretted it. He was sitting against a large rock on the side of the highway. He hoped he'd had enough sense to shut it off.

He looked at the bottle as if it was a bad dream. He tried to open it but dropped it instead. Had he been warmer and sober he might've caught it. He did try, but it was too late. He could only watch as it fell and smashed on the rocks.

"Fuck!"

He looked up and went brain dead. His head hurt, his mouth felt like shit, and he was cold.

He looked in his toolbox hoping another would magically appear. When it didn't, got in his truck, turned it on and turned up the heat. He checked the time. He'd been there for almost twelve hours. He laid his head back and prayed for carbon monoxide poisoning.

Brenda was still up, but getting very sleepy. She was lying on the couch, and every few minutes or so she'd look outside. She didn't think he was serious when he said he might overnight on the highway. She looked at the phone and wondered if she should call Jake. She laid her head on the pillow, prayed for dreamless sleep, pulled the comforter around her and minutes later she was sleeping.

He was suffocating, and his breathing was coming in gasps. He was also hot and sweating. He woke up and started coughing, then leaned forward and hit his head on the steering wheel.

"Fuck!" he moaned.

He raised his head and got his bearings, then opened the door and almost fell out. The cool air was a relief. He regained his breathing, then looked around to see where he really was. *What 'a fuck am I doin' here?*

He looked south and wondered if he should just drive and get the hell out of the region and maybe the whole fucking country. He felt like shit and probably smelled like it too. He began thinking of excuses, but his muddled head could not come up with a plausible one. He looked around for the caribou, hoping he could have a good excuse. He got back in his truck and hoped he had enough gas to get back to town. *Maybe not. Maybe I can tell her I ran out of gas.* He checked his tank and knew he had enough. *Maybe I can poke a hole in my tank. Maybe I can say I broke down. I did, but only in body and mind.* He turned the truck around and slowly drove back to town. *What the hell am I scared of? It's my house, my life and my choice. She don' like it — tough.*

Brenda was sleeping when he walked up the steps carrying two water containers. He dropped them outside the door, then went back to his truck and got his Thermos. He'd stopped at one of the small streams and washed in the ice-cold water. He still felt like shit, but a well-washed and wide-awake shit. He walked in just as Brenda was getting off the couch.

"Where were you?" she asked.

"Out an' about," he said and grinned.

"I thought you were jokin' about staying up in the hills."

"Had you worried?"

"Yeah."

"Sorry."

She was looking at him with suspicion. "See anything?"

"One ol' wolf," he said, then lied. "Seen couple caribou an' walked to them, but they were too far." *That's why I look like shit.*

"You look pretty rough." She smiled as she went and hugged him.

He put his arms around her and closed his mouth, hoping she didn't kiss him. He needed a wash, shave and some mouthwash. *Maybe I drink some 'a that.* "Didn't sleep too good," he said. *I was too passed out.*

Brenda turned on the coffeepot while he had a shower. He was out in five minutes, still feeling like shit, but a well-showered shit. He took the cup of coffee she gave him and hoped he wasn't shaking. He was. "Cold up there," he said.

"Want breakfast?"

"Yeah."

The phone rang. He hoped it was Jake asking him to go back into the hills. It was Jane and she wanted him to do her a favour. He hung up and went to the kitchen.

"That's Jane," he said. "Wants me to pick up Joanne in Helena. Wanna come?"

"Bertha asked if I can help her cook for tomorrow," she said. "When you gonna leave?"

"Gotta gas up," he said. "Be ten by then. Two an' a half hours down.

Should be back around four or five. Need anything?"

"Not really." She put a plate in front of him.

He looked at it: bacon, eggs and toast. He hadn't realized how hungry he was.

"Snowing up there?" she asked.

"Not yet," he said. "Soon, though. You sure you don' wanna come with me?" He knew she'd committed herself to helping Bertha, but it didn't hurt to ask.

"No," she said. "You go ahead."

She took her plate into the kitchen and began running the water.

He followed and took a travel cup from the cupboard and poured his coffee into it. She was still in her nightgown and looked enticing. He put his arms around her waist and rose to the occasion. *At leas' 'at still works.*

She turned and held him, then wondered if he'd stayed in town. She knew then she was not ready to trust him. *When?*

He kissed her, and one thing led to another and he proved to her he was normal. That's all I have to do. *Fuck her an' things get back to normal.*

For the first time since New Year's Eve the church was full. Everyone knew the remains of Michael Lazarus would be dug up later and there was an air of excitement. It was as if they were going to be doing something sacrilegious. Something illegal.

James arrived at the Helena airport just as the Boeing 737 was landing. It was twenty years since he had seen Joanne. *Where does all 'a time go?* He stood in the back of the terminal and spotted her.

Joanne wondered if James would look the same. The last time she'd seen him, he had on a black leather jacket and cowboy boots. Boom! Boom! Boom! She turned. *Hasn't changed. Wonder if he's got the same grin.* Boom! Boom! Boom! He grinned. *It's him, all right.* He put his hand out and she expected a large hand full of scars and calluses, but it was soft and gentle. She held it. *What other secrets do you carry?*

She thought about Michael and how quiet he'd been.

"How's Aberdeen?" she asked as they pulled onto the highway.

"Same ol'," he answered. *We're on the road to hell.*

"What do you do?"

"Work for the Band now an' then. Trying to become a painter."

"Houses?"

"Canvas. Wanna become the nex' Picasso or Van Gogh. Not crazy 'nough, leas' not yet." *Got lots 'a time though.*

She smiled. "Have you ever lived anywhere else?"

"Not really. Went to college in Yellowknife for couple years. That's about it."

"Really? What you take?"

"Business."

"Really?" she said.

He looked at her and smiled. "Not as nuts as people think I am."

She grinned. "Married?"

"No thanks, not yet."

"Kids?"

"None."

"Were you and Louise married?"

"No."

"What happened?"

Fucked up. "Broke up."

"When?" she asked, genuinely surprised.

"A million years ago," he said. "Right after high school."

"Wow? I thought you two would be married an' have a million kids."

"Can't have no kids."

"Why not?"

"Had a vasectomy."

"You're kidding. Why?"

"Almost got hauled into court once."

She looked at him and wondered if he really was nuts. She decided he wasn't. He was just like . . . *Like who? Like Michael.* "What's gonna happen now?" she asked. "About the abuse."

"I've no idea," he answered.

"Someone's gotta do somethin'."

"Ain't gonna be easy. Happened long 'go."

"That doesn't take away from the fact it was wrong. Someone's gotta do something."

Me, I'm gonna kill him.

As they drove into Aberdeen, they could see the people at the cemetery.

"Wanna go up?" he asked.

"Gotta do it sooner or later."

The first person they saw was Jane, who welcomed her daughter home. They then watched as the coffin that contained the remains of Michael was removed and carried to the church.

After it was over, Jane got into his truck. "Mussi," she said.

"No prob."

"You're gonna take him up tomorrow."

It wasn't an order, nor was it a question. It was just a statement of fact.

Twenty-Two

Old Ways and New Beginnings

Monday, October 11th, 1999
The old wolf ate, but his heart wasn't in it. He saw the caribou to the north, then slowly walked to the ridge and waited. For what he didn't know. He just waited.

The community was up early and people were calling to make sure they had a ride or to offer rides. There was an air of cooperation not felt since the good old days. Those with trucks picked up food from houses and most would pick up wood along the highway.

It was overcast and fall was definitely in the air when more than thirty trucks, vans and one old bus began the three-hour journey into the hills with over two hundred people.

James led the procession with Jake, Mary and Brenda and Michael's coffin in the back. They arrived at the spot where they'd seen the caribou and started piling the wood for the fire that was to send

Michael home. The People made smaller fires to keep warm and the teakettles and the food were brought out.

After everyone had arrived, Chief David stood and spoke of Michael's life and death. "We all know why he came up here," he said of Michael's last ride into the hills. "That part is not over, at leas' not for some of us an' it might never be over for others. We still have a long way to go." *A long way.* "In the last few days, we've seen something happen in our community. We've seen People disclose an' we've seen the drum return if only for one night. I wish I can tell you it's going to be like this forever, but we all know it isn't. Not unless we work together to keep it."

Bertha then spoke of Michael's last visit and the letter. It wasn't easy and she cried many times, but she did get through it.

Afterwards, Chief James, Chief David's predecessor, spoke about the Old Ways and about the last time the People sent someone to the Old People in these hills. That someone was his dad, Chief Francis. He looked at the Reverend Andy as he spoke and remembered how the minister of the day had tried to stop them, but the People couldn't be stopped. At least not on that day. *This one is different. This one understands.*

Martin then thanked the People for attending and helping out. "My wife an' I knew about the letter for a long time, but we didn't know what to do. We now know there are others an' he was not alone. I only hope his soul will find peace, wherever that is."

When all was said that had to be said, the Reverend Andy led the People in a prayer while Martin and Jane lit the fire, and the People watched as an old tradition was reborn from the flames. They stood in silence, and most wished him well on his journey to find the peace he couldn't find on this side. The north wind fanned the flames and Michael was slowly returned to the land.

As the fire burned, Old Pierre and the Elders started drumming and started singing an Old Prayer Song. It rose from the crowd and drifted over the land.

James and Jake stood next to his truck and watched in silence. As the fire burned, James removed the gun from his truck and walked to the edge of the crowd, and Jake followed. They looked to the south, and as the People watched, James fired one shot into the heavens to pave the way for Michael's journey. *It's over for you. For me, it's jus' beginnin'. Will I make it? Who knows? Time enough to worry about it.* He held out the gun to Jake, who did the same.

Louise's heart went out to them. She looked at the fire and wondered if she'd ever forgive Michael. *Maybe someday.*

The People watched the fire slowly consume the remains of Michael and stood as the wind carried his ashes into the mountains. As the Elders were slowly ending the Old Song, the sky began to clear and the sun broke through. The People basked in its warmth. In a few months it would be gone, but it would return. It always did. There was a silence that no one had ever heard and a calmness that everyone enjoyed. They lifted their faces as if drawing energy from the sun.

The old wolf had been sitting on the ridge watching. When the drums started, he stood as though something was calling to him. Whatever it was, he didn't stop to ponder its origin. He went on instinct. He circled, then slowly came into the herd from the north. The herd moved up over the ridge and into the sunlight.

One by one, the People watched as a thousand caribou in their full autumn glory came over the ridge and onto the flats. They slowly walked to the highway and, as their ancestors must have done at least ten thousand times, they witnessed the return of the caribou to the Blue Mountains.

Chief James stood with his wife and Old Pierre and Dora on the side of the highway. "The caribou are home again," he said in the language. "Mussi."

The People slowly returned to the fires, elated. They ate whatever food they'd brought, and the stories and jokes sprang forth as if it were some sort of tradition. It was.

Later the People watched as Martin walked to the fire and offered a piece of meat for Michael's long journey back to the Old People. No one had to explain this to them. They knew what he was doing, and over the next hour they all did the same in their own time and in their own way.

As darkness approached, the Elders talked about the good old days when the caribou stretched as far as the eye could see.

Chief James remembered those days and smiled. "It's time to bring the caribou home," he said.

Without a word, Old Pierre brought out the drums, and for the first time in fifty years, the People sang the Old Songs in the mountains for the caribou. They sang loud and lifted their voices to the heavens. All those who could understand the words stood around the fires and joined in. Even those who didn't understand still joined in. The caribou stood as if hypnotized.

Liz and Sarah took part as if it were all a dream. They joined James and Jake and said nothing.

James realized he was thirteen going on fourteen when they were born. They didn't have to put up with what he and Jake and thousands of others had to endure. He could sense their uneasiness. "How's it goin'?" he asked.

They looked at him and pictured him in the community hall screaming his heart out. *Was this the same man?*

"I don' know what to say," Liz said.

James grinned. "You don't have to say nothin'," he said. "I'm still the same ol' me. Nothin's changed. At least not yet. I'm still movin' an' life goes on." *Or doesn't.* They had tears in their eyes. *What can I say? What can I do?* He said and did nothing. Nothing had to be said or done.

Later, Joanne walked up to James, Chief David and Jake. She wanted to say something but didn't know what. *What do you say? We were just kids.* "I never knew my brother that well," she said. "He was always quiet, like he had a secret." She looked at the fire. "I guess he did," she said. "I want to thank you for what you've done." She looked at James. *Are you the one? Are you the one that's going to settle this?* "What's going to happen?" she asked him.

I'm gonna kill the son of a bitch. "I don't know."

James wished he could do something, but he was no hero. He was no knight in shining armour. He was still insecure about his future and what it held, if it held anything at all. He now knew what he had to do: he had to leave. Either that or stay and die, and he had no intention of dying. At least not yet. He looked at Chief David. *What happens now?*

Chief David was also looking at him. He too was wondering what would happen now. He looked at Jake. *Will he be the one? He started it. Albeit in a roundabout way. How many more were there? How many that weren't in the hostel? How many more found their way into his dark room while they visited the hostel?* He felt a tug and looked down at his daughter. He held her in his arms and the tears came.

Wanda stood by his side and looked at James and Jake. She'd known them all her life but she didn't know them. They were strangers. She knew they drank and partied for the last twenty years and that's all. She'd heard David talk about how intelligent James was, but she could never picture it. He was silent, almost dangerous, but he'd stood up when it counted. He stood up in a crowded community hall to tell David he was not alone. So had Jake. She was wondering if Jake would ever grow up when she realized he *was* grown up. He was older than she was. At that moment, she felt she was a million years older. "Jake?"

Jake looked at her.

"I just want to say thank you," she said. "For standing up with my husband." She felt the tears coming. "For my children."

Jake smiled, then wiped his tears.

James said nothing. He looked at Chief David, then at his daughter and son who'd joined them. *How old is he? Thirteen? Fourteen? I was younger when it happened.* He looked at Wanda. "They'll have a better life than we did."

Later, as the People were preparing to leave, Louise came over with Caroline and introduced her to James and Brenda.

Caroline smiled at James. "My mom's got your picture," she said.

"Caroline!" Louise was embarrassed.

"Well, it's true."

James looked down at Caroline and said, "I got a picture of your mom too."

"Where?"

He took her hand and placed it on his heart. "Here."

"You made my mom cry," Caroline said.

James stood. *I love you.* "Louise?"

She looked at him.

"I'm sorry."

"It's okay."

No, it's not okay. "I'm sorry," he said again.

This time she smiled. *It's okay. I love you, too, but I'm married an' tomorrow's my anniversary. But you don' need to know that. Twenty years 'a misery.* She took Caroline's hand and disappeared into the crowd.

James wondered if she was real. *Maybe she was a dream. Maybe she was always a dream.*

Brenda wondered what kind of couple they'd have made had they been married. *Would they still be together? What about us? Will we make it?* She looked at him standing there in his big, black boots and black leather jacket and smiled. *Of course we will.*

James smiled at her, then reached out to see if she was real. She held his hand to her face and was about to tell him she loved him, but didn't. *Why? Why can't he say it?*

They all turned to see Bertha carrying an old envelope that contained a secret. She walked over to the fire and placed the envelope in the flames and another secret was laid to rest. She looked at Jake and smiled. *He'll be okay.* She looked at James. *What about him? Is he strong enough? Will he make it?* She turned to the hills and offered another prayer to the Old People. *Help him.*

After everyone had left, James, Jake, Brenda and Mary stood and watched the dying flames. In a few days the ashes would be scattered by the winds and Michael would be part of the land, part of the water, as it should have been in the first place.

James looked at the gun. *Was it a gift or was he trying to tell me somethin'?*

Old Man Abraham Lazarus had bought it in the 1940s and it had provided for an entire family. It travelled the land of the People through the good times and the bad times. It rang in the New Year. It rang in many New Years. Old Man Abraham left it to his oldest son to carry on the tradition. He did. Benjamin left it to his oldest son to do the same, but Michael found a new tradition. He also found peace in these mountains. The gun was prepared to take the life of James Nathan, but it wasn't his time. *At least not yet and maybe never. Who knows?*

James stood next to his brother and both knew it was time to say goodbye to the past and move into the future and whatever it held. *New beginnings? New horizons?* He looked at the gun and for the first time in his life he fully realized he'd never have a son to pass it on to. *This tradition will die with me. Should I let it?* His mind was made up for him. By whom, he had no idea. He held the gun out to Jake.

Jake looked at the gun, then at James.

"I don' know why he lef' it to me," James said.

Jake took the gun, then looked at his own. It didn't have the same history as Old Man Abraham's, but they had time. He held it out to James.

James took it. *Another gift? Another tradition?* Then, for the first time in his life, he spoke the language. "My brother," he said. "I'll always be here for you."

It was an eternity before Jake answered. "So will I," he said, also in the language.

They then did something they'd never done in their lives. They hugged each other like brothers and held nothing back.

"I love you, *my brother*," James said.

"I love you too."

The old wolf watched the four people get in the truck and leave. As they were driving away, he approached the fire and basked in its warmth. Then he looked to the hills and the mountains and then at the stars that were now appearing in the night sky. He lifted his head and howled like his kind had done since the last ice age. He then laid his tired body down beside the fire and went to sleep for the last time.

Far away and long ago, something happened. Michael watched the truck drive into the night, then he watched the old wolf lie beside the fire. He stood there for a long time, then turned and followed the way into the hills and darkness.

Part Three

The Real World

Twenty-Three

The Week After

James woke up on Tuesday morning feeling he'd slept forever. He had a strange desire to drive into the hills again. It was something he couldn't explain. Perhaps it was the desire to be alone. Perhaps it was the desire to see if the events of the previous day were real. Perhaps it was the desire to finally do it. Whatever the reason, he left at eight, after telling Brenda he was going to see if he could get a couple of caribou. She didn't really believe him, but she didn't try to stop him either. She had to trust him, and forever at that.

Three hours later, he was approaching the site where they'd sent Michael back to the Old People. Like so many times in the past, he couldn't remember the drive up. He knew he'd stopped to get some wood, but the rest of the drive was a blur. He'd been thinking again, or time-travelling. About what, he couldn't remember.

He slowed, then got out of his truck and saw the old wolf. Almost without thinking, he gathered what wood was left in the area and put it on the fire, then walked back to his truck. He put on a pair of gloves, then carried more wood to the fire and placed the wolf in the flames.

He watched it burn and wondered again if this was all a dream. He wondered if his life was nothing more than a dream and would he wake up? His body sagged and he let loose a scream, then dropped his head.

After a few minutes, he stood and wondered why he still felt like doing it. Why did he still feel he was going crazy? He waited, but as always there was no answer. He thought about the events of the last few days and wondered why he'd said and did what he'd said and did. He came up with an answer: Jake saw a nightmare on television and brought it back from the Dream World.

He knew there was no changing the past. At least not yet and maybe never. Not unless the USS *Enterprise* time-travelled back from the future to pick him up in a valiant effort to change the course of history for his People. He looked up and waited, but they didn't come.

He looked at the fire and the wolf and wondered what was real and what was the dream. He thought about Brenda and Yellowknife and new beginnings and knew he had to get out of there and get a life.

On Tuesday, Louise and Caroline passed James's truck on their way to work and school, but they did not look at him. As far as Louise was concerned, he was history. As far as Caroline was concerned, he was just a picture in her mom's bedroom. Louise realized she had worked for the last twenty-four years and was six years from retirement. By then she'd be fifty and life might as well be over.

On Wednesday, the news about the workshop was old news and the story about the exhumation of Michael Lazarus was nothing more than rumours that no one believed and even if they did, they didn't care. Injuns returning to the Old Ways was nothing new. The two reporters from Helena missed out on the drum dance, the exhumation and the dream in the hills. They weren't invited. Come to think of it, no one was. It was something that just happened.

James and Bella signed the legal papers on Friday, then he, Brenda and Jake left for Yellowknife and what they hoped was a new beginning and a better way of life. They all had jobs except for James, but he hoped he'd have a calling as an artist. Mary had already lined up a job as a secretary in January. It was part-time, but like Jake, it could turn into something permanent.

Friday night was a typical night in Aberdeen. The bootleggers did well that night. Things were slowly returning to normal.

Meanwhile, Leon and Jeff were soon forgotten. It was as if they'd never existed. They were nothing more than mounds of dirt in the cemetery. Sam Hunter was also forgotten. He'd never existed. He was a mound of dirt in the cemetery.

Twenty-Four

The Geographic Change

James, Brenda and Jake arrived in Yellowknife late Saturday night and stayed in a townhouse that Brenda had rented. They'd decided to take their time before buying. Actually, she made the decision. She did ask James, but he said, "Whatever."

Jake moved in at their insistence, but they didn't see too much of him. He worked long hours and called home every night for the first week until Mary told him to stop it on account she cried every time they hung up. He then called every other night and sometimes in between.

James wondered what Jake and Mary talked about. He and Brenda woke up in the morning, said good morning, then she went to work. When she came home, they said hi and that was about the extent of their conversation.

Ernest and Margaret Austin moved to Yellowknife at the end of October and stayed with Clara. Clara's life was far from the hell she'd left a million years ago in Aberdeen. She was full of life and definitely in love with her second husband and looked forward to Larry joining them in December. It never dawned on her that he could get a couple of years. At least not yet.

At the end of October, Chief David called James. "I'm gonna do it," he said.

"Do what?" James asked.

"Lay a formal complaint."

"When?"

"Today."

"How long you think it'll take?"

"Don' really care, long as it gets done."

It took James a few seconds to make up his mind and even then he wasn't one hundred percent sure. "I'll do it too," he said.

"What about Jake?"

"He's out, but I'll talk to him when he gets in."

"Good enough for me."

"What do I do?"

"No idea. I already tol' 'a Sarge an' he's expectin' me."

"Do I just go in an' tell 'em?"

"Why don' you gimme couple hours. I'll ask the Sarge to call Yellowknife an' tell them to expect you."

"Good idee. Don' wanna make 'em think I'm crazy. Bad enough people think I'm crazy at home."

Later, James almost decided against it, but he kept picturing the shower room and dark rooms. He wanted nothing more than to exorcise his demons once and for all.

The next day, after they relived their nightmares for the Yellowknife RCMP, James felt like having a few to drown his miseries. He didn't.

Jake, on the other hand, told Mary what he'd done, then went to sleep.

James woke at four in the morning and looked for the fucker, but he was gone. It was then he realized that he'd have to meet his nightmare for the first time in thirty years. There was no way around it and there was no turning back.

The Sarge wondered what was going to happen once the shit hit the fan. He had a list of people to interview, but he wasn't sure how many would come forward. He hadn't known Michael Lazarus, but he'd met enough of them to know what he must've gone through. Or so he thought.

After two weeks, James still wasn't getting any job offers despite his education and his experience.

Brenda started working. She was glad to be home and renewed old friendships and made new ones. She invited some of them over to meet James, but he just sat and time-travelled or daydreamed. They did not have the same taste in friends, and most of hers only saw a tall, dark, handsome and very silent man who had a hard time smiling.

He tried painting, but his paintings looked like something Picasso would've done when he was hungover and in a sour mood. He painted what he knew would sell and sold them for next to nothing. Had he tried, he could've sold them for a whole lot more, but his mind wasn't where it should have been.

Three weeks after they arrived, Jake found a small house that needed some work. He put a down payment on it, then went for a mortgage on the rest. He moved in soon after and started fixing it up.

The day after Jake moved out, James learned that shacking up for the night and living together were two totally different things. He and Brenda had their second disagreement. It was over his lack of a job and a future and a lot of things. He drove to the airport and looked at the highway leading out of town and thought about leaving. He was homesick and lonely.

Brenda was wondering if he had left when she heard him drive up. She met him at the door. "I'm sorry."

"Me too," he answered.

Then they did the only thing they could: they fucked.

"Are you happy here?" she later asked.

James had an answer, but he didn't say it.

"I'm not gonna hold you," she continued. "You're not obligated."

He still said nothing.

"Is it me?" she asked.

"It's not you. It's me. I've got some stuff to work out." After a few seconds, he said, "Can I ask you something?"

"Sure."

"Why me?"

"What?"

"Why me?"

"I don't know," she said.

Brenda came home on Monday to find supper prepared and James sketching and thinking. "What's on your mind?" she asked, then regretted it. Something *was* on his mind.

"Thinkin' of goin' home for while."

"Will you be back?"

He stared at the sketchpad.

"I'm sorry," she said.

"Don't be," he said. "Who knows? Maybe after I get my shit together . . ."

"James?"

"Yeah?"

"I love you."

"Me too."

"How come you never say it?"

"Say what?"

"You never told me you loved me."

"I didn't?"

"Not once. You always say, 'Me too.'"

She was right. He tried to remember the last person he'd said that to. He thought about a small hotel room in Helena a million years ago and a beautiful woman named Myra.

"James?"

"Yeah?"

"You okay?"

He smiled. "Yeah."

"Why don't you ever say it?"

"Never said it to anyone, 'cept Jake, an' only once."

"You ever tell Louise when you were with her?"

"I don' think so."

"You've never said it in your life, before Jake?"

"Never."

"Why?"

"I don' know."

"Why don't you just say it?" she asked.

"You want me too?"

"I don't want you to say it 'cause I'm askin'. I want you to say it 'cause you mean it." When he didn't say anything, she didn't push. "Let's take it one day at a time. Works better that way."

"I'm sorry."

"Don't be," she said. "Where you gonna stay?"

"I'm gonna ask Ernest if I can use his house."

"People are gonna ask about you — about us."

"Tell 'em to mind 'eir own business."

"I'll tell 'em you're huntin'."

He was about to tell her that was a lie, but didn't.

The next day, he went to see Ernest and Margaret, and they gave him their house keys and told him it was his for as long as he needed it. Somehow they knew he'd never be back. At least not for good.

James packed a few personal effects as though he'd be coming back.

He called Brenda at work. "I'm gonna leave now," he said.

"I love you," she said.

After a few seconds, she said, "Call me when you get there."

"I will."

"James?"

"Yeah?"

"Look after yourself."

"I will."

"James?"

"Yeah?"

"Call me," she said and almost broke down.

"I will."

James then called Jake at work.

"You comin' back?" Jake asked after he'd told him of his plans.

"Prob'ly not."

"Whatcha gonna do?"

"Get back in 'a taxi business, paint, work, whatever."

"Need a ride home in a few weeks."

"Let Mary know an' I'll be down."

He drove out of Yellowknife and went brain dead to take his mind off the drive, his dismal past and his uncertain future.

Twenty-Five

The Return Home

James's first stop in Aberdeen was at Mary and her parents. He dropped off some parcels Jake had sent.

"How's he doin'?" Mary asked.

"Peachy."

They laughed, but he noticed she was concerned. "He's doin' okay," he said. "No need to worry 'bout him. He'll be home in couple weeks."

"When you goin' back?"

"Couple weeks to pick him up."

He also went to see Chief David.

"Grace got a new job in Helena an' I'm lookin' for a band manager," Chief David said.

"No thanks, leas' not now."

"Whatcha gonna do?"

"Gonna start paintin' again. See if I can make a livin' or least die tryin'." He wished he hadn't used the word "die."

"How you holdin' up?" Wanda asked.

"So far, so good," he said. "How's Louise?"

"She's at her parents'. You know where that is."

James did visit Louise on Remembrance Day. Her parents were glad to see him and were even happier that he was sober. Louise looked like she wanted to hug him, but she didn't. She didn't even shake his hand.

"Where you were?" Caroline asked him.

"Yellowknife."

"What for?"

"Visitin'."

"Who?"

"My brother."

"Who's 'at?"

"Jake."

"Wait here," she said and ran into her mother's bedroom.

"Want some tea?" Louise asked.

"Sure."

"See?" Caroline said as she returned. "My mom got your picture."

"Caroline!" Louise screamed.

But James already had the photo. It was an old black-and-white taken while they were in the Helena hostel. It was yellow and faded. "You got a camera?" he asked.

She nodded and looked away, then caught herself and looked at him.

"Get it," he said, then wondered why she always looked away.

She went to her room and brought back a camera while he sat between her parents and held Caroline on his knee.

"Take a picture of this," he said.

"How's Jake?" she later asked.

"Okay."

"And how's Brenda?"

"She's okay."

"How long you here for?"

"Don' know yet."

He's not goin' back. "So what're you gonna do?" she asked.

"Don't know. Might start up my taxi. Do some paintin'. Who knows? What about you? How've you been?"

"Still gettin' a divorce, still workin'." She watched for a reaction, but it was like he wasn't listening.

Having nothing else to talk about, he left and decided to get some painting done. He had not called Brenda since his return and it never crossed his mind. Come to think of it, she hardly ever crossed his mind.

Meanwhile, George Standing got back into business. He drove to Helena and picked up a couple of cases, then sold to only those he could trust. Things were almost back to normal. Normal, abnormal, whatever.

James kept a low profile over the next few days. He did call Brenda, but they didn't have much to say. On Sunday, Sarah invited him to Liz's for supper. Sarah asked, "What're you doin' back in 'is place?"

"Gotta fin' a job an' a life."

"What's wrong with Yellowknife?"

"Ain't nothin' 'ere for me." He wished he hadn't said it like that.

"What about Brenda?"

"She's gonna stay an' work."

"You goin' back?"

"No idea," he said.

He spent the next week coming up with ideas for paintings, but on Friday he had had enough. He needed a drink.

He drove around town looking for a bottle, but the only person who had any booze for sale was George Standing.

George was in the process of exorcising some demons by getting drunk when James knocked on his door. "Come in," he yelled. He was surprised to see James. He thought about Myra, then thought about kicking the shit out of the fucker, but he was no match for the big son of a bitch.

"Hey, George," James said, then smirked. "Got any?"

"Nothin' for you."

"Why not?"

"You know why."

Over the last few years, George had done some reading and learned he had rights. One of these rights was to lay charges against James Fuckin' Nathan if the fucker so much as swore at him. He also had two secrets and today he let loose one of them. "You think I don' know about you an' my wife?" he said.

James stood and said nothing.

"She told me 'bout it, you fucker." Then he said it. "She was pregnant."

"You're full 'a shit," James answered.

"Get outta my house, you asshole."

Two hours later, James was in a familiar hotel room in Helena with a bottle of vodka and a case of beer. He looked at the bottle, then at Myra sitting on the armchair. Almost without thinking, he poured a drink then drank it.

After his third drink, he thought about blowing George Fucking Standing into oblivion with the rest of his fucking demons. He thought about Myra and wished she were here. She wasn't.

He remembered what she'd told him in this very room a million years ago. They were both drunk, but he remembered. "George molested his sister," she said.

"How you know?"

"I know."

"None 'a my business."

"None 'a mine either."

He never thought about it until now. He didn't want to think about it, but he did. He didn't want to believe it, but the more he thought about it, the more he believed it.

He guzzled another. He thought about what George said about Myra. He didn't have to think too hard about that one. It was time, it had to be.

He couldn't remember the next few drinks. He couldn't remember taking his clothes off. He couldn't remember passing out. He couldn't remember falling off the bed. Things were returning to normal.

Edward and Rachel William passed away within three days of each other and were buried in the cemetery as they had requested. James helped with the gravedigging but did not attend the funeral, nor did he attend the feast.

Twenty-Six

Secrets, Lies and Truths

Brenda was at home in Yellowknife during the last week of November. Since James had left, she'd time to think about her life and their relationship. He'd called only twice and they didn't have much to say. She came to the conclusion that despite the fact she was in love with him, he wasn't in love with her and he never would be. He was in love with Louise, even if he denied it. She decided the only thing to do was give him his freedom, but it wasn't an easy decision. She thought about being alone for the rest of her life and wondered if sex was enough of a reason for staying together. It wasn't. In the end, she had to come to terms with it and deal with it. She called him soon after. "Do you know why I'm callin'?" she asked.

"I think I do."

"What do I say?"

"Nothin' much to say. That's just the way it is."

"I never meant to hurt you."

"Of course you didn't."

"I'll always care for you."

"Me, too," he answered. "I'll be down in couple weeks. We'll talk."

James hung up, then thought about his future. He had none to think of, none was looming on the horizon.

Larry Hunter's trial was rescheduled until June, and he was ordered to remain in custody. He'd never been in a hostel in his life, but had he been, he would have realized jail was almost similar. Routines.

James arrived in Yellowknife on Wednesday, December 15th, and stayed at Jake's. He called Brenda the next morning and told her he was coming over to pick up his odds and ends. That evening, she met him at the door and held him like she was never going to let go. She thought if she could just lock her door and never open it again, things might be okay.

She watched him take his few belongings out to his truck. When he came back in, she said, "Sit down. I got somethin' to tell you."

James sat and listened as Brenda told him the reason she dropped out of school.

"You ever tell him?" he asked.

"No."

"Why tell me?"

"I don't know," she said. "I had to tell someone."

"Who else knows?"

"My parents an' her adopted parents."

"Where're they?"

Brenda shrugged. "Don't know."

"You gonna look?" he asked.

"Not likely. Not unless she wants to meet." She then thought about Raymond. "Did you ever wonder why he did it?"

"Thought about it, but not for a long time."

"And?"

"I don't know," he said. "You ever ask?"

"Thought about it, but never did."

"He's got a big family."

"I know," she said. "I've seen them but never talked to them."

"You should."

"They might . . ."

"It's not your fault," he said.

"I know, but that doesn't make it any easier. Maybe if I'd stayed? Maybe if I'd told him?"

"But you didn't and you can't change that."

"I know," she said. "What about you? What're you gonna do?"

He shrugged. "Go home an' look for a job an' paint."

"You *are* good, you know."

"So they tell me."

"You are and you can make a living at it."

"I hope so."

"You will."

"Thanks."

Brenda looked at the walls and ceiling. "James?"

"Yeah?"

"Can I ask you a question?"

He shrugged. "Sure."

"Are you in love with Louise?"

James looked at her and said nothing.

"Are you?" she asked again. "And please be honest with me."

"I think I've always been in love with her," he answered. "Does that bother you?"

"Not as much as I thought it would. You gonna tell her?"

"Who knows?"

"I think she still loves you."

"She tell you?"

"No, but I think she does."

He looked at his hands.

"You need someone, James."

"I know."

"I don't think you do."

"Got this far."

"And where're you?" she asked. "You've been alone all your life. You can't be alone too much longer or you'll . . ."

"Or I'll what?"

"Or you're gonna end . . ."

"I won't."

"I don't believe you," she said. "You've said you've tried it."

He looked away. He was uncomfortable, and she knew it.

"Tell her," she said.

"I will."

"You won't. I know you. You're gonna wait for her to say it and she's probably waiting for you too. God, you're both so stubborn."

"I've got things to do," he said.

"Like?"

"The investigation is still goin' on."

"When's that gonna be over?"

"A couple months. Who knows?"

"If you don't tell her, I will," she said. "Either way, you have to know."

"And what about you?" James said.

"What about me?"

"What're you gonna do?"

"About what?"

"About your daughter?"

"I think I'm gonna tell my ex," she said. "He deserves to know."

"And Michelle?"

"I don't know if I'll tell her."

"Why not?"

"I've thought about it and I can't. She's gonna always want to know where she is."

"You still love your ex?"

"Yeah."

"So you weren't really in love with me?"

"I was and I am, but it's different."

"How?"

"I can let you go," she answered. "It's not easy, but I have to. You're in love with Louise and I'm not her."

"I'm sorry."

"Don't be. That's just the way it is. Or so I've heard."

He grinned at that one. "You gonna tell your ex?"

"I don't know."

"So you and I are not being honest," he said, "with the one we love."

"I guess we aren't."

"I'll tell her, but only in my time."

"I guess I can't be a hypocrite," she said.

"I don't know. I'm just talkin'."

"But it does make sense. You are making sense."

He laughed. "Thanks."

"I guess I will have to tell him."

"Better than not knowing."

"My words exactly," she said.

James looked out the window into the darkness. "I've thought about telling her a million times and I've done it a million times," he said, "in my mind."

"And what happens?" she asked. "In your mind?"

"She either tells me to fuck off, or we . . ."

"Either way, you'll know."

"Guess so."

"James?"

"Yeah?"

"I'm gonna tell my husband, I mean my ex."

"That's good."

"Then I'm gonna wait for the trial to be over and then I'm gonna tell her if you haven't."

He smiled.

"I'm not joking," she said.

"I know. I was just hoping you were."

"I'm not."

"Well, I've got to go."

"James?"

"Yeah?"

"How come we never talked like this before?"

"Like what?"

"Honestly."

"Don't know," he said. "Anyhow, I've gotta go."

"So this is goodbye?"

"Not really," he said. "We'll see each other now an' then."

He gave her a hug and walked out into the night.

Twenty-Seven

Weddings and Vows

James and Jake arrived in Aberdeen on Saturday. Mary and her parents were glad to see them.

Two days later, on December 21, Jake and Mary were married. James was the best man and Alfred and Danny were the groomsmen. Louise was the maid of honour while Sarah and Liz were the bridesmaids.

The feast that followed was spectacular and the dance that followed was packed. Despite never having jigged in public when he was sober, Jake found out that jigging was genetic. The women kept him on the floor for fifteen minutes and he enjoyed every minute of it.

James tried to disappear, but Mary slung his ass onto the floor and the women did the same to him. The People hooted and hollered when his and Louise's turn came. He later wondered if the whole town knew. Or were they hoping?

The next day, Brenda called Jake and Mary from Calgary and apologized for not being able to attend. She asked about James.

"He's up in 'a hills," Jake answered.

Brenda wondered if Martin was going to find another body up in the mountains.

Up in the Blue Mountains, James was cutting wood and contemplating the meaning of life. He wondered if he would have the courage to sit in a crowded courtroom and tell his story. He wondered if they'd look at him differently. He wondered if it was all a dream. He wondered if he should just eat a bullet and fuck it.

Twenty-Eight

Myra's Revenge

James woke up Christmas Day and called Jake and Mary and wished them a Merry Christmas. They invited him for Christmas dinner and he said he'd be there. He hung up and burst out crying. After a few minutes, he got up and looked outside. It was cold and dark. He felt as if he was the last person Earth. He needed a drink.

That afternoon, he went to Jake and Mary's for dinner, then over to the Chief's house. He saw Louise and Caroline and wished them a Merry Christmas and nothing else.

He stayed in that evening and did some sketching, but his heart was not in it. He still needed and wanted a drink. He thought about what he'd heard that day.

What everyone saw or heard that Christmas Day in Aberdeen was three children who were taken from their parents' house by Const. Adrienne Taylor and the social workers. They'd been left alone without food and without much of a Christmas. Martin and Jane took them in, and five days later they would be sent to Yellowknife to what everyone hoped was a better life.

Rumour was their parents had spent all their money on bootlegs and had spent Christmas in jail. The former was speculation, but the latter was true. They had plenty of company in the cells that night.

One of the persons who kept them company was Daniel, who realized he might be going to jail for a long time. He'd slapped Doreen and this time she'd called the cops. He was thinking about what he should do and he had three options. First, he could go with the flow and end up in jail. Second, he could get her to drop the charges and he'd be free until the next time. Third, he could borrow a gun.

The day after Christmas, there were five assaults, two break and enters, and three more windows were smashed on the new school. Twelve people spent the night in the cells. Things were slowing down, but just barely. Daniel persuaded Doreen to drop the charges after he promised he'd never do it again, and they got on with life.

Two days after Christmas, six young people were thrown in jail for underaged drinking and no one really gave a shit. Thomas assaulted his wife and she had to be sent to the Helena Hospital and he was put jail for the night. His sister took their children and kept them until Thomas was released.

Three days after Christmas, George Standing went to Helena to pick up more booze. Sales were good and fifteen people spent the night in jail. Things were picking up.

James went to Chief David's house that evening and had some left-over turkey and decided to look for some fish and soon. David told him about the number of people being thrown in. "I really don' give a shit about the parents," he said. "I just worry about the children."

It had not been a good Christmas. But it was normal.

James had never seen it sober and didn't like what he saw. He needed that drink more than ever. He drove to Helena that night and got the same hotel room and dreamed of Myra. He wished he could've stayed in that dream. He woke up at four o'clock the next morning and was once again standing naked in front of the mirror with a bottle of vodka in one hand and a cigarette in the other. He didn't remember too much after that. Things were more or less normal.

Four days after Christmas, James was on his way home when he tuned in to CBMP and listened to Liz and Sarah play some hurting music. Chief David then got on the air and talked about the number of people being charged for this, that and everything in between. James could sense the desperation in his voice.

Ten miles out of Aberdeen he stopped and looked for his gun. He was tired. He wanted to get drunk, then walk into the trees and disappear.

He checked his time and it was almost eight. He got in his truck, then drove by Aberdeen and away from a way of life that was slowly killing him.

One hour out of Aberdeen, he had an idea and turned his truck around.

As he was driving into the unknown, he thought about his past. He'd drunk with people who'd neglected their children. At the time he thought nothing of it because he had more important things on his mind, like getting drunk and laid. But he'd seen enough children neglected because people like George Fucking Standing sold booze to their parents. He'd seen enough fucking killings, suicides and beatings. He had had enough of George Fucking Standing and his lies. He loved Myra, and George Fucking Standing had killed her. He might not have done it in the eyes of the law, but he'd done it in the eyes of James Fucking Nathan and that's all the law that mattered.

He arrived at George's house at ten and was now going on instinct. He walked in without knocking to find George sitting on his sofa getting ready to drink another night into oblivion.

George wondered if the fucker was drinking. "Get 'a fuck outta my house, you asshole!" he screamed.

James waited for him to say the magic word, and he did.

"Get outta or I'll call 'a cops!"

"Why don't you?" James said quietly. "Maybe we'll tell 'em about you. Maybe we'll tell 'em about you an' your sister."

Someone smacked George Standing upside the head with a two by four, at least that's how it felt.

"Myra told me, you asshole." James grinned like he really didn't give a fuck what happened now.

George felt like he was going to have a fucking heart attack. *The bitch tol' him!*

"I came here to kill you, you son of a bitch!" James said. "But I won't. I'm gonna do somethin' worse. I'm gonna let you live."

George stared at him.

"Know what I'm gonna do?" James said. "I'm gonna talk to your sister about bringin' you up on charges. Maybe you'll do time with well-hung motherfuckers that have no love lost for a child molester."

George felt the sting of every syllable.

"That's what you are. Nothin' but a fuckin' bootleggin' child molester."

The two men weighed their options. George had none. James had two: he could stay and kill the son of a bitch or he could leave. He left.

Five days after Christmas and two days before the new millennium, James woke up feeling normal: like shit. He spent the day wondering what the fuck got into him. It was none of his business. Or was it?

Jake came around that evening and said nothing for a long time. "You drink?" he finally asked.

"No," James said.

"Good. You look like shit."

"It's jus' 'at time 'a year."

"Know what you mean."

"You still goin'?"

"Gotta. Nothin' here for us. Nothin' was ever here for us."

James woke up the next morning feeling worse than ever. He went up to Liz and Sarah, hoping they'd invite him to the Saloon. They didn't. They invited him up to Louise's.

At midnight, James drove the three of them and Caroline up to watch the fireworks and to see if they'd disappear at the stroke of midnight as a result of the Y2K bug. Nobody really cared if it was a new millennium. It was a new year and that's all that mattered.

After the fireworks, James found himself alone with Louise and a sleeping Caroline. He drove them home and carried Caroline into her bedroom. As he was putting her down she opened her eyes.

"What a faker," James said.

She smiled. "You gonna stay with us again?"

"We'll see."

He came out of Caroline's bedroom and Louise was making coffee. He knew there was no way out, he'd have to stay for coffee. He fell asleep on the sofa.

Louise watched as he drifted off into the Dream World, then she covered him with a blanket and went to sleep with Caroline.

"Is James gonna sleep over?" Caroline asked.

"He's sleepin' on the sofa."

"Good," she said. "I wish he was my daddy."

"Me too."

James woke up on New Year's Day just as Louise and Caroline were getting up.

"Want breakfast?" Louise asked.

"Just coffee, then I gotta check my place."

They felt uncomfortable and were glad Caroline was there.

"You got any kids?" she asked James.

"No."

"Why not?"

"Ain't got a wife."

"My mom's gettin' a divorce."

"Caroline!" Louise said.

"Well, you are."

"I know, but . . ."

James smiled.

"You goin' to the feast tonight?" Louise asked to change the subject.

"Yeah," he said, then got up. "Gotta go."

She watched him leave and wondered why he always seemed to be in a hurry to get away from her.

James went home and made a fire in his woodstove and fell asleep again. He was awakened by a million demons knocking on his door. Had he been in a better frame of mind, he wouldn't have answered it.

Wanda and fifty women walked in yelling "Happy New Year!" and he went deaf. Wanda, Liz, Sarah and five other women held him down while Louise, Mary and the others covered him with baby powder and a ton of cheap perfume they'd all gotten for Christmas.

Liz snapped a few memorable moments. "Nex' year's Christmas card," she said as she closed his door.

He was about to turn on the shower when the phone rang.

"Don' answer your door," Jake said, then burst out laughing and hung up.

Two days later, James loaded Jake and Mary's belongings into his truck. After a million goodbyes, they drove out of Aberdeen.

That afternoon, Kevin and Greg went looking for some booze and banged at George Standing's door until it opened. They found him sitting in his armchair with a bottle of rye on the table and a gun on the floor and wondered if this was fucking real. They took whatever money and booze was lying around to their apartment, then walked to the RCMP and reported what they'd found.

Adrienne went to investigate, but there was nothing to investigate. It was suicide, plain and simple. It was also plain and simple that George Standing was a poor shot since they later estimated that it had taken him more than a few hours to die. He'd been dead for four days and no one noticed or gave a shit — same difference.

James, Jake and Mary arrived in Yellowknife late that night and called home. They were told about George, but it was just another nightmare. Or maybe this was the Dream World and tomorrow they'd wake up and everything would be back to normal. But this was reality and things *were* normal.

James decided it was none of his business. But it was and there was no denying it. He'd killed him as sure as he'd held the gun to his head and pulled the trigger. He put the secret with his others and got on with life. Or what was left of it.

On Tuesday, as James was about to leave Yellowknife, they received word that Martin was in the hospital for more tests. They visited him and found most of the Aberdeen crew sitting around looking miserable.

On Wednesday, George Standing was laid to rest. Few people attended and no one cried, least of all Clara, who did not attend and who would inherit everything. She would sell everything and make an anonymous donation to the Aberdeen Alcohol Society. There is no such thing as anonymity in any small northern community. Everyone would know she made the donation, but no one really cared. That too is another trait in most small northern communities.

On Friday, James decided to leave Yellowknife. On the way out of town, he decided to have one for the road.

He woke up the next morning at Jake and Mary's wondering what the hell he was still doing in Yellowknife. He dragged himself out of bed and walked into the living room feeling normal: like shit.

Mary and Jake were on the sofa drinking coffee.

"How you feel?" Mary asked.

"Like shit."

"Good."

His head started pounding. "Where's my truck?"

"Outside," Jake said.

"Did I drive it here?"

"No, I did."

"How'd you fin' me?"

"Tradition."

"So, you're not gonna gimme shit?"

"For what?" Jake asked. "Bein' human? I think we should congratulate ourselves. We've done pretty good considerin'."

"Actually, I went to Helena a couple times."

"So you had a drink," Mary said. "You're old enough, but nex' time leave your truck here or I'll kill you."

He decided to stay another day and went comatose. The next morning, he stopped in to see Martin, then drove out of the city and arrived in Aberdeen fifteen hours later.

He spent the next week painting and wondering if anyone knew about his visit with George. A few days later, he realized that no one really gave a shit. They had other, more important things to not give a shit about.

Martin was sent home soon after. He would never return to Yellowknife.

Twenty-Nine

The Appearance

On Tuesday, January 18th, 2000, the Winnipeg RCMP paid a visit to Tom Kinney at his place of work. He looked at them as if it were a fucking dream and never said a word when they told him why they were there. He never said a word when they told him he was under arrest. He never said a word when they read him his rights. He never said a word when they asked him if he understood those rights. He just nodded. Tom Kinney made the news that night, and would be in Helena in a few days to be formally charged.

James was listening to the news since Adrienne had told him what was going to happen. She also mentioned that only three of them had laid charges. He thought there'd be more. He pictured them arresting the fucker and in his mind Tom Kinney hadn't aged.

That night Jake called to say he was returning for the appearance.

Later, James thought about going for a drink but didn't. That night, his dreams tormented him. It was so real that he woke up at four in the morning, jumped off his bed and looked for the fuckers, but they'd buggered off into the Dream World. He stayed up and felt like shit for the rest of the day.

On Wednesday, Tom Kinney was flown to Helena for his first court appearance. Tom Kinney made the news that night and was the topic of discussion over thousands of cups of coffee in Aberdeen, Helena and the rest of the territories.

James listened to the news that evening and his mind went into overdrive. He thought about making a collect phone call to Saddam to see if he had any surplus Scuds that he could lob at the cells in Helena to expedite the fucker on his way to hell. He thought about sneaking into Helena, waiting on some grassy knoll and putting a bullet through the fucker's head as he drove by in the RCMP vehicle. He thought a lot about killing Tom Kinney. *Everyone's gonna know.*

Jake and Mary arrived late that night and stopped in to see him. He still looked like shit. They were worried about him but didn't say anything.

On Thursday, Bertha called James, Jake and Chief David into the community hall for a pep talk on the trial.

"What're we gonna talk about?" David asked.

"Your experience."

"You already know."

"I know, but you're gonna have to get up on the stand an' tell the whole world about it."

The three men looked at the ceiling and wondered if the fuckers were getting ready to pounce on their sorry asses and drag them into the great beyond.

"Tell me again," Bertha said.

That night, the three men relived their nightmares. It was easier this time, but just.

Just when James thought he had it beat, Bertha turned to him. "Tell me about Myra," she asked.

A ton of bricks hit him. "What?"

"Tell me about Myra."

"What about her?"

"Tell me."

"Nothin' to tell."

"Tell me anyway."

He looked at Jake and wondered who the fuck told her. He looked at Chief David and by the look on his face he didn't know.

"She tol' me," Bertha said.

James looked at the floor.

"She was in love with you."

James picked that moment to remove himself from his body and went nuts. He picked up a chair and screamed and threw the chair against the far wall. He looked at the ceiling hoping the fuckers came and took him right then and there. He wanted to run. He couldn't. He wanted to kill someone, but there was no one left to kill. He wanted to die, but his gun was at home. He wanted to lay down on the floor and disappear. He couldn't. He just went nuts.

After a few million years, he sat and looked at the ceiling. "I was in love with her," he said. "I wanted her to leave with me, but she wouldn't."

His audience said nothing.

"She'd still be 'live if we left."

"You don' know that," Bertha said.

"I know."

Bertha waited.

"She was pregnant," he added.

"I know," Bertha said.

He looked at her. "How much you know?"

"Too much."

He pictured Myra walking to Bertha's house in the cold and dark, searching for answers and finding none. He pictured her walking home to George and telling him she was pregnant. "How much?" he asked.

"I know it wasn't alcohol poisonin'. I can't prove it, but I know she did it."

"I thought about that for many years an' wondered if she did it." He was surprised at his calmness. "Guess I always knew it. I wanted to kill George an' I think I did."

No one said a thing for a long time. They just looked at him and waited for him to tell.

"I went to George after Christmas an' ask for a bottle," he said. "That's when he told me 'bout her bein' pregnant. Why, after all 'ese years?"

No one offered an answer.

"I told him somethin' that might've made him do it."

"What did you tell him?" Bertha asked.

He realized she didn't know about George and Clara. "Nothin', jus' the truth."

"What truth?"

"I can't tell you."

"You think he done it 'cause 'a what you tol' him?"

His silence was his affirmation.

"He did it," David said. "That's all that matters an' it doesn't."

Bertha wondered if they could handle the court case. She knew David could, but was Jake's silence a sign of something deeper? He still looked like a kid. She knew James was a ticking time bomb. She didn't know what he was capable of. "You'll be okay?" she asked.

"Yeah, no problem."

He lied. But then you already knew that.

The dreams came that night and they were bigger and scarier than ever. Things were normal. Things were fucking normal.

The next morning, James had some serious reservations about driving to Helena for Tom Kinney's court appearance. It was the first time he'd be looking the fucker in the face in thirty years. His mind was made up for him when the telephone rang.

"Martin an' Jane want a ride down," Mary said.

"I'll pick 'em up in a couple."

"We're gonna take Bertha down. David says he's gonna take Wanda, Louise, Caroline an' Abraham."

He picked up Martin and Jane and made the trip in relative silence.

Ten miles out of Helena, Jane turned to him. "James, you're okay?"

He nodded. "Yeah. Just gettin' nervous, 'at's all."

"It's only his firs' appearance," Martin said. "The big one's still comin'."

"Don' do nothin' crazy," Jane said.

He looked to see if she was teasing. She wasn't. "No prob," he answered.

They arrived at a packed courtroom. He watched the clock as it crept closer to two. At first he couldn't believe it was him. The fucker was a million years old. He wasn't big and fat, he was short and skinny and his beard was gone. His hair was white and sparse. They watched the old man slowly walk into the courtroom handcuffed and wearing a bulletproof vest as though someone was waiting on a grassy knoll. He turned to face the bench, then sat and disappeared into the chair.

James felt his breathing increase. He willed the little fucker to disappear into oblivion with the rest of his nightmares. But the old man sat and never moved.

After thirty million years, the judge entered the courtroom and they all stood. James kept his eyes on the fucker in case he made a break for it. He hoped he would, so he could jump the fucker and break his neck to stop him from fleeing justice. Maybe he'd even crack a few ribs.

Tom Kinney was charged with more than a dozen sex-related offences dating back to the sixties. He pleaded not guilty to every one with no hesitation.

Martin remembered the morning he'd taken his children to the hostel and met Tom Kinney for the first time. He'd shaken hands with him and looked him right in the eyes. "You're new so I'm gonna tell you just once," he said. "You touch my kids, I'll kill you." Tom Kinney thought he was joking. The pressure on his hand told him he wasn't.

Martin thought how easy it would be to walk up and choke the old man dead. He would later say that if he'd had a gun, he would've sent the fucker to hell. It was the first time anyone heard Martin swear.

The judge set the trial date for April. The defence attorney attempted to get the bail waived and to get Tom Kinney released on his own recognizance, but the judge didn't bite. "Bail is set at one hundred thousand dollars," he said.

After the judge left, there were a few seconds of silence.

"Tom."

Everyone turned to see who would dare talk to this man.

Tom Kinney stared at this Indian who looked like he'd just stepped off a postcard: tall, dark and dignified. He also saw three of the biggest, angriest Injuns he'd ever seen.

"Michael was my nephew," Martin said.

Four RCMP officers led Tom Kinney to the back door. On the way, he tried to smile, but it looked like a smirk, and all hell broke loose. James Nathan went nuts. The scream that came from the pit of his soul sounded like it passed through hell on its way out. People jumped and two old women almost fainted. "You fuckin' asshole!" he screamed, then tried to follow the old man.

"I'm gonna kill you!" James screamed. "You son of a bitch! I'm gonna kill you!"

The remaining five RCMP officers backed up just in case he attacked.

"We could lay charges against you," one of the rookies said.

"Why don't you?" James screamed.

They took one more step back.

"Why don't you fuckin' do it?" James stepped closer to the rookie and they stood nose to nose. "Where the fuck were you when that bastard stuck his cock up my ass!"

The whole room was silent.

"I dare you," James whispered.

After a few seconds, he felt her hand on his arm.

"James."

He turned, looked at her and immediately felt calm. They walked into the light and a whole shitload of reporters.

"How do you feel now that he's behind bars?" one asked.

"Can you tell us the details?" a rookie reporter asked.

James looked at the rookie, then said, "Why don't you get 'a fuck outta my way." They did.

"Gimme your keys," Abraham said. "I'm drivin'."

James didn't argue. He was exhausted and sat between Abraham and Louise and held Caroline on his lap. Ten miles out of Helena, his head fell against Louise's shoulder. He was sleeping.

"Mommy?" Caroline asked. "Is he gonna be okay?"

"Yeah, he'll be okay."

"Is he crazy?"

"Of course not. He's just . . ." *What?* "He's just hurtin'."

They drove to Aberdeen to Louise's house.

"Come in," she said to James, and he didn't look for a way out.

"You gonna be okay?" Abraham asked.

"We'll be okay," Louise answered.

James didn't miss the "we."

Inside, Louise turned the radio on and made tea.

James Nathan made the news that night. They told of his outburst in the courtroom and his promise to kill Tom Kinney. They played his one-liner and beeped out one word, but the listeners got the gist.

"Hey, that's you!" Caroline shouted.

Was 'at me? Do I sound like 'at?

"You okay?" Louise asked.

"Sometimes I think I'll never be okay," he said, then wished he hadn't.

"James, you gonna stay with us again?" Caroline asked.

"You want me to?"

"Yep."

Someone was watching him. He couldn't see them, but he felt it. He held his breath and waited. He opened his eyes and she looked like a dream. The dream spoke. "I love you."

He closed his eyes, for how long he didn't know. When he opened them, she was gone. He got up, put on his jacket and was gone when she came out of the bathroom.

On Sunday, James drove Ernest's snowmobile into the hills. He told no one where he was going and he left no note. He parked on a hill and took out the gun. It wasn't *the* gun. It was Jake's. Same difference. He loaded one shell, then sat back and thought about life and death and looked for a reason to die. Tom Kinney. Demons, dreams and nightmares. Uncertain future. No future. Lost future. Lost youth. Lost family. No family. He looked for a reason to live. Only one came to mind, but she was just another dream.

He pulled the hammer back and heard the click. He put the barrel under his chin, put his thumb on the trigger. He closed his eyes and thought if he could just push that fucking trigger it would all be over. One nanosecond of pain followed by an eternity of nothing. Something stopped him. *Who're you?*

He sat there for a long time before coming to the conclusion that he couldn't do it. If he did, Tom Kinney would win. He looked up at the land, and on the very spot Michael had surrendered to his demons, so too did he surrender. But to his heart, if only for the day. He arrived home around midnight.

On Tuesday, Tom Kinney's family came up with the money and he was released. Tom Kinney made the news that afternoon. James was listening and the memories returned as though it were a fucking rerun. He tried to drive them from his mind, but they kept coming. He willed them to disappear. They wouldn't. He jumped into his truck and sped north to Helena.

He looked in his rearview mirror and the memories were still there. He saw the old white man in the courtroom. He saw the same man thirty years ago. He could feel his hairy arms and hairy hands. He could smell the foul stench of his body and breath. He could smell his cock. He could feel his cock in his hands. He could feel his cock in his mouth. He could feel the pain as Tom Kinney forced his cock into him. He wanted to cry. He could hear his breathing. He could hear him moan. He could smell his semen. He could hear the promises and lies. He saw the young boy walking down the hall. *Is that me?* He saw the young boy walking into the shower room. He could see the shower room. He could sense someone watching him.

Thirty years of hell followed him into Helena, where he got a hotel room, then bought a bottle. He was going on nothing more than instinct.

That afternoon, he sat in his room and fought a whole shitload of demons, dreams and nightmares. He sat and willed Tom Kinney to kill himself. He willed so hard he fell asleep and woke up at eight. On a planet with six billion people, he'd never felt so alone in all his life.

He looked at the bottle. He filled a glass then smelled it. It brought back memories. "Aw, fuck it," he said, then drank it. It was as though it wasn't him. It was the old James.

He felt the warmth as the alcohol slid down his throat and spread to all parts of his body. He poured himself another and drank it. He poured himself another. He drank it, then went to the lobby and bought a pack of cigarettes and looked around to see if there was anyone he knew. The lobby was deserted. He walked into the lounge and saw no one he knew.

He was starting to feel better, but there was no one to share it with. He went up to his room and poured himself another and lit a cigarette. He tuned in some country music and listened without hearing. He guzzled the drink. He looked at the bottle and it was half empty. He was getting drunk and he knew it, but he didn't care. He filled the glass, and guzzled.

It was twelve o'clock. He thought about picking up another case of beer and one of his old sluts. He poured himself another drink and guzzled. He poured and drank another. He passed out shortly after.

The next morning, the family of Tom Kinney found him hanging from the ceiling of his apartment and wondered if they would get their bail money back.

James woke up on the floor feeling like someone had crapped in his mouth. He looked for Jake. He wasn't there. He felt like he had the clap. He looked for Angie, but she too had disappeared into the

Dream World. *Good.* He looked at the bottle. It had enough for one normal drink. He wasn't normal. He was fucking abnormal.

He took a shower and felt a little better, but not much. He looked at the stranger in the mirror. He looked at the bottle. He lit a smoke and took a long drag. He turned on the radio and fell asleep. It was noon when he woke up.

Jake called from Yellowknife that night. "You hear?"

"I heard."

"It's over," Jake said. "You okay?"

"I'm okay. I think I willed the son of a bitch to do it."

"I think we all did."

On Friday evening, James packed his few belongings in his truck and went to see Martin, who was getting thinner and weaker but still kept up a brave front. James did not tell him he was leaving. He did not tell anyone. He stopped in Yellowknife the next day and told Jake and Mary he was going to Alberta to look for work. Then he disappeared.

Thirty

Missed Opportunities

In February, Louise turned forty-four and wondered where James was. She hadn't seen him for two weeks. Liz and Sarah helped her celebrate her birthday and she learned that James was now in Alberta.

James turned forty-four in April and called Jake in Yellowknife. He told Jake he was living in Canmore, Alberta, and working wherever he could and doing some painting and carving for the tourists in Banff. He did not tell him he was doing quite well at it. He also did not tell Jake he'd not had a drink since forever. Or at least it seemed that long.

Sergeant Thomas Simpson arrived in Aberdeen and looked forward to the best years of his life and his career.

On Wednesday, April 26th, Jake turned forty-four and was in heaven and in Mary just as much. James called and wished him a happy birthday, then asked about Brenda and learned she and her husband were getting back together. He asked about Martin and was told he wasn't doing well. He did not ask about Louise.

Sgt. Thomas Simpson was now wondering what the hell he was doing in Aberdeen.

Larry Hunter pleaded guilty to three charges of manslaughter and was sentenced to five years. Clara and Daryl attended his trial, and then got on with life. Or what was left of it.

Chief David called for an election in July, but no one ran. He decided to stay on for another term. Apathy.

In early September, James called Jake and learned that Martin was not going to last the week. The next day, he pulled into Yellowknife, picked up Jake and Mary and drove to Aberdeen. They went to see Martin, but there was not much to see.

Two days later, Martin quietly passed away in the presence of his wife and family. By Monday, the entire region had heard, and tributes began pouring in. Most referred to him as Chief even though he'd never been.

Six hundred People made the pilgrimage into the Blue Mountains and returned Martin's body to the land and his soul to the Old People as he had requested.

James, Jake and Mary left soon after. He dropped them off in Yellowknife, then continued on to Alberta, but not before learning that he was going to be an uncle: Mary was pregnant.

Thirty-One

More Confessions

In December, Brenda and Earl visited Aberdeen and Brenda went to see Louise. "I've got to tell you something," she said.

"Yeah?"

"Do you know that James is in love with you?"

Louise waited for the punch line, but it didn't come. "He tell you?" she asked.

"Yes, he did."

"When?"

"Last winter in Yellowknife when we broke up."

"Why did you break up?"

"He didn't love me," Brenda said.

"Why are you tellin' me this?"

"I told him I was going to if he didn't. Did he?"

"No."

"Louise?"

"Yeah?"

"Do you love him?"

"I don't know," she said. "He's so unstable an' . . ."

"And what?"

"He's been with so many others."

"He loves you," Brenda said again.

"Then why doesn't he tell me?"

"Why don't *you* tell him?"

Louise had no answer.

"You're so stubborn," Brenda said. "Him too. You love each other and you're both waiting for each other to say it."

"He wasn't my first, you know," Louise said.

"So?"

"It meant a lot to me."

"I don't think that matters to him."

"It matters to me."

"It shouldn't."

"I was raped!" Louise blurted out.

"What?"

"I was raped," she repeated. "When we were in the hostel." There was a long silence. "It was Michael. We went out once an' he raped me."

"You tell anyone?"

"Only you."

"Why not?"

"Who could I tell?" Louise cried. "I wanted James to be the first an' he wasn't."

"I don't think he has to know. An' even so, I don't think it matters to him."

"How do you know?"

"I had a baby," Brenda said. "It didn't bother him."

"You were married."

"I mean I had a baby while I was in school. I left the hostel because I was pregnant. I had Raymond's daughter."

Louise said nothing for a long time. "Where's she?"

"I don't know. I gave her up."

"Why you tellin' me?"

"I don't know. I just said it."

"Who else knows?"

"My parents."

"Did he know?"

"Raymond? I don't think so."

"Why not?"

"I was young," Brenda said. "I didn't know what to do."

"I was young too."

They sat there for a long time not saying anything.

"So," Brenda finally said. "You gonna tell him or are you gonna wait for him?"

"I don' know where he is."

"Geez, Louise, ask Jake for his number!"

"What if he changed his mind?"

"Geez," Brenda said. "Find out!"

They both sat for a few minutes, then Louise said, "'Geez, Louise'? Long time since I heard 'at one!"

Brenda and Earl left Aberdeen shortly after and got on with life in Calgary.

Thirty-Two

New Beginnings

On Wednesday, February 14th, 2001, Louise turned forty-five and was legally divorced and waiting for husband number two, but only she knew that.

James called Jake from Vancouver, where he was taking jewellery classes and getting a tan. Or so he said. He told them he would not be able to attend the birth of his nephew, but he'd be up and soon at that. He did not tell them that he was into his fifteenth month of sobriety and he'd done it on his own. They did wonder how he knew they'd have a son.

On Thursday, April 26th, James called and wished Jake a belated happy birthday and learned he was an uncle. Matthew Joseph Noland was born the day before. Jake asked when he was coming up and was told soon.

Two months later, Mary turned thirty-five and heard the phone ringing. She answered it.

"Hey, young lady, is your mommy home?"

"James! Where are you?"

"Walking up the steps with your husband and my nephew."

She looked out the window and there he was with a cellular to his ear and Matthew in his arms. She ran out and hugged him. "Why didn' you tell us you were comin'?"

"Wanted to surprise you."

They were surprised at how well he looked. He told them he'd been doing quite well as an artist and not only dabbled in painting but was also into carving and jewellery.

"So where are you gonna stay?" Mary asked. "I mean for good?"

"No idea," he said. "Might go back to the West Coast. Who knows?"

"You ever goin' home?" Jake asked.

"Not likely. Nothin' 'ere for me."

Jake asked, "Where's your ol' truck?"

"Canmore. Rustin' in peace. Why? You thinkin' of buyin'?"

"Yeah," Jake said. "Was thinkin' of a minivan. Easy on gas an' lots 'a room."

That night, Jake suggested they go hunting.

"Where?"

"Up the Teal or in the hills."

"Sure, why not?"

James left the next day without much fanfare.

Two days later, Jake and Mary were at home when a new minivan pulled into their driveway.

"You Jake Noland?" the driver asked.

"Yeah," Jake said cautiously. "What's up?"

"Need your signature on these documents."

"What for?"

"A James Nathan bought this minivan and asked us to deliver it to you today. It's used, but it's the best on the lot."

Thirty-Three

The Calm and the Storm

One month later, James drove into Aberdeen. He visited Chief David and Wanda and told them what he'd been doing over the last two years. They were amazed he hadn't had a drink for almost twenty months and seemed to have his shit together. Wanda was playing bingo and let out a groan as Liz told her audience to stand by for a possible bingo.

"You come close?" David asked.

"I had one number lef'," she answered.

"Yeah, right! You an' a million other people."

They laughed at that one.

"So," James said to David. "You comin' with us?"

"Sure, why not?" he said. "Tired 'a fish."

The phone rang and Wanda answered it.

"You get close?" Louise asked.

"Not even. You?"

"Not my night. Who's 'ere?"

"Just me an' David an' 'a kids, and James."

"He is?"

"Yeah. You wanna talk to him?"

Louise almost said yes, but didn't. "Tell him I said hi. Maybe I'll be up later."

Wanda hung up. "Louise says hi," she said to James.

James thought about going up for a visit. He didn't.

The following Thursday, James was sitting on the bench by the river near his dad's cabin at the Redstone. The colours still amazed him.

"God, I wish I could take 'ese mountains back with me," Jake said.

James laughed. "Gonna paint a picture of this," he said, meaning the river and the mountains and hills.

"Give us a copy when you're done," Mary said.

"You got it."

"When you wanna head down?" David asked.

"Whenever," James said.

"Like to go down now?"

"Sure."

They'd shot four moose, and that would last a few weeks until the caribou returned. Not that they'd eat it all in a few weeks. Most of it they'd give away to the Elders and the rest of the community.

"What about you young people?" James asked. "Whatcha gonna do?"

"I'd like to stay one or two more days," Mary said. "Not gonna see this country for a long time an' we can make some drymeat."

Jake grinned. "I can live with 'at."

"Tell my mom an' dad we'll be down in a couple days," she said to James.

"Will do."

"Hey, James," Jake said. "Le' me borrow your gun?"

"Where's yours?" James asked as he handed Jake the gun.

"In my van."

"What kind 'a Injun are you? Forgettin' your gun."

They both laughed at that one.

James went to Ernest and Margaret's home and had a good shower, then fell asleep feeling better than he had in years. He was tired, his dreams were gone, and he no longer carried any secrets. Or did he?

The next afternoon James began working on another painting. Later that day he took a drive into the hills to the site where Michael and Martin were sent back to the Old People. He filled some water containers and returned late that night. He parked near the Saloon and watched people going in while others staggered out. He wondered if he should stop in to see Karen's tits and smiled at the thought. He didn't. He drove to Simon and Bella's and carried two water containers and came face to face with Louise.

"Hi," he said.

"Hi." She almost looked away, but didn't. She smiled.

"No sign 'a Jake an' Mary?" he asked Liz, turning towards her.

"Diddly," she answered.

"Prob'ly tomorrow."

Louise was looking at him out of the corner of her eye. When she saw him looking she busied herself with Matthew.

"Hi, James." Caroline said to him. "Where you were?"

"Alberta."

"What you were doin'?"

"Livin' an' workin'."

Matthew started crying, so Louise picked him up and carried him into one of the bedrooms. When she came out James was gone.

Louise watched him leave and thought about getting up and going after him and telling him she loved him once and for all and let the chips fall where they may. *Maybe later.*

The next morning, James looked at the overcast sky and the rain on the window. If Jake and Mary left around nine or ten, they should arrive around three or four. More than likely they'd stop at his dad's cabin and that meant they'd be here at seven.

He spent most of the day taking photos of people and places he hoped to paint. At six, he went to the dock.

Two hours later, Liz and Sarah pulled up in Jake's minivan.

"No sign 'a them?" Liz asked and shivered in the cold autumn evening.

"Diddly," he answered.

"Maybe they're gonna camp 'nother night?" Sarah said.

"Could be."

"Wanna go for a cold one later?" Liz asked.

"No thanks," he said. "Gotta watch the figure."

"Your figure's all shot to hell," Sarah said.

"Bite me!"

"You wish!"

"As if!" he said, and they all laughed. "Haven't had a drink in almost two years," he added.

"You're shittin' me," Liz said.

"No. It's been twenty months, three days an' four hours, but who's countin'?"

"You serious?" Sarah asked.

"Yep."

"Wow!" they both said in unison.

"Why?" Liz asked.

"Tired," James answered. "Tired of it all." He checked his watch. It was almost nine and getting dark. The wind was also picking up. "Well, I guess they'll be down tomorrow," he said. "I'm gonna call it a night."

"What if they come when we leave?" Liz asked.

"Leave their van. Put the key under the front left wheel."

James removed the gun from Jake's minivan and put it in his truck. Then he drove Liz and Sarah to Simon and Bella's and told them he'd check the dock again in the morning. He then drove home and had a good night's sleep.

It was six o'clock the next morning when James, Chief David and Abraham started up river.

"Prob'ly broke down," Abraham said to no one.

The wind on the river was cold and they kept an eye out for a fire, or for Jake and Mary paddling. Fifteen miles up, Abraham pointed to the southwest bank. James expected to see them standing beside the boat. He didn't see anything until they were about two hundred feet from the bank, then he saw the overturned boat. He looked for them on shore, but he didn't see them. He looked up river then down and then at the boat, hoping it wasn't theirs. He looked at Abraham and David and hoped they'd tell him this wasn't real. They didn't. It was.

David steered the boat up river and they watched for anything on shore that might indicate they were okay, but they found nothing. No footprints, no clothing, no nothing. They went back down river and did the same thing, but again saw nothing. They returned to the boat, turned it over and beached it, but there was no sign of them.

"Let's go back," Abraham said. "We'll get John Harley's jet boat an' check further up."

They returned to town and Abraham called John Harley and he didn't need anyone to draw him a picture. He hooked his jet boat to his truck and drove up to the dock.

Chief David went home and told Wanda what they'd found, then he and Bertha went and told Simon and Bella.

"We'll find them," Chief David promised, then got the hell out of there and drove up to the dock to find the men waiting for him.

An hour later, they were thirty miles up river and it was getting dark.

"We have to go back," Abraham said.

John slowly turned the boat around, and they returned to the community to find a whole shitload of trucks on shore waiting for any news. From the looks on the faces of the men, the people knew they'd found nothing, and deep in each and every heart they knew the worst had happened. They didn't want to think about it, but they did.

Wanda and Louise watched from David's truck and knew what was going on. Louise looked at James and was frightened at what she saw.

James climbed into his truck, started it and turned up the heat. He looked at Jake's van and saw Liz at the wheel with Sarah, and Simon and Bella in the back. He heard Matthew crying.

He didn't remember the drive. He didn't remember going into Ernest's house. He didn't remember Liz making a fire. He didn't remember Sarah making tea. He didn't remember falling asleep.

He did remember waking up at four o'clock wondering if this was a fucking dream. He walked into the living room and found Liz and Sarah sleeping on the sofa and wondered if they were partying. He prayed it was a nightmare. The tears, the rage and horror returned. They wracked his body.

He grabbed his black leather jacket, put on his boots and left like a ghost in the night. He drove up to the dock and got out.

"You fucker!" he screamed. "You fucker!"

He wanted to kill. He wanted to run. He wanted to do something — anything. He did the only thing he could. He went nuts.

How the fuck do you describe something like this? Words can't describe shit like this. It was like watching your children being led down a long hallway knowing their hair was going to be shaved or cut. It was knowing they were going to be stripped and their clothes burned. It was knowing their brown bodies were going to be scrubbed by white hands. It was knowing white lips were going to mutter "Dirty fuckin' Indians" one or two million times under their breath. It was knowing they were never going to speak their language again. It was knowing they were going to be forever ashamed of who you are. It was knowing they were going to be forever ashamed of who they are. It was knowing they were going to cry that night. It was knowing it was going to sound like a million porcupines screaming in the dark. It was knowing all this and knowing there was not a thing you can do about it. Not one fucking thing.

The tears came and there was no stopping them. He closed his eyes and let them come and come they did. After a million years, he opened his eyes and he was still here. At that moment, he did the only thing he could. He went on instinct. He had nothing left to go on.

Two hours later, he stood alone beside the highway in the Blue Mountains like he'd done so many times before. His tall, dark figure looked foreboding against the dark clouds. His black leather jacket glistened like blood-soaked armour from another time. His scowl told everyone and everything to keep their fucking distance. He looked like Death ready to go on a rampage.

He looked at his parked truck still running and wondered how he got there. He looked at the hills and mountains in their autumn splendour and at the gravel highway that cut across the land like a rip in a painting. It was as though he was seeing it for the first time. It looked like a dream, and who knows, maybe it was.

He spread his hands, then slowly lifted his head to the heavens as if to ask a question. What came was something he didn't expect: the hate, the rage, the anger and the sorrow. They burst from his tormented soul and ripped a hole in his chest and were given a voice. They sounded like a million deaths rolled into one. They spread out over the land of his People, shook the sky, then echoed off the distant mountains and disappeared into hell, where they belonged.

After a lifetime, he looked to the sky again and asked the question. Six billion people must've looked to the sky at one time or another. Six billion people must've asked it at least once in their lives.

Why me?

He waited for an answer. Six billion people must've heard it at least once in their lives. It was silent. It was nothing. He felt as if he were the last person on this cold, desolate planet. He then realized he had one option left and no alternative but to take it.

He took the gun from the truck and loaded one bullet, then returned to the side of the highway. He closed his eyes, then lifted his head to the heavens. This time he asked the Powers That Be to take him instead. They didn't. He told them he'd do anything they wanted. They wouldn't. After another lifetime had come and gone, he told them to fuck off. They did.

He thought about his reason for being here now in the mountains.

He thought about the people he'd lost. Mom. Dad. Raymond. Myra. Martin. Jake. Mary. He thought about the people he'd killed. George. Tom. Michael? Then it came to him.

He was alone. He'd always been alone. He'd always be alone. He then did something he'd thought about and tried for a million years. But this time, he knew he'd do it.

All in one smooth motion, he got down on one knee, put the barrel in his mouth, then pushed the trigger. He watched the hammer fall and closed his eyes. He tensed, waiting for the explosion. After a million years he heard it: metal on metal. It was the loudest sound he'd ever heard. It shook his whole body and deafened him.

He let go of the gun and took a deep breath. He relaxed. It was then that he heard it: the peace and the silence.

He waited for his demons, dreams and nightmares to come for him. He waited for his ultimate journey to hell.

A few seconds later, he wondered if it was over. *Is this it? Is this death?* He opened his eyes and saw the same mountains and the same sky. He looked at the gun, then looked around for his body. He found nothing. "Fuck!" he shouted to the heavens.

He loaded another bullet, pulled the hammer back, put the barrel to his head and pushed. This time there was no explosion. This time there was only the sound of metal against metal.

He opened his eyes. "Why are you fuckin' with me?" he screamed.

He waited for an answer that he knew would never come. Instead it hit him like a slap in the face. There was no God and there were no Old People. Shit happens and there's not a fucking thing you can do about it. He sank to his knees and willed his demons to return and drag him to the fiery pits of hell. *I do not belong here. I never did.*

After a million years and a billion lifetimes, he heard them coming. He heard them in the wind that now sounded like a hurricane. It sounded like a million trucks tearing up the highway. They screeched to a halt. They walked up to him. Their footsteps were magnified a billion times. He dropped the gun and closed his eyes. He raised his head to the sky and surrendered to the Powers That Be. And for once in his life, he surrendered totally.

Then they spoke to him. But it was not what he expected. It was the last voice on earth he thought he'd hear. It was the voice of reason and of hope. It was the voice of love and compassion.

"James?"

On a cold September morning up in the Blue Mountains, at a site that is considered special and will in years to come be considered sacred, James Nathan slowly opened his eyes expecting to see hell. What he saw was heaven on earth and his only reason for remaining on this plane of existence. And for one brief instant, it all made sense. And sometimes that's all you need: one brief instant.

Louise looked at him with a million years of tears in her eyes and said the words he wanted to hear more than anything. "James, I love you. I've always loved you. I'll always love you . . . forever. We'll get through this."

At that moment, he surrendered to the unseen force. He opened his arms and she moved into them like she belonged. She did. He held her like he was never going to let her go — ever. He buried his face in her neck and held the young girl he'd held so many years ago and revelled in the joy. Then he said the words she'd never heard him say. "I love you."

After another million years, he picked up the gun and threw it into the heavens and it disappeared forever. Some traditions were never meant to be. Some traditions are best laid to rest.

He looked out over the land of his People: the land of his father and his grandfather. He wondered if this was still a dream. He felt her hand on his arm and turned. She was real and this wasn't a dream.

James's journey had come full circle, and the future had unfolded as it should.